Praise for the Culinary Mystery Series

Fortune Cookie

"The mystery's personal this time as Sadie confronts painful memories and makes a surprising discovery in her quest for answers. **A story chock-full of humor and tenderness**—and of course plenty of yummy food. Sadie Hoffmiller is the real San Francisco treat!"

—Jennifer Moore, author of *Becoming Lady Lockwood*

Rocky Road

"Another fabulous installment of the Sadie Hoffmiller series. **The further I got into the story, the more complex it became** . . . definitely a rocky road of a plot!"

—Heather Moore, author of *Heart of the Ocean* and
the Timeless Romance anthologies

Baked Alaska

"Sadie is a well-loved character with plenty of genuine issues which add depth to her personality. I love that **Josi's books are clean and well-rounded with a bit of humor, plenty of mystery, and nail-biting suspense.**"

—Rachelle Christensen, author of *Diamond Rings Are Deadly Things*, *Wrong Number*, and *Caller ID*

Tres Leches Cupcakes

"Kilpack is a capable writer whose works have grown an[illegible] taken on a life of their own. ***Tres Leches Cupcakes* is an** [illegible] **ptivating addition to her creative compil**[illegible]

—Mike Whitmer, *De*[illegible]

Banana Split

"In *Banana Split*, Josi Kilpack has turned a character that we've come to love as an overzealous snoop and given her the breath of someone real so we can love her even more. **This is a story with an ocean's depth's worth of awesome!**"

—Julie Wright, author of *Spell Check*

Pumpkin Roll

"*Pumpkin Roll* is different from the other books in the series, and while the others have their tense moments, **this had me downright nervous and spooked**. During the climax, I kept shaking my head, saying, 'No way this is happening.' Five out of five stars for this one. I could not stop reading."

—Rachel Holt, www.ldswomensbookreview.com

Blackberry Crumble

"**Josi Kilpack is an absolute master** at leading you to believe you have everything figured out, only to have the rug pulled out from under you with the turn of a page. *Blackberry Crumble* is a delightful mystery with wonderful characters and a white-knuckle ending that'll leave you begging for more."

—Gregg Luke, author of *Blink of an Eye*

Key Lime Pie

"I had a great time following the ever-delightful Sadie as she ate and sleuthed her way through **nerve-racking twists and turns and nail-biting suspense**."

—Melanie Jacobsen, author of *The List* and *Not My Type*

Devil's Food Cake

"Josi Kilpack whips up **another tasty mystery where startling twists and delightful humor mix** in a confection as delicious as Sadie Hoffmiller's devil's food cake."

—Stephanie Black, four-time winner of the Whitney Award for Mystery/Suspense

English Trifle ✓

"***English Trifle* is a delightful combo of mystery and gourmet cooking**, highly recommended."

—*Midwest Review Journal*

Lemon Tart ✓

"**The novel has a bit of everything. It's a mystery, a cookbook, a low-key romance and a dead-on depiction of life**. . . . That may sound like a hodgepodge. It's not. It works. Kilpack blends it all together and cooks it up until it has the taste of, well . . . of a tangy lemon tart."

—Jerry Johnston, *Deseret News*

"***Lemon Tart* is an enjoyable mystery** with a well-hidden culprit and an unlikely heroine in Sadie Hoffmiller. Kilpack endows Sadie with logical hidden talents that come in handy at just the right moment."

—Shelley Glodowski, *Midwest Book Review*

WEDDING CAKE

OTHER BOOKS BY JOSI S. KILPACK

Daisy

Her Good Name

Sheep's Clothing

Unsung Lullaby

Culinary Mysteries

Lemon Tart

English Trifle

Devil's Food Cake

Key Lime Pie

Blackberry Crumble

Pumpkin Roll

Banana Split

Tres Leches Cupcakes

Baked Alaska

Rocky Road

Fortune Cookie

Wedding Cake recipes

Download a free PDF of all the recipes in this book at josiskilpack.com or shadowmountain.com

WEDDING CAKE

A CULINARY MYSTERY

JOSI S. KILPACK

SHADOW MOUNTAIN

Visit us at ShadowMountain.com

Library of Congress Cataloging-in-Publication Data

Kilpack, Josi S., author.
Wedding cake / Josi S. Kilpack.
pages cm
Twelfth and final book in the Culinary mystery series. See the Josi S. Kilpack website.
ISBN 978-1-60907-932-1 (paperbound)
1. Hoffmiller, Sadie—Fiction. 2. Cooks—Fiction. 3. Weddings—Fiction. I. Title. II. Series: Kilpack, Josi S. Culinary mystery.
PS3561.I412W43 2014
813'.54—dc23 2014013541

Printed in the United States of America
Lake Book Manufacturing, Inc., Melrose Park, IL

10 9 8 7 6 5 4 3 2 1

To Jana Erickson

The woman behind the curtain at Deseret Book and Shadow Mountain who has watched over this series with a careful eye from start to finish. Much of this series' success is directly linked to her efforts in making it the best it can be. I am blessed and grateful—as is Sadie—to have her.

Author's Warning

Do not read this book until you have read the first eleven books in the series!

Up to this point, each book in the Sadie Hoffmiller Culinary Mysteries has been a stand-alone volume, meaning they could be read in pretty much any order without giving away the mystery of prior books in the series. Granted, this got a bit trickier as the series progressed, and there are several characters who didn't show up in later books because doing so would give away another story. However, with book twelve, the gloves are off.

I am excited to bring back some of my favorite characters who have waited so patiently for me to get to this point so that I can catch you up on their stories and lay to rest any lingering questions. Because of that, I really, really, really, really, really mean it when I ask that you not read this book until you have read all the other ones. It's brimming with spoilers, and I would hate for your experience with those other stories to be ruined. Plus, if you wait to read this one, you'll better understand the threads that come together to make this story happen.

If you have *not* read the prior volumes, please do so before you turn the next page. ☺

If you *have* read the prior volumes, then happy reading! I hope you love Sadie's last ride. It's a doozy.

Josi

Chapter 1

Dead birds were the antithesis of a wedding day, which should be all about hope and goodness. That's why Sadie was making tiny tulle bags of birdseed for her wedding guests to throw instead of rice. She'd heard that rice could distend a bird's stomach, resulting in death if they ate too much, and though she'd never read scientific proof of such a thing, she didn't want to take the chance.

Two days, she thought as she finished tying a gossamer bow on one of the favors. *Two days and I will be Mrs. Peter Cunningham.* Her whole body shivered in excitement and anticipation of what lay ahead for her. For them.

Sadie's phone rang, and she pivoted from the kitchen counter to the kitchen table where her phone vibrated against the lacquered top.

She glanced at the caller ID and smiled before answering. "Hi, sweetie."

"Hey, Mom," her daughter, Breanna, replied. There was a lot of noise in the background, and Sadie imagined her daughter—tall, dark, and beautiful—standing in a corner of the Heathrow airport in London, plugging one ear. "We're checked in and will start boarding in about twenty minutes."

"Wonderful." Sadie allowed a break from the myriad wedding details and sat in the worn brown recliner in her living room. It was her favorite place in the house, and she settled into the squishy softness of its embrace with a sigh indicative of her long day. Forty-eight hours—well, forty, really—and she would be Pete's *wife*. She could hardly believe that after three years of what could only be classified as a tumultuous dating relationship, they were finally getting married. "What time do you land in Minneapolis?"

"Around four o'clock in the morning your time," Breanna said. She stifled a yawn, reminding Sadie that it was about 2:00 a.m. in London right now—8:30 p.m. here in Colorado. Since it was July, the sun was just setting, casting orange shadows through the big front window of Sadie's house. The red-eye flight from London to Denver wasn't the best itinerary available—in fact, it might have been the very worst—but it had allowed Liam, Breanna's husband of only six weeks, to attend an important event in London that evening.

"I hope you'll be able to sleep on the plane," Sadie said.

"I'm not worried about that," Breanna said. "I'm *so* tired. The flight is nine hours, which will give me plenty of time to rest before the layover. We should be to Garrison by noon or so."

"Wonderful," Sadie said, hoping the jet lag wouldn't be too bad and they'd be recovered by the time the ceremony took place. "Pete swapped out the bed in your old room for a queen-sized bed from his house. It's got new sheets and everything." Sadie liked Liam quite a lot, but he'd grown up wealthy and privileged, and she worried that her modest home wouldn't meet his expectations. "I even bought new towels." They matched the bedspread and the new curtains

Sadie had put up; she'd been going for an English countryside look and then worried it would look pretentious.

"Don't stress too much," Breanna said with a smile in her voice. "We're looking forward to staying at the house and having more time with you. Shawn's there already?"

"He flew in this morning," Sadie said, smiling in anticipation of having both her children—and Liam—under her roof at the same time. It didn't happen very often, what with Breanna living on another continent and Shawn finishing up his degree at Michigan State. "He's at Pete's bachelor party right now."

"Oh, a *bachelor* party. And you're not spying on them?"

They joked for a bit about what the men might be doing. Sadie kept to herself that she knew *exactly* what they were doing: barbequing Omaha steaks, drinking imported beer, and playing poker until midnight at the home of one of Pete's police department buddies. It had only taken a quick scroll through Pete's text messages and eavesdropping on a couple of conversations when he thought she was occupied with something else to assure her that she had nothing to worry about on this last night of "debauchery"—not that her investigation meant she didn't trust him. It was just a habit, good or bad, depending on the circumstances of its employ.

It had been an intense few weeks. Pete's house had sold and would close after their honeymoon. He had been spending a lot of time preparing for the move, and Sadie was glad he'd gone ahead with a night of cards and food with his buddies. Sadie's house still had the realty sign in the front yard, so they would be living here for now. After the honeymoon, they would step up their efforts to find a new place of their own and then, maybe, she would lower the price on her home to encourage it to sell in the unpredictable market.

"Well, I better go," Breanna said on the phone. "If I use the restroom now and don't drink too much water on the flight, I might be able to avoid the horrible bathroom on the plane *and* sleep straight through."

Sadie said good-bye with a smile that stretched all the way to her toes. Sixteen hours from now she would get to hug her daughter and new son-in-law. And twenty-four hours after *that,* she'd be making vows to the man she had come to love so much. Still grinning, Sadie pushed up from the chair, then flinched slightly at the tugging pain in her right side, just below her ribs.

Three weeks ago she'd been stitched up following *the* most harrowing experience of her life, which was saying a lot based on the number of harrowing experiences she'd survived in recent years. She'd healed better than the doctors had expected, but she was still sore and had to be careful about moving too quickly. Sadie credited her quick healing to the level of endorphins running through her bloodstream as the wedding plans had picked up speed.

Sadie returned to the kitchen and finished tying up the rest of the birdseed packets. When the last bow was tied, she put the tiny bundles in a basket and set it by the front door next to the monogramed napkins so that she'd know right where they were when she was running around crazy in the hours before the ceremony.

She scratched "birdseed favors" off her to-do list and looked at the next item: "update guest list." She sat down on one of the kitchen chairs and pulled the guest list in front of her. There was a purple check mark next to the guests who had responded that they would be in attendance and a black X next to those who had RSVP'd that they couldn't make it. Sadie had expected most of their out-of-state friends and family wouldn't be able to attend the ceremony, but she'd loved all the phone calls of congratulations and catching up that sending the invitations had garnered. Everyone was so happy for her and Pete, and she loved hearing the well wishes over and over again.

There were a few names unmarked on her list, including Ji, her recently discovered nephew. He wasn't sure he could get away from his restaurant in San Francisco but hadn't yet said he *wouldn't* be there. She still held hope that he, and perhaps his daughters, would be able to attend.

There were half a dozen other guests she hadn't heard from, and she considered whether or not she should follow up with them. She didn't want to put anyone on the spot, but what if their invitations had been lost in the mail? She'd feel terrible if they learned about the wedding later and believed she hadn't included them. Or what if they'd tried to get in touch with her but called an old phone number, not realizing she'd put her new number on the invitation? If they hadn't received the invitation at all, they might not even have her new number.

There was still time to make a few calls tonight—at least to those not on the East Coast—but was it worth the possibility of an awkward conversation if they simply hadn't cared enough to respond? She tapped her pen on the paper—*decisions, decisions*. She needed to give North Hamptons—the reception hall where the wedding would be held—and the caterers a final guest count by noon tomorrow.

Her phone's text message alert chime interrupted her thoughts. She picked up the phone and noted that though the texter came up as UNKNOWN, the area code indicated it was someone local.

Unknown: Hi, Sadie.

Sadie: Hi, who's this?

Unknown: You don't know? I'm hurt.

Sadie: Your name didn't come up on my contact list so you'll have to tell me. ☺

Unknown: Think about it for a minute. Do you really not know who this is?

Sadie furrowed her brow as she remembered some advice Pete had given her almost two years ago when she'd disconnected her landline, forwarded her mail to a PO Box, installed an alarm system for her home, and gotten her first private cell phone number, which she only shared with select people.

"Don't answer any calls or texts from unknown numbers," Pete had said. "I'll look them up, and when you know who it is you can decide whether you want to call them back. Don't take any chances."

As time had moved forward, Sadie had bit by bit given up the protective measures. She felt a little silly for thinking about Pete's advice now since she'd sent her new number out with her wedding invitations to dozens of people—this unknown caller was surely one of them. But that didn't sit quite right. Most of the people in her life knew that she'd had some difficult times; they wouldn't play with her anxieties, would they?

Her phone chimed again, and she regarded it an additional moment before picking it up.

Unknown: You're not even going to guess? I thought you'd missed me.

Annoyed at the interruption but determined to get to the bottom of it through proactive measures, Sadie took the phone with her across the room where she sat down at her desk and opened her laptop. She typed the unknown phone number into the Google search bar and scrolled through the links until she found one that would give her the origination information about the owner of the phone number.

The link didn't give names, but it did tell her that the number was registered through an AT&T wireless store in Fort Collins, Colorado—the closest large city to Garrison—and that the account had been opened in 2002. Not only was the caller someone local, it was someone who'd had the same number for more than a decade. That should give her some comfort, but it didn't give her as much as she'd have liked.

Someone local would *definitely* know of the struggles Sadie had had since they were the reason she'd lived away from home for several months. Why would they tease her?

"This is ridiculous," Sadie said, standing up from the desk and heading back to the kitchen table and her to-do list for tomorrow. She wanted to make sure it was complete before she turned in for the night.

Ridiculous or not, however, her anxiety was triggered, and she felt tense. In search of a remedy, her eyes were drawn to the pan of rice pudding still on the stove; she crossed the room toward it. Shawn had requested his favorite meal for lunch today—Evil Chicken—and she'd made enough rice to make rice pudding for dessert with the leftovers. Shawn had left for the bachelor party before the rice pudding was ready, so she'd enjoyed a bowl herself and had been waiting for the rest of it to cool before she put it in the fridge. She really shouldn't have a second bowl, especially this late at night, but she knew the creamy dessert would help her calm down and focus—good food always did.

Sadie took a bite of the still-warm perfection while expertly pushing the feelings of tension from her mind. It was all about compartmentalization and she was not going to give the obnoxious texter more power than he or she deserved. Especially when so many other things needed her attention.

She scanned the longer to-do list for the wedding to see if she'd missed anything, then set it aside and looked at the shorter list she'd made just for tomorrow. Had she left off anything that would need her attention? In fact, she had! With a smile, she wrote, "Clear out space in bathroom for Pete" and felt her stomach flip-flop at the thought of how soon they would be sharing the master bathroom. The master bedroom.

Holy moly, this is happening!

The chime of another text message shattered her glitter-tipped thoughts, and Sadie's eyes snapped to her phone still on the computer desk. The tension returned. She looked at the clock—it was just after 9:00 p.m.—then reminded herself that this newest text could very well be from someone else. Perhaps one of the guests who hadn't yet confirmed their attendance. Or maybe it was Pete texting to tell her he loved her.

Sadie pushed away from the kitchen table and walked toward the phone. The screen had gone black by the time she reached it. She picked it up and slid her finger across the screen to wake it up.

Unknown: Didn't I tell you that you'd never be free of me?

Jane!

The name came unbidden to Sadie's mind, and her breath caught in her throat. Her heart began to race, and the tenuous optimism she'd felt faded fast. She'd become so used to not thinking of the woman who had threatened her life in Boston—it had been almost two years, after all—that it was a shock to suddenly jump to that conclusion. She immediately tried to dismiss it.

There were several people who held Sadie responsible for the consequences they'd faced after being caught in a variety of criminal behavior—it could be one of them. But Jane was the only one who had gotten away, so to speak. And Jane *had* said those exact words: "You'll never be free of me." Wouldn't it be just like her to wait until two days before Sadie's wedding—on an evening when Sadie would be home alone—to make good on that threat?

Sadie took a deep breath in an attempt to calm herself. Pete would want her to call him about this. She began toggling to the keypad on her phone.

Did I lock the doors after Shawn had left for the party?

She told herself, again, not to overreact. It was probably nothing. A moment later, the squeak of a floorboard froze her in place. Her head snapped up, but her eyes stared blankly at the cabinets in front of her.

This is not happening two days before my wedding!

Sadie felt the warmth of another person standing behind her at the precise moment something suddenly covered her eyes. She screamed, dropped her phone, and grabbed at the hands that were blinding her and pulling her backward.

A throaty whisper in her ear nearly paralyzed her. "Guess who?"

Rice Pudding

1½ cups milk
1 (12-ounce) can evaporated milk
2 eggs, slightly beaten
1 tablespoon cornstarch
½ teaspoon salt
⅔ cup sugar
2 cups cooked rice
Dash of nutmeg
Dash of cinnamon
Dash of cloves
1 teaspoon vanilla
½ cup raisins (optional)

In a small saucepan over medium-high heat, combine milks and cook 10 minutes, stirring constantly until scalded. Be careful not to let milks boil. (You can also heat milks in a microwave-safe bowl for approximately 1½ minutes.)

Crack eggs into a small bowl and mix with a fork. Set aside.

In a 3-quart saucepan, whisk together cornstarch, salt, and sugar. Add hot milk mixture, whisking constantly until well blended. Reduce heat to medium and stir consistently until mixture thickens slightly. (It's okay if it comes to a boil, but reduce heat if mixture becomes frothy and risks boiling over.)

Trade whisk for a wooden spoon and add rice. Bring to a full boil, stirring consistently. Remove from heat.

Pour approximately ½ cup of the hot mixture into the eggs, stirring rapidly to combine. Return egg mixture to hot milk and rice mixture and stir until mixture thickens. If the mixture doesn't thicken within a minute or two, return to heat for another minute. Stir in spices and vanilla. Adjust spices to taste. Add raisins, if desired.

Pudding can be served warm or chilled. Store leftovers in the fridge.

Note: To plump raisins, either put them in a colander over a pan of boiling water or put them in a microwave-safe bowl, cover with water, and heat for 30 seconds; drain.

Note: This recipe works great with cold rice from the fridge.

Makes 6 servings.

CHAPTER 2

Sadie threw her elbow back as hard as she could and hit solid flesh, then she kicked backward, and spun to the right, successfully pulling out of her attacker's grasp. She ducked to avoid being grabbed again and was able to take a few steps away when her attacker didn't put up a fight. She turned and crouched down, ready if they came after her.

"Gosh, Mom," Shawn said, looking at her like she was crazy and rubbing a spot just below his ribs. "That hurt."

Sadie's brain registered that it wasn't Jane standing in front of her. Her relief took center stage for half a beat before she straightened, balled her hands into fists at her side, and glared at her son. "What on earth are you thinking sneaking up on me like that!"

"I was thinking it would be *funny*," Shawn said. He looked down and lifted his shirt, obviously looking for an injury he could use to evoke sympathy. He revealed less stomach than Sadie had ever seen on her massive boy. She'd noticed his weight loss when he'd arrived that morning but hadn't realized how much of a difference it had made to his overall physique. "You have some freaking pointy elbows, Mom. I'm surprised I'm not bleeding."

"I'm not sure I would feel all that bad if you *were* bleeding," Sadie said, still angry. "You scared me half to death."

"Which could have been *funny* if you hadn't gone all ninja on me." Shawn put his shirt down and smoothed the fabric. "What's your deal?"

Sadie turned to the cabinet and got out a bowl instead of answering him right away. In light of the fact that it wasn't Jane who'd broken into her house and attacked her, she felt silly for having thought it in the first place.

Shawn had a history with Jane from when she'd pretended to be interested in him in order to get closer to Sadie. The pseudo relationship was embarrassing for Shawn, and she knew he didn't want to revisit the memories. Shawn had probably sent the texts all along, but her pride kept her from asking for confirmation; she wasn't in the mood to hear him gloat over the fact that he'd totally had her going.

Sadie dished up some rice pudding and handed him the bowl. He'd asked her to save him some for when he got home, and now it seemed a perfect change of subject.

"Can I just have half of that amount?" Shawn asked.

Sadie looked at the brimming bowl, a bit hurt. "You love my rice pudding."

"Too much," he said, patting his flattened belly. "It's way past seven o'clock at night, and that's, like, pure carbs and sugar. After having Evil Chicken for lunch—which was awesome, by the way—and steaks for dinner, I need to draw a hard line."

Sadie scooped half of the pudding back into the pan, only slightly mollified by his explanation. At least she could share the leftovers with Breanna tomorrow; she loved Sadie's rice pudding, too. "You've never turned down my cooking in your life."

"I'm finally eating the way I know I should. Except if I were really being careful I wouldn't be eating this at all and I wouldn't have asked for Evil Chicken in the first place."

Sadie handed the half-full bowl to her son who took it with a grateful smile. Shawn was part-Polynesian and part-African American, which explained his large build, dark coloring, and tightly curled, medium brown hair. In the past he'd worn his hair in a fluffy, picked-out Afro but had recently cut it rather short. The conservative style made his face look thinner and his jaw stronger. In a word, he looked more like a "man" than he ever had before.

Sadie would never have guessed she'd miss the frothy hair or the long braids of his youth but in a way, she did. Maybe it was harder for her to see him so grown up because of the relationship he'd developed with his birth mother, Lorraina, over the last year or so. Sadie hadn't come to terms with the idea that she and Lorraina were sharing him now. When he was younger, she had been the only parent in his life.

"You're looking really good," Sadie said, as they headed to the table. She gathered her papers into a stack and set it aside so that neither of them accidentally spilled rice pudding on any of her precious lists.

"Thanks," Shawn said before taking his first bite. The way he savored it, holding it in his mouth for a few seconds before chewing and swallowing, made Sadie feel better about him having a smaller portion. "Lorraina's doctors suggested I work on eating better as we prep for the surgery."

"Four weeks from now, right?" Sadie had learned about Lorraina through a bizarre set of circumstances on an Alaskan cruise several weeks ago. Lorraina had fallen ill on the cruise and had been in a hospital in Anchorage ever since where doctors were monitoring her recovery until she was strong enough for a living liver donation from her only biological child, Shawn, whom she had given up for adoption at birth.

Sadie was proud of him for being willing to donate part of his liver, but she was still a little jealous of the relationship he shared with Lorraina, hurt that he'd kept it from her for such a long time, and worried about her baby boy having major surgery. They were taking part of his liver, for heaven's sake. That wasn't like donating blood where a granola bar and some orange juice was sufficient for recovery.

"The surgery's scheduled for a month from yesterday," Shawn said. "Did I tell you I was able to get out of my lease early?"

"No," Sadie said, though he'd told her he was going to try. The lease was supposed to extend through December. Shawn updated her with the specifics of how he'd negotiated the shortened term and went on to tell her his plans from here on out. After the wedding, he would fly back to Michigan long enough to take the final exam for his last class. He would then pack up his apartment and bring everything to Sadie's house to store it for a little while.

"And then you'll go to Anchorage from here?" Sadie asked when he finished.

"Yeah, I fly out on August seventeenth. The hospital arranged for me to stay in a guest house that won't cost me much. Can you still come up in time for the surgery?"

"Absolutely," Sadie said, so glad that he trusted her to not let her petty feelings get in the way of being a part of this experience. She was determined to prove herself worthy of his confidence. "And how are things with Maggie?"

Shawn glanced at her over his spoon and his whole face lit up. "Amaaaaazing," he said in a breathy word that made her smile.

For the next ten minutes, he updated Sadie on the state of his relationship with Miss Maggie Lewish from Sacramento, California. Other than the time they'd spent together on the cruise, the rest of their relationship had taken place online, but it seemed to be getting pretty serious despite them living twenty-five hundred miles apart.

"I applied for some jobs in Sacramento last week," Shawn said. Sadie put down her spoon with a clink. He smiled sheepishly as he continued, "Actually, I *only* applied for jobs in Sacramento."

Sadie's arms broke out in goose bumps. This *was* serious. She opened her mouth to ask about his long-term expectations of this relationship when her phone chimed with a text message. The sound reminded her of the text messages she'd received earlier in the evening. She looked at Shawn, who was scooping another bite of rice pudding from his bowl and, therefore, not sending her a cryptic text from someone's phone he'd borrowed at the bachelor party earlier. Somehow her brain had built up an entire theory without having asked him a single question about it.

"What?" Shawn asked when he noticed her watching him.

"Um, were you sending me text messages earlier?"

"Earlier like this morning when we were meeting up at the airport and you had the wrong terminal?"

"No, earlier like when you were supposed to be at the bachelor party and then took five years off my life instead."

"No offense, Mom," Shawn said, looking back at his bowl as he scraped a final bite from the edges. "But that was *not* a party. It was a bunch of old guys playing poker without money and talking about fishing lures. Bo-oring."

Sadie attempted a smile to cover her sinking stomach at the realization that it wasn't Shawn behind the earlier messages. The text reminder chime sounded again, and she looked around for her phone before remembering that she'd dropped it when Shawn had played his practical joke. She searched the kitchen, finally locating the phone underneath the lip of the cabinets next to the stove. Good thing she'd invested in a top-of-the-line protective case. She'd been through enough phones in the last couple of years to know better than to take any chances. Before picking up the phone, she took a deep breath and braced herself.

Unknown: I don't like it when you ignore me.

"Mom?"

Sadie's heart rate increased again, and she looked up to see Shawn watching her. His forehead was wrinkled in concern. "You okay? Why did you think I was texting you?"

"I've been getting these weird messages tonight."

Shawn crossed the room to her. "What do you mean, weird messages?"

Sadie gave him her phone and watched him scroll through the messages. She wanted to say something like, "I'm sure it's not a big deal," but she couldn't make herself do it.

"Do you think it's Jane?" Shawn asked when he finished. Him jumping to the same conclusion Sadie had without her saying so both validated her concern and increased it that much more. The phone chimed again, and Shawn's eyes darted to the screen. He stiffened and Sadie stepped beside him so she could see the latest message.

Unknown: Tell Shawn hi for me. It's been a long time.

Chapter 3

It was midnight before Sadie slid the key into the door of room 233 of the Carmichael Hotel in Garrison. Ironically, it was in the parking lot of this same hotel that Sadie had first met Jane Seeley more than two years ago. Sadie had had no idea at the time how much Jane would change her life and resented that Jane was doing it again.

After Sadie had called Pete about the texts, she called the police department as well. Everyone agreed it wasn't safe for Shawn and Sadie to stay at the house tonight. Despite the fact that Sadie had spent several months in hiding following Jane's threats, locking the front door behind her tonight was more painful than her other exoduses. The weight of Jane returning at what should be such a happy time left her feeling overwhelmed.

A subdued Pete and Shawn followed her into the hotel room, each of them burdened by their own thoughts. Sadie flipped on the light and took in the gold coverlets on the two queen-sized beds, the blue and gold patterned carpet, and the walnut dresser and desk. *Home sweet home*, she thought sarcastically as Pete gently pushed her to the side in order to inspect the room.

"I don't think Jane is in here," Sadie said, closing the door behind Shawn who was texting on his phone, his duffel bag slung over his shoulder. He hadn't been in town long enough to unpack. Sadie, on the other hand, had been given five minutes to throw whatever she could into an overnight bag. Such unorganized packing had done little to improve her mood.

"Don't start," Pete said, and although she suspected he was trying to make a joke, they were all too tired for him to pull it off. He opened the closet, peeked into the bathroom, and then checked the window, pulling the blackout curtains tightly together after ensuring the window was locked and barred. Only when he was satisfied that the room was safe did he turn around. They held each other's eyes for a few moments across the space of the room while Shawn dropped his bag and sat heavily on the bed closest to the door, seemingly oblivious of the mood of the room.

"This was the best option, Sadie," Pete said.

Shawn looked up from his phone, glancing at Pete and then Sadie as though just now noticing the tension.

"I'm not saying it wasn't. This just isn't where I want to be." She wanted to be in her own bedroom in her own home. She wanted to steal one more bite of her rice pudding. She frowned. She'd forgotten to put the rice pudding in the fridge. Her jaw tightened with the realization that she'd have to throw it all away once she got back home. It was mostly eggs and milk and couldn't sit out all night. One more thing Jane had ruined for her. "Will I be able to go back home tomorrow? I have so much to do."

"We'll know better in the morning," Pete said. "Finding Jane is the department's top priority tonight."

"What if they *don't* find her?" Shawn asked. "What will happen with the wedding?"

"We'll know better about that in the morning too," Pete said, and Sadie closed her eyes as she processed his words. Could the wedding really not happen? She imagined the cake drying out in the freezer of Rachel's Bakery, the beautiful ivory dress she'd found at a boutique in Denver staying in the closet of her home unused, and the phone calls she'd have to make to all the guests telling them not to come. Part of her tried to insist that the wedding wouldn't be affected, that she wouldn't give Jane the satisfaction, but the rest of her knew she might not have a choice.

The cell phone used to send the text messages Sadie had received had been traced to a woman in town who said she'd lost her phone at the grocery store earlier that evening. A missing cell phone wasn't something you called the police about, and it wasn't a fancy smart phone that could be locked with a password. It was the perfect device for Jane to contact Sadie with undetected.

The police had also traced the text messages through the cell phone tower closest to Sadie's house but Sadie had already known that Jane must have been close enough to see Shawn come home from the party. That particular tower covered half of the town so it didn't really narrow things down as to where the police should start looking.

Lost in thought, Sadie didn't notice Pete had crossed the room until he was only a few feet away from her. "It's going to be okay," he said.

"Is it?" Sadie replied, irrationally irritated by his attempts to pacify her fears. "I spent over a year in hiding because of that woman."

She'd stopped hiding about nine months ago, finally easing back into a normal life not ruled by fear. She didn't want to give that up.

"The police are doing everything they can," Pete said. "And you're safe—that's what matters the most. You need to have confidence that she isn't smarter than everyone else—even if she thinks she is. We're going to find her, Sadie."

Sadie's irritation faded enough for her to feel bad about spouting off when she knew how much effort was going into protecting her. "Thank you for everything you've done," she said. "And be sure to thank the department. I feel so . . . responsible for all—"

"You're not responsible," Pete cut in. "And we *are* going to find her." He leaned in for a quick kiss before reminding both Sadie and Shawn that he was only a phone call away and that an officer would remain posted outside their door. Sadie wondered if Pete would be up all night helping with the case despite the fact that he had retired from the police department a few months earlier. She hated this so much.

After the door was locked and the chain engaged, Sadie lifted her suitcase onto the dresser and unzipped it. She was in the process of double-checking the items and attempting better organization of her things when she thought about Breanna. Her hands slowed as she considered that her daughter and Liam would be arriving in Denver twelve hours from now. Maybe the police would have found Jane by then, but if they didn't . . .

She looked at Shawn, whose eyebrows were pulled together as he continued texting—probably with Maggie. She hated that he was in the middle of this as much as she was, and she wasn't sure she could handle the increased pressure of Breanna being in the same position.

After a few more moments of consideration, Sadie turned away from her suitcase. She knew what she had to do, as much as she despised doing it.

"Can I borrow your phone?" she asked Shawn. The police had taken her phone in order to download the texting history. She hoped they didn't read the ones between Pete and her—the personal nature of their messages would embarrass everyone, not just Sadie and Pete.

"Uh, sure," Shawn said. "Just let me finish this up. Are you making a call or sending a text?"

"Text." Breanna wouldn't get it until her flight landed four hours from now, but Sadie hoped to be sleeping by then. She was exhausted and knew she'd need rest before she faced whatever tomorrow might hold. Shawn opened a new text message and handed the phone to Sadie.

Before Sadie typed out the message she felt a rush of resentment, regret, and just plain anger that any of this was happening. It was so unfair that Jane had hijacked such a happy time for all of them and turned it into her stage. Pete's words came back to her, that Jane wasn't smarter than everyone else. Sadie had to believe that was true. Despite her own pessimistic thoughts, she had to believe the police could catch her, put an end to the shadow Sadie had been living under, and bring Jane to justice for the things she'd done in Boston. Accepting that belief system, rather than a more fatalistic one, made it easier to type the message to her daughter—not a *lot* easier, but a little.

This is Mom. Stay in Minneapolis. Jane is here. Shawn and I are at the Carmichael. I'll call with details in the morning.

Chapter 4

It took half of a sleeping pill and twenty minutes of soothing rain sounds from an app on Shawn's phone before Sadie fell asleep. She used her headphones to not disturb Shawn but woke up around five o'clock tangled in the headphone cord; she thought it was a rope for a frightening few moments. She couldn't breathe, couldn't think of anything other than the fact that she was trapped, that Jane had somehow found her. The terror kept her frozen until she awakened enough to realize she was as safe as she'd ever been.

After disentangling herself from the headphone cord and thinking calming thoughts until her heart rate returned to normal, she put her legs over the side of the bed and sat up in hopes it would help clear her head from the leftover fog of the prescription medication she hadn't used in months.

The silver dawn of morning peeked through the gaps around the curtain, outlining Shawn's mountainous form in the other bed. She stretched and blinked and only then did she remember *everything.* The subconscious hope of a new day was smothered and choked.

Sadie closed her eyes and wished she was still asleep even as her mind slogged into wakefulness and anticipation of the day looming before her. She reached for Shawn's phone, unplugged the headphones, and checked Shawn's text messages for anything from Breanna or Pete. She purposely did *not* read the text from Maggie as it was none of her business—though it sorely tempted her.

There was one text from Breanna.

Breanna: What?!? Call me when you can. Be safe.

Sadie looked around the hotel room and thought about the police officer posted outside her door. She *was* safe. Pete and the police were making sure of it, but if they'd found Jane during the night, Pete would have made sure she knew it. Since he hadn't, Sadie had to assume that Jane was still out there.

She went into the bathroom so she could call Breanna without waking Shawn. Breanna answered on the second ring, and Sadie explained the situation before all but forbidding Breanna and Liam from coming to Garrison. They had already missed their scheduled flight per Sadie's instructions but they could catch another one, Breanna said. She obviously wanted to come, but Sadie was relieved that she didn't argue.

"What does Jane want?" Breanna asked in a frustrated tone.

Sadie opened her mouth before realizing she didn't have an answer to that very simple question. "I don't know," she finally said.

Before—in Boston—Jane had wanted Sadie's attention, approval, and . . . friendship; paltry things in light of the lengths Jane went to in order to earn them, as though her manipulations could make a difference. From the first time Sadie had met Jane, she'd never trusted her entirely, not even after Jane saved Sadie's life in Portland. There had always been something that held Sadie back, a kind of cunning on Jane's part that kept Sadie wary. Frustrated that Sadie wasn't relying on her more, Jane had increased the stakes in an attempt to drive Sadie to include Jane in what was happening. When Sadie still didn't turn to Jane for help, Jane had staged Sadie's abduction and positioned herself as the rescuer—certain that would earn Sadie's loyalty. Things had not gone according to Jane's plan and the night had ended with a knife at Sadie's neck and a threat that had rung in her ears ever since. What Jane had wanted back then was impossible now, which made it difficult to guess at her possible motivations for coming back now.

What does she want? Sadie had no idea.

"Mom, at least let us come as far as Denver," Breanna asked. "We can stay there until you give us the all clear to come to Garrison, but at least we'll be close instead of halfway across the country. Maybe we can even help. Liam offered to hire a security company to work the wedding events; his mom does that all the time. I don't want to be so far away."

"I don't know," Sadie said, wavering. She *wanted* Breanna here—her daughter had strength and calmness Sadie could certainly use about now. "I'm worried someone might get hurt." Jane had hurt Mrs. Wapple in Boston, which gave precedence for Sadie's fears.

Breanna followed Sadie's line of thought perfectly and easily argued the point Sadie hadn't said out loud. "Mrs. Wapple was some crazy woman who dug for potatoes in her flower beds. Give us some credit at being a bit more savvy than she was."

Sadie let out a breath. She didn't know what to say but Breanna saved her from having to speak.

"We're coming to Denver." Breanna wasn't one to be so instantly decisive, which showed how strong her feelings were. Sadie heard some muffled whispers and imagined that Liam had been waved toward the ticket counter to work out the details of finding a new flight. "I'll call you when we get there. Have you talked to Pete this morning?"

"If they'd found her or discovered anything important during the night Pete would have called or texted me."

"Maybe you should call him and make sure."

Sadie considered that but felt sure Pete had been up most of the night helping with the investigation. She didn't want to disturb him in case he'd managed to catch a little sleep. "I'll call him in a little while," she said, scrubbing a hand across her forehead where the first taps of a headache were growing stronger. "I'm going to shower and organize my thoughts. Let me know what time you'll be landing in Denver, okay?"

"Hang in there, Mom. Everything's going to work out."

They ended the call, and Sadie retrieved her clothes from her suitcase—quietly so as not to wake Shawn—closed the bathroom door behind her, and turned on the shower. A minute later she stepped under the hot water and felt the physical and mental relaxation the warmth inspired.

For the first time since working so hard to forget that night in Boston, Sadie went back to it in her head. She needed to remember everything about Jane to be clear about what she was up against. That night was something Sadie had wanted to forget so it was difficult to pull forward. She forced herself to do so, however, and put herself back in the art gallery on Newbury Street.

Sadie had been in the office of the Bastian Gallery when she saw what she thought was a ghost coming toward her face. The ghost had turned out to be a rag doused with chloroform and it had rendered her unconscious. Sadie remembered waking up in the trunk of a car. She remembered Jane letting her out of the trunk and then driving past the police station, promising Sadie she'd take her there after she blamed someone else for Sadie's abduction. Sadie jumping out of the car. Hiding at the pond. Listening to Jane search for her in the fog and . . .

Sadie's mind shut off the memory like an old-fashioned movie reel running out of film.

She turned her face up into the water before going back into the memory. She started with the ghost again and tried to stay in the memory, which kicked her out a second time when her anxiety levels got too high. Frustrated but determined, she turned around so the water hit her back, and she closed her eyes again, pictured the ghost, and put herself back there. Trunk. Darkness. Cold. Rescue. Doubts. Drive. Fear. Panic. Her hand on the handle of the door when she thought about jumping from Jane's car. Jump . . . and she was kicked out again.

Sadie growled at her inability to see this through and turned the water off. The bathroom had steamed up from such a long hot shower, and a sucking kind of silence filled the room. The vapor settled and moved around her—a warm version of the cold fog that had appeared that night in Boston, both blinding and protecting her.

Sadie put herself back into the memory and scrolled through everything again, determined to find a balance between feeling the emotions she'd felt that night and not letting them overwhelm her in the present. Driving. Passing the police station. Pete. Jane's confession. Fear. Panic. The sign to Jamaica Pond. Her hand on the door. A red light. A turn. Rolling on the concrete. Crawling into the fog and trees. Hiding. Jane's attack. Pete. And then . . . "You'll never be free of me, Sadie! Never."

The words sent a shiver down Sadie's spine that was quickly followed with confirmation of just how true those words had proven to be. Jane's threat had changed so many things for Sadie, sending her into a state of anxiety, and to both Hawaii and then New Mexico as she tried to learn how to feel safe again.

The Boston police had conducted a thorough manhunt for Jane after the incident in Boston but other than confirming her as the person behind the seemingly mystical things that had been happening to Sadie and Pete, the police had come up empty-handed. Jane Seeley was not her real name but an alias she'd been using for approximately three years—a very good alias that hid her true identity. "Jane Seeley" had disappeared as soon as she'd run away from Pete that night, and she never used her debit card, cell phone account, or driver's license again.

Though Pete had insisted Sadie take extreme precautions and had kept his eye on databases and records, the police hadn't found so much as a shadow of the woman known as Jane Seeley. There was a warrant for her arrest and fingerprints in the national database that would be matched should she be arrested anywhere in the country. If that happened, then she-who-they-called-Jane would go straight to jail for the crimes committed in Boston. But she had to be found first, and that hadn't happened in nearly two years.

Now, Jane was back—just as she'd promised—and drowning out every beautiful thing in Sadie's life. Once again, she was a hostage.

Sadie stepped out of the shower and dried off, deep in thought. She dressed and considered the optimistic possibility that the text messages might be the extent of Jane's interference. Jane had to know the police department would be on high alert due to the threat against Sadie—someone who was so closely tied to one of their own: Pete.

What if Jane had sent the texts and then left town to save herself, believing the texts would be enough to send the wedding into a tailspin? She might be miles away by now knowing that everyone was scrambling into a defensive position. She must have a life established somewhere else to return to. She could then play this game with Sadie all over again sometime in the future. The very idea of having to deal with this level of stress and frustration again made Sadie groan out loud. The Garrison police department had been searching for Jane for hours—maybe she was too far away to be found.

Sadie wiped away some of the condensation that had built up on the mirror and looked at her reflection as though consulting all the versions of herself before making a decision on what to do. She thought of the other cases she'd been involved in—cases about someone else and their troubles. She had taken countless risks to solve those mysteries; she'd been determined and smart, and she'd helped to find resolutions. Now, it was *her* trouble she was dealing with, and she was hiding in a hotel room. It felt so counterintuitive for her to hide while everyone *else* tried to fix this. Meanwhile, what about the wedding? With everyone so intent on finding Jane, would Sadie and Pete choose to postpone the wedding? Was Sadie willing to give Jane that much power?

"I am not," she said to her reflection and felt buoyed by the proclamation. Her thoughts shifted just enough to feel strong again. Did a few text messages truly warrant the amount of attention they'd all given to the situation? Was Jane's taunting worth all of this? Jane had once told Sadie that she knew how people thought; she'd nearly bested Sadie before by anticipating how Sadie would react to a given situation. But Sadie had outsmarted her, and then, through her healing from the psychological toll Jane and Sadie's other cases had taken on her, Sadie had become stronger than ever. More assured. More capable. So why was she running scared now?

The deeper Sadie reflected, the more invigorated she felt by the reminders of what she had done in the past. Jane had thought she had the upper hand before and she'd been wrong. She'd made mistakes that had proved her undoing; like Pete said, Jane *hadn't* been smarter than everyone else. The Sadie who Jane had attacked at Jamaica Pond in Boston was not the same Sadie that Jane had taunted last night. This Sadie would not give up her wedding so easily. She would not hide. Resolved and relieved to have an empowered direction, Sadie wrapped a towel around her still-wet hair before leaving the bathroom.

"Shawn," she said as she gathered moisturizer, hair products, and makeup from her suitcase. She hadn't brought everything she used on a typical day, just enough to make herself presentable.

"Huh-hmm," Shawn mumbled from the other bed.

"It's time to get up."

He rolled onto his back. "Wh-what?"

"It's almost six but we need to get going."

"G-go where? What?" He sat up, bracing himself with his elbows while blinking toward her in the semidarkness.

"We're going home," Sadie said. She'd found everything she needed to finish getting ready. "I've got so much to do today—getting ready for the barbeque tonight, packing for my honeymoon, double-checking everything to make sure every T has been crossed."

"Wait, did they find Jane, then?"

"Not yet," Sadie said with a flutter of anxiety in her stomach. "But nothing is going to happen as long as I'm hiding in a hotel room. And I'm not giving up my wedding so easily."

Chapter 5

Sadie's idea was easier to come up with than to actually put into action. Pete had driven her and Shawn to the Carmichael last night, so after they were packed up and ready to go, she asked for a ride home from the officer posted outside her hotel room door. The officer called his superior, Detective Malloy, whom Sadie had met on her first ever murder investigation involving her neighbor four years ago. Sadie and Malloy had never really seen eye-to-eye, and the officer posted at the hotel ended up driving them to the police station so that they could "discuss it" in person. Pete was called, and Sadie and Shawn both tried not to act or feel like children sent to the principal's office.

An hour after first explaining her reasoning to Malloy, she was explaining herself to Pete—the person whose opinion mattered the very most—and hoping he would back her up. He sat in one of the chairs in Malloy's office with his arms folded over his chest and that blank detective expression on his face while she explained why reacting with such defensiveness may very well be working against them and why it would be best for her to go back to her normal routine.

"All she did was send some text messages, and if what she

wanted was to make everyone scramble, she's certainly achieved her goal. If she's still around, I want her to see that she isn't pulling my strings. And if she does get close enough, we can throw her in jail, and I won't have to worry about her coming back. If she's already left town, then I don't want my wedding affected more than it already has been." She opened her mouth to say more, but Pete's expression never changed, and she realized she would only be repeating herself. She closed her mouth and kept her chin up.

Shawn had been amused by everyone arguing with her in the beginning, but she could feel his tension as they waited for Pete to respond. Pete wasn't a police detective anymore—he'd retired two months ago—but the Garrison police department listened to him more than they would ever listen to a retired schoolteacher who had muddied up more than one of their cases. Never mind that she was also the reason those cases had been solved. She was a wild card for them, someone who followed her gut rather than their guidelines.

Because of his relationship with the officers working this case, including Detective Malloy whom Pete had worked with for years, Pete's response carried weight unparalleled to anything else Sadie had on her side. As the seconds ticked by, she felt her chest tightening. He knew more about police procedure and criminal mindsets than she ever would, but he didn't like the way Sadie tended to put herself in dangerous situations, which meant he might side with Malloy's more cautious approach. She could appreciate Pete's protective feelings toward her—he loved her and wanted her to safe; how could she not appreciate such things?—but she hoped, hoped, hoped that he wouldn't let that part of his nature get in the way of what she believed to be the best course of action.

"Jane held you at knifepoint, Sadie, and she assaulted Mrs.

Wapple and her sister. She is not a benign criminal, and we don't know anything about her actual history."

"Except that she's never been arrested. If she had, her fingerprints would be in the database."

"Not every crime justifies fingerprinting," Malloy cut in.

Sadie ignored him and kept her eyes on Pete. "Violent crimes do and there was no match to her prints. That means something."

"It means that she's never been *caught* in a violent crime," Pete said. "It doesn't tell us anything about what she may have done or what she may be capable of doing now."

"Didn't the profile you developed suggest that she *wasn't* out to kill me?"

When Sadie had been in Hawaii—recovering, sort of, from Jane's attack in Boston—Pete had sought the help of a retired FBI friend to come up with a criminal profile of Jane. There had been several key points that suggested Jane's manipulations and scare tactics were not motivated by a desire to kill Sadie. She could have killed her that night in Boston and didn't. She could have killed Mrs. Wapple or her sister, but she didn't cause any permanent damage to them either.

When Sadie had first heard the supposition that Jane's intentions weren't fatal, it had brought her little comfort as her imagination had built Jane into a veritable demon with supernatural abilities. Sadie had come a long way since then, though, and relied on the comfort that profile provided them now.

"The profile did suggest that," Pete confirmed. "But it was a limited report due to the limited amount of information they had to consider. You know that."

Malloy cleared his throat, and she reluctantly shifted her gaze to his round face. He wore plain clothes now that he'd been promoted from patrol officer to detective, and she decided she preferred him in a uniform. It gave him an air of distinction that his too-tight collar and rumpled jacket did not. He'd put on some weight since she'd first met him and didn't carry it well.

"We've only been looking for this woman for twelve hours," Malloy said. "And having *you* involving yourself in this investigation will be an extra complication."

Sadie bristled at his tone. She knew what he meant: another citizen in a similar situation could be trusted to go home and be still. Sadie would not be still. She would react to anything that happened and wouldn't necessarily consult with the police for permission before she moved. She sat up a bit straighter and was preparing an argument, when Shawn stood up. His large presence in the small room felt even larger due to the fact that everyone else was sitting.

"Well, I'm going home," he said, turning toward the door.

"What?" Malloy said a split second before Sadie could say it herself.

Shawn faced Malloy, though he glanced at Pete long enough to see that he had everyone's attention. "My mom's house isn't a crime scene, no crime has even been committed other than the stolen cell phone, and that bed at the hotel sucks." He turned to Sadie. "Are you coming with me, Mom?"

Everyone was silent for a moment, then Malloy straightened in his chair. "This investigation is all about keeping your mother safe. To return home when we have expressly asked that she stay out of the way and allow us to do our job compromises her safety and—"

"Look," Shawn said with forced calmness, zeroing his attention on Malloy. "We both appreciate what you're doing, but I think you're forgetting that my mom isn't some Sunday school teacher who doesn't understand what's what. In the last four years, she has put over a dozen people in jail, found missing persons, discovered frauds, uncovered conspiracies, solved several murders, saved lives, and managed to break a few noses in the process. To not consider any of those things is . . . dumb, and with this threat targeting her, I think she has the right to be heard in regard to how she'd like to handle things. That she's talking to you at all is merely because, at her core, my mother is a well-mannered woman. She doesn't *need* your help—heck, she's not even asking for your help—she's simply asking that you support her instincts, which have proven to be right time and time again."

Sadie blinked back tears of pride and gratitude as his words reverberated in the silence of the room. She had no idea he felt this way about the things she'd done these last years, especially since it was only six weeks ago that her skills were put to use poking around in his business, which he hadn't liked very much. That he was proud of her and saw her as strong and capable was an enormous boost of confidence.

When no one spoke following Shawn's monologue, he turned to her. "Are you coming with me, then?"

Sadie glanced at Pete, who had yet to react, and felt her stomach tighten. She didn't want to discount what Shawn had said—especially since she completely agreed with him—but neither did she want to be at odds with Pete. Not now; not on this. Pete held her eyes but gave no indication of his feelings. Frustrating, but she couldn't base her actions on his. She stood side-by-side with Shawn, though she didn't even reach his shoulder.

"We *would* like your help," Sadie said to Malloy. She let her eyes flicker to Pete, disappointed that he maintained his blank expression. "And I'll be careful, but I will not be held hostage like this. I don't know what Jane's intentions are or if she's still here, but I won't hide anymore. I don't feel like I can defend myself if I take a position of fear, and if Jane really is back—if she means to take this as far as she did in Boston—I need to be able to defend myself."

Another silence. Finally, Pete gave the slightest nod, filling Sadie with relief and confidence, though she didn't know why he couldn't have given her such a signal earlier.

"And I'm willing to help her do what she needs to do," Shawn added.

There was another silence until Malloy spoke up. "I agree that your mother has done some impressive things," he said to Shawn, as though Sadie weren't there at all. "But she has also crossed more than one line and created more than one complication in past investigations. She is not a member of law enforcement; she is not trained on how to proceed in situations such as this. I will reiterate that in order for us to *properly* investigate—"

"Yeah," Shawn cut in with a nod, then looked at Sadie as though Malloy hadn't spoken at all. "So, I'm gonna go. You comin'?"

Sadie looked at Pete and worked hard to contain her relief when he stood and faced Malloy. "We don't need to work against each other on this," Pete said. "I'll keep you informed of what we might come across."

"You're going to support this," Malloy said. Sadie couldn't decide if he sounded more disappointed or surprised.

"I haven't worked with many officers who have a success rate like Sadie's, and I can't argue with her wanting to take a less defensive tack. All we have are some text messages, and there was nothing discovered last night to give us additional leads to follow up on. There has been no blatant threat, and if this situation can be defused without aggressive interaction, we should explore that possibility. We're supposed to get married tomorrow, and with Sadie's willingness, I'd like to continue toward that goal."

Sadie worked hard to keep her expression neutral in the wake of Pete's words.

After a few seconds, Malloy made a disgusted noise and shook his head. "Fine," he said, putting up his hands as though in surrender. "Do it your way." He shooed them toward the door, and they all turned except for Sadie.

"I, uh, need my phone back," she said. She'd checked her purse in at the front desk that morning—standard procedure—but the police had taken her phone last night and she needed to make sure she didn't leave without it. Jane had the number; maybe she would contact her again.

Malloy glared at her as he got up from his desk and left the room without comment. Pete, Sadie, and Shawn met him in the hall a minute later where he handed Sadie her phone—completely dead.

"Thank you," she said. Malloy said nothing, went back into his office, and closed the door with a snap.

Pete reached for his car keys and looked between Sadie and Shawn. "I'll drive," he said. "And while we drive, I'll go over the controls we'll put in place to keep you safe. Deal?"

Sadie stopped trying to hold back her grin. Boy, did she love this man. His support, especially in the wake of Malloy's *lack* of support, meant so much to her. She held his eyes and nodded quickly. "Deal."

Chapter 6

The drive wasn't long enough to adequately cover Pete's suggested "controls" so he continued even after they'd arrived at Sadie's house, unlocked the front door, and disabled the alarm that started beeping as soon as the door was opened.

Sadie plugged her cell phone into the charger she kept in the kitchen and set about throwing out the rice pudding that had sat out all night—mourning every bit of it.

When that was done, she went to work on the things she'd planned to do today, starting with breakfast. She'd promised Shawn yesterday that she'd make her mother's cheese blintzes this morning, and she was glad to be able to fulfill that promise.

"So, will you agree to those stipulations?" Pete asked as Sadie dropped the first spoonful of lumpy batter on the preheated griddle.

"No," Sadie said casually. She actually hadn't listened that closely after the first few minutes because it had become apparent that Pete was being ridiculous. She sensed he knew it, too, since each stipulation had been accompanied by a long explanation of why it was important. Too much justification usually signaled a lack of confidence. "If I can't go anywhere or do anything then I may as well have stayed at the hotel."

Shawn spoke without looking up from texting on his phone. "Except there was no way to make ugly cheesy pancakes at the hotel." He had called cheese blintzes "ugly cheesy pancakes" since he was little; an apt description.

Sadie gave him a withering look, which he didn't see because he was still focused on his phone. She focused on shaping the batter into an imperfect circle with the back of the ladle. "I came home to get some work done, Pete, and to live my life; not to be a prisoner in my house."

"But we can't compromise your safety, and I can't be here every minute."

"Jane isn't going to take me out with some sniper shot from the bushes," Sadie said. "But I *will* agree to have someone with me everywhere I go, and I *will* tell you if anything strange happens—so long as I can get ahold of you."

Pete frowned. "You're really going to go about the day as though nothing is different?"

"Yes," Sadie said with a nod, giving him a strong look she hoped would further convince him she was not going to be passive about this. "If Jane is still here and bent on making trouble, she'll contact me again. If she's gone, then she's gone."

"And if she wants to hurt you?" Pete asked.

"Honestly?" Sadie said in an attempt to prepare him for the truth she knew he didn't want to hear. "If that's her intent I can't hide long enough or go far enough away to stop her—not forever. I didn't stop hiding because I felt safe, Pete, I stopped hiding because I would prefer an encounter rather than living in fear of one. If she's come back to exact some kind of revenge, I want it to be the very last time I ever have to deal with her."

He held her eyes for a minute. "You understand why that's hard for me to support, right? If something happened to you, Sadie. If she hurt you or worse . . . I can't imagine how I would live with that."

Sadie flipped the blintzes, feeling the weight of Pete's words. "I know that, but you understand what I'm saying."

Pete made a grunting, growling sound, something he did when he was frustrated. It also meant he *did* understand what she was saying. He knew what it had cost Sadie to hide—not just physically, but emotionally too. He'd seen how the paranoia and anxiety had taken their toll and knew how frightening it was for Sadie to consider a return to that shell of herself.

Pete didn't answer, Shawn continued texting, and Sadie removed the first batch of blintzes to a plate before putting the next set on the griddle.

"Are we still going to have the barbeque?" Pete asked as she finished making the fourth imperfect circle. "Are we going to invite everyone over here despite the fact that Jane might not have left town?"

Sadie moved a little slower shaping the last pancake and frowned, considering Pete's point. Continuing on as though nothing had happened wasn't only about her. It might put other people at risk. She'd felt that sense of responsibility when she told Breanna to stay in Minneapolis, but her thoughts hadn't expanded to include the rest of their families.

"I hate to cancel it," she said. Pete's family had a special meal they used to make whenever they went camping: Frikadeles with Ruskumsnuz. It was Swedish and was basically fried meatloaf topped with creamed peas and potatoes. Pete's kids had offered to make it for the family dinner that would be held in Sadie's backyard. Plus it was an opportunity for their families to get to know each other better before the formalities of the actual wedding day. Sadie let out a breath as she considered both options—cancelling the dinner and disappointing so many people, or the possibility of Jane using the event to do something to the people Sadie and Pete cared for the very most. It was one thing to argue Jane's prints not matching those of a violent criminal when Sadie felt it was only herself she put at risk with such optimism.

Pete interrupted her thoughts before she'd drawn a conclusion. "It's only 9:30 in the morning. We have several hours before we need to make a decision one way or another, but it's something we should keep in mind. Maybe we just let things sit as they are for now and hope we find Jane before then."

"I agree," Shawn said, putting down his phone as though he'd been an active participant in the discussion all along. "Besides, if we're going to act as though nothing has changed, we can't cancel something as big as the family dinner. Plus, that meatloaf stuff sounds good." He pushed out from the table and stepped behind Sadie to get more plates out of the cupboard.

"Wait and see" wasn't the best solution, but it was a temporary resolution Sadie was willing to agree with.

"By the way," Shawn said as he put the plates down, "I told Maggie to take her original flight to Denver. Bre and Liam will already be there and the three of them can hang together until we give them the green light to come up." Shawn put two of the blintzes on his plate and sat down at the kitchen table where Sadie had set out a variety of topping choices. Shawn went with the ranch dressing and diced ham.

"So, for right now the plan is that we're going to go about the day and hope Jane has either left town or that she'll make herself known when she sees us acting as though nothing has happened?" Pete asked.

"Yes," Sadie said, though she felt she'd been abundantly clear about that at the police station. "I have so much to do today."

"Like what?" Pete asked as she took his plate to the table. "What can we help you with?" He poured salsa on his blintzes; for not having eaten them before, he was a pretty quick study.

"I need to decide how to handle those guests who haven't RSVP'd yet, double-check the favors to make sure I have enough, and get the backyard set up for dinner." She flipped the blintzes and continued through her list. "I also need to call everyone involved in the wedding to make sure we're on the same page, and then I need to clear out some space for you in the bathroom and pre-pack for—"

"Pre-pack?" Pete cut in, looking up at her, pausing with his fork partway to his mouth.

Shawn cleared his throat. "It's what obsessive-compulsive people do a few days before they go anywhere," he said authoritatively. "They put everything they're going to take into their suitcases to make sure it fits, then take out most of it since they still have to use it again before they *actually* pack. Neurotic, but you'll get used to it. My mom's president of the association of pre-packers."

Sadie glared playfully at her son, and he smiled back. She finished the batch she was working on before using a rubber spatula to scrape the remaining batter out of the bowl for the last two blintzes—the ones she would eat with jam. She preferred the salty-sweet flavors though she liked them with ranch dressing too. "I also need to make a batch of my lemon-almond shortbread and—"

"You're baking stuff?" Shawn cut in. He was between bites, which Sadie appreciated as she had a low tolerance for bad table manners. "I thought you weren't doing a reception. You're having a catered lunch instead, right?"

"Yes, but I wanted to make something for the family barbeque tonight."

"Aren't Pete's kids in charge of that?"

"Well, yes," Sadie said, feeling defensive. "But I wanted to contribute."

Both Shawn and Pete continued to stare at her. "It's the day before your wedding, Jane's out to get you, and you're going to spend it cooking?" Shawn said.

"I'm going to spend it taking care of all these little details that need to be taken care of. My shortbreads are one of those details; it's my part of this wonderful family dinner that Pete's kids are working so hard on." She gave Shawn a pointed look. "When you get married, you can choose to do it however you please." She immediately pointed her spatula at Pete before he could say anything. "Don't say a word. You love my shortbreads—that's why I'm making this particular recipe."

Pete closed his mouth and smiled before looking back at his plate. "Indeed I do love your shortbreads," he said wisely.

Sadie gave Shawn a triumphant look and was turning her blintzes over when Shawn's phone rang with the theme song from *Hawaii Five-0.* He put the bite on his fork into his mouth, then scowled at the phone when he picked it up, chewing quickly.

"What?" Sadie asked, instantly on guard. "Who is it?"

Shawn shrugged and swallowed simultaneously. "Don't know the number," he said before pushing the button and putting the phone to his ear.

"Hello," he said while Sadie and Pete exchanged a look. The number Jane had used last night had been an unknown number—could this be her?

"Yeah, this is Shawn Hoffmiller. . . . Yes . . . yes . . . what?"

The alarm in his voice didn't make Sadie feel any better and when he pushed back from the table and stood, Sadie was downright worried. There was still half a blintz on his plate.

"Yeah, I can log in right now," Shawn said, turning toward the computer desk where Sadie's newest laptop was set up. She'd been through a few the last couple of years.

"What is it?" Sadie asked, quickly removing the blintzes from the griddle and following him. "What's going on?"

He ignored her even though she was right behind him. "It'll take me a minute," Shawn said into the phone. He sat in the desk chair, and Sadie hovered behind him.

"Shawn," Sadie said, tapping him on the shoulder, nearly ready to burst with all the questions she had. "What's going on?"

He moved the phone away from his mouth. "There's something wrong with my bank account," he said in clipped words. "Fraud department."

"That's terrible." Sadie patted him on the shoulder and relayed the news to Pete. What lousy timing. Whatever they'd flagged on his account, it probably had to do with his travel and making charges so far away from his usual locations. That the call wasn't Jane-related made her feel much better.

She returned to the kitchen and set about preparing her blintzes.

She'd defrosted her last pint of peach freezer jam two days ago in anticipation of this very meal, and she made quick work of spreading the perfect amount on her breakfast. She brought her plate to the table and sat down across from Pete, while casting a sympathetic look toward Shawn at the desk.

"What do *you* have going on today?" she asked Pete.

"I have a final load of things from the house to put in your garage," Pete said, cutting another bite. "Brooke's husband is coming over with his truck so he and Jared can help with that. Jared and his family should be here around noon. After we get that settled, I'd told my kids I'd take all of them to the Happy Hut for lunch."

Sadie raised her eyebrows at the mention of the arcade-slash-pizza parlor in town. Pete hated that kind of thing. "The grandkids will love it," she commented, realizing that because he hadn't invited her to go it was likely his last hurrah as a single grandpa with his family. It made her feel a little left out, but she understood it all the same. Since their conflicts in San Francisco over the increasing reality of their marriage, she had given Pete a wide berth in regard to what he and his family needed to do to be at peace with all the upcoming changes. Besides, she had too much to do to make time for poor quality pizza anyway.

"I didn't make any of those authorizations," Shawn said loudly. Sadie could only see him from behind, but he was obviously upset. "No, I didn't give my PIN number to anyone. I'm not an idiot."

Authorizations? As in, more than one? A sense of dread formed in her stomach. This call from the fraud department wasn't about some charge made at a fast-food place in a state where he didn't usually buy his hamburgers. She and Pete shared a look, and she knew he was thinking the same thing.

She got up from the table and went to stand behind Shawn again, looking over his shoulder at the computer. The entire screen—top to bottom—was full of transactions categorized as cash withdrawals. She scanned the column of numbers and let out a breath as she saw $400 repeated over and over again all the way down the page.

"Yeah, I'm near a branch I can go to," Shawn said a few moments later, his voice calmer but forcibly so. "I'll go in right now and fill out the paperwork. . . . Sorry for losing my cool. . . . Right. . . . Thanks for understanding. Okay. Bye." He put the phone down next to the computer before scrolling down the screen, showing more and more transactions.

"Sixteen withdrawals for $400 each," Shawn said. "All made between eleven thirty last night and one o'clock this morning at half a dozen different ATMs in Garrison."

"Oh my gosh," Sadie said. She hesitated to express her fears out loud, not wanting them to be true, but she knew Shawn had to be thinking the same thing. "Do you think it's Jane?" Twenty-four hours ago the thought wouldn't have crossed Sadie's mind, now it felt like the only explanation.

"How could she have my PIN number?" Shawn shook his head as he scrolled back to the top. "Whoever it was drained my entire account and overdraft. The bank didn't freeze it in time."

"How is that possible?" Sadie asked. "Aren't there automatic controls?"

"Yes, but the daily limits reset at midnight, and the lady in the fraud department told me that actual physical withdrawals aren't flagged as readily as online transactions are, since that's where the vast majority of fraud happens." He scrolled back up to his account balance—$12.34—and groaned. "I'm supposed to move across country and make my flight arrangements for Anchorage and I'm completely broke."

"We'll get it figured out," Sadie said. "I mean, aren't there fraud protections on the account?"

"Yeah," Shawn said, but didn't sound relieved. He stood up. "But I have to fill out some paperwork verifying that I didn't make the withdrawals myself and then I have to file a police report because of the amount taken and then it's thirty days before they'll be able to settle anything. The amount taken mandates a complete investigation." He shook his head and clenched his jaw. "I can't believe this."

"I'll call the department and have an officer meet you at the bank so you can file the report simultaneously," Pete said, joining the conversation. "The bank probably needs to have the police report before they can initiate their internal investigation."

"That'd be helpful." Shawn picked up his phone and faced Sadie. "You're okay without me for a while? I don't know how long this will take."

"We're okay," Sadie said. "Do you want me to come with you?"

"No, I'm fine," Shawn said, letting out a breath. "How could Jane do this? How did she get access like this? I used my card yesterday and everything was fine. She couldn't have gotten a replacement card and PIN, could she? I've heard of that happening before but wouldn't that deactivate *my* card?"

"I don't know," Sadie said with a shake of her head. She really wished she did, though. "I'm sure the bank can look into that, right?"

Shawn nodded. "I'll let you know how it goes. Can I borrow your car?"

"Of course." Sadie gave him the keys and a quick hug, then

watched him leave before turning to Pete. "She is such a mean person," she said, renewed anger at the situation.

"It might not be her," Pete said diplomatically. Sadie gave him a withering look, and he shrugged as though to say he was just doing his job by suggesting possible alternatives.

No longer hungry, Sadie gathered the dishes from the table. She rinsed them in the sink before she put them in the dishwasher.

"So, I guess we know she didn't leave town after stealing the phone or sending the text messages last night," Pete said.

Sadie nodded. Jane would have had to have stayed in town at least until 1:00 this morning. And she had more than six thousand dollars of Shawn's hard-earned money in her pocket now. "The ATMs might have cameras, right? How many ATMs are there in Garrison?"

"Twenty-five or so," Pete said.

Sadie frowned. "That many?"

"At least. And they don't all have cameras, but I would guess most of them do."

"People might have seen her at one of them."

Pete nodded. "They're all in public places."

Sadie turned to face him, her hands on the counter behind her. "You know the woman whose phone was stolen, right?"

"I know her name and address, but I'm not the one who interviewed her." He pulled his phone from his pocket. "I better get Malloy in on this."

"I want to talk to the woman who owned the phone," Sadie said, ignoring his comment. "I want to know if she saw anything. She had the first opportunity to have seen Jane. Then maybe we can find other people who might have seen something too—"

"The police already interviewed her," Pete reminded her. "And that makes her part of *their* investigation."

Sadie waved that away. "I'm not going to mess anything up for them. I just want to know when she last had her phone. Maybe she saw Jane and doesn't know it. If we can get even basic impressions or possibilities, it will be easier to match with whatever comes of the ATM part of this investigation."

Pete leaned against the counter opposite her and folded his arms over his chest, phone still in hand. "I don't want to be stepping on Malloy's toes any more than we already have by going after his contacts, especially when I'm asking for his help with Shawn's situation."

"It's not stepping on his toes if he's done talking to her," Sadie clarified.

Her phone rang from where she'd plugged it in on the kitchen counter. She let Pete ponder her comment while she unplugged her phone from the charger. The call was from Rachel's Bakery—Rachel was doing the wedding cake.

"This is Sadie," she said when she put the phone to her ear. Pete looked at her expectantly, but she waved him away and shook her head to indicate that this wasn't a phone call that would be of any interest to him. Likely Rachel just had a question about the cake. She was very efficient and it didn't surprise Sadie in the least that she'd called before Sadie had a chance to check in with her. Pete started typing a text message—probably to Malloy. Sadie frowned and turned away from him. They did not see eye to eye on Malloy.

"Hi, Sadie. It's Rachel."

"Hi, Rachel. How are you?"

"I'm fine," Rachel said, her voice a little tight. "But I wanted to confirm the change with the cake before I adjust the schedule for my day."

"Change with the cake? What do you mean?"

"I just got off the phone with Julie, your niece." Sadie's hand tightened on the phone. She didn't have a niece named Julie. "She said you wanted to pick up the cake today instead of having me deliver it tomorrow. I'm calling to verify that so it's all official. According to the contract you signed, you'll remember that I usually require those kinds of changes to be made in person but if it's really necessary I'll do my best."

Annie's Savory Cheese Blintzes

1 cup flour
½ teaspoon salt
⅛ teaspoon fresh cracked pepper
1 cup grated cheddar cheese
2 tablespoons butter, melted
1 cup sour cream
1 cup cottage cheese
1 tablespoon sugar
4 eggs, well beaten

Heat griddle to medium-low (245 degrees F. on an electric griddle). In a large bowl, mix the first four ingredients together with a fork until combined. Add the remaining ingredients; use the fork to mix well. Batter will be lumpy.

Drop ¼ cup batter on hot griddle, using the back of a spoon or ladle to spread it out like a lumpy crepe. Cook 4 to 5 minutes on one side—watch for top to dry out—flip, and cook 3 to 4 minutes on the other side until the center is cooked through.

Note: You can cook blintzes in a preheated waffle iron. Use ¼ cup batter per well-greased square. Re-grease waffle iron between each batch to keep batter from sticking. Cook 5 to 6 minutes before removing blintzes from waffle iron.

Makes 10 blintzes.

Serve with savory or sweet garnishes, including:

Parmesan cheese
Salsa
Fresh tomatoes
Fresh basil, chopped
Balsamic vinegar
Olive oil

Salt and pepper
Salsa
Ranch dressing
Ham
Bacon
Syrup
Jam
Fresh fruit
Fruit pie filling
Whipping cream

Chapter 7

When did you speak to her?" Sadie asked as heat filled her chest and head. Jane wasn't wasting any time this morning. Pete must have heard the tightness in Sadie's voice since he looked up at her.

"Just a minute ago," Rachel said. "I have to completely restructure my day in order to get your cake ready for pickup this afternoon."

"Do you have the number she called you from on your caller ID?" Sadie asked.

Pete lifted his phone, his thumbs poised to type in the number.

"Yeah, but . . ." Rachel said, sounding confused. "Didn't you ask her to make the change?"

"No," Sadie said simply. How much should she explain to Rachel? "Could I get the number she called from?"

"Right now?" Rachel's confusion was increasing.

"If you don't mind."

"Is everything okay?"

Sadie hesitated. She wanted to explain things to Rachel since Jane had involved her, but it wasn't a situation that could be addressed in a quick explanation. "Would it be okay if I came over and talked to you in person?" Sadie said, looking at Pete as he nodded his approval. Like her, he always preferred a face-to-face meeting when possible. "I'll explain to you what's going on, and then maybe you could tell me more about the conversation you had with this woman."

"Your niece?"

"Um, it wasn't my niece," Sadie said.

"Oh. Well, yes, it's fine for you to come down," Rachel said, sounding equal part curious and concerned. Sadie would plan out what to tell Rachel during the drive over; there was always a question regarding how much to tell the innocent bystanders involved in a situation through no fault of their own.

"Can I get that number first, though?"

Rachel gave her the number, and Sadie relayed it to Pete, who put the phone to his ear as soon as she finished. Was he calling the number? It wasn't the same one from last night; Sadie recognized that much. Pete hadn't wanted Sadie to interview the owner of the stolen phone since the police had already talked to her. Would he be okay with them preempting the police about this second number? Assuming it was stolen like the first one had been. Sadie told Rachel she'd be at the bakery in about ten minutes, and then finished the call about the same time Pete ended his.

"It went to voice mail for somebody named Brian." He was already dialing another number on his phone. "I'm going to have Malloy track it."

"Won't that make it part of *his* investigation?" Sadie didn't want to give up anything they didn't have to.

"I can talk to him on our way to the bakery," he said, stepping around her question. He headed for the door and put the phone to his ear, leaving Sadie no choice but to follow him. She grabbed her own phone and put her lists into her purse in case she needed them before she came home. Maybe she could make some of the calls on her list while they were out and about. If she was going to complete everything on her to-do list she would need to be efficient.

For the first part of the drive, Pete talked with the officer who was running the search, then asked the officer to call him when he had the information as well as to send someone over to Shawn's bank to write up the police report about that situation. He hung up and put his phone in the middle console.

"They'll call me back," he said unnecessarily, then glanced at Sadie. "What exactly did she try to do? Pick up the cake?"

"I didn't get into the specifics with Rachel over the phone. Jane had to know that Rachel would verify the change, though, right? Was she doing this to make sure I knew she was still around?" Did that mean Jane had anticipated Sadie's suspicion that Jane might have left town or was this part of her plan all along? She hated thinking Jane knew her well enough to guess her thoughts correctly but took an odd comfort in the fact that Jane was still in Garrison. It meant she could be caught, and they could put all of this to an end.

"Maybe either option would have worked," Pete said thoughtfully. "If Rachel *hadn't* alerted you to the change, Jane could have interfered with the cake delivery. Since Rachel *did* alert you, you're following up on it instead of working on the other things you needed to do today. Either way she causes trouble."

"And the day's just started," Sadie said.

They passed the bank where Shawn was currently trying to

mitigate the problems with his account—Sadie's car was parked near the front door—and she felt another surge of frustration. Shawn was applying for jobs on the West Coast, moving across the country, and planning a trip to Alaska to save his birth mother's life. Having problems with his account could cause all kinds of trouble for him, even if Sadie loaned him the money until the bank got things worked out.

Knowing that Jane had orchestrated something so cunning was disturbing. It had to have been planned out in advance, which meant that Jane being here was premeditated and focused. The headache that had first bothered Sadie when she woke up made a strong comeback, and she lifted a hand to her forehead, wishing she'd thought to take some Tylenol when she was at the house. Maybe she had some in her purse.

Pete reached over and squeezed Sadie's free hand as though he sensed the increasing heaviness of her spiraling thoughts. Sadie appreciated that he knew her well enough to both read her thoughts and know how to comfort her. They shared a smile of shared purpose and hope. "We could very well have her tracked down in time for lunch," he said.

"Wouldn't that be wonderful?" Sadie said, allowing herself to enjoy that possibility while pulling her purse onto her lap in search of the Tylenol. Past experience made it difficult to be so hopeful, and yet this was her wedding day—or, well, tomorrow was her wedding day—and weddings were all about hope and futures and happiness.

Oh please, oh please, oh please, she prayed silently as they drove toward the downtown section of Garrison where Rachel's Bakery had been for more than a decade. She found some Tylenol—thank goodness—but had to swallow it without water, which was not her preference. She leaned back against the seat and took a breath. *Please let all of this be wrapped up by lunchtime.*

Chapter 8

The officer Pete had been working with at the station called back as they pulled up to the curb in front of the bakery, so Pete stayed in the car. The bell above the door announced Sadie's arrival, and by the time she reached the glass case full of delectable goodies, her stress levels were telling her to have one of each. She thought of the cookies she'd planned to make at home—would she really have time to bake? And if they didn't find Jane in the next few hours, would she need them at all?

There was a full tray of Rachel's sugar cookies with pale pink frosting in the case, which Sadie knew from experience were delicious. Maybe she should buy them instead of making her lemon-almond shortbread recipe but that would defeat the purpose of having *made* something for the barbeque.

Rachel entered from the back of the bakery, her dark hair piled on her head and covered in a barely noticeable hairnet. She wore her signature white shirt and pants with a pink apron bearing a calligraphy *R* on the front—her logo. "Hi, Sadie," she said, resting her forearms on the top of the glass case. "I got to thinking about something after we talked. Are you *tracing* that number I gave you?"

"The police are," Sadie said.

Rachel's eyebrows went up reminding Sadie that most people didn't trace calls on a regular basis. Sadie gave Rachel the condensed version of the situation, which caused Rachel's eyes to grow even wider. Most people didn't deal with stalkers much either.

"What can you tell me about the caller?" Sadie asked, segueing rather smoothly, she thought, into why she was here.

Rachel nodded, ready to do her part now that she knew what they were dealing with. "It was a woman—like I told you—but with a deep voice."

Sadie remembered Jane's masculine demeanor and smoking habit that could be heard in her voice. "And what exactly did she say?"

"Well," Rachel said, looking thoughtful, "she said she was your niece, Julie, and helping you with some of the final details. I didn't think too much about it, people double-check on things all the time, even though you seem a bit more hands-on once I thought about it." She offered an apologetic smile, and Sadie waved it off, encouraging Rachel to continue. "She asked how the cake was coming, and I told her that things were going well; the basket weave was done, and I was waiting for it to set before I added the flowers." She paused to smile. "It really did turn out beautifully. Want to see it?"

"I'd love to," Sadie said, distracted by the offer. Rachel moved to the side of the counter and lifted a latch that allowed her to pull open a hip-high door, allowing Sadie to pass through.

"What else did she say?" Sadie asked as she followed Rachel toward the swinging doors that separated the two halves of the shop. Sadie was reminded of Blackburn Bakery in Santa Fe, New Mexico, and was excited to see the back of Rachel's Bakery too. She loved behind-the-scene views of places like this; it made her feel like she'd gotten a backstage pass.

"She said she'd be picking up the cake for you and asked when it would be ready. I told her it would be ready this afternoon. I always try to finish my cakes a day in advance." Rachel gave a self-deprecating shrug as she pushed open the door and ushered Sadie through. "But wedding cakes aren't something you can just store in the fridge next to your leftover sausage gravy, ya know? So I asked her why the change since I was planning to deliver it tomorrow, and she said you were storing it at North Hampton overnight and she wanted to pick it up for you at three. That was downright weird since you rented North Hampton for tomorrow, not today. Besides, why would they let you bring the cake early? Why would you pick it up instead of having me deliver it? Do you have any idea how many cakes get ruined in transport? Plus, the Iversons—do you know the Iversons over on Powell?"

"Ruby and Kent?" Sadie scanned the baking area for her cake but didn't see it. Instead she saw pans of unfrosted éclairs and half a dozen cakes about four inches in diameter and eight inches tall—Rachel's famous Triple Chocolate Stack Cake. They were baked but had not yet been drizzled with Rachel's equally delicious ganache. It was a recipe Rachel wouldn't share—Sadie didn't blame her for that—but Sadie had come up with a version on her own that was pretty darn close, even though it relied on a mix, which she was certain Rachel's recipe did not. "Ruby was the assistant librarian for years, wasn't she? And isn't Kent a carpenter?"

"That's them," Rachel said, smiling at the shared acquaintance. "They're having their fiftieth wedding anniversary dinner at North Hampton tonight." She pointed to the chocolate cakes, which must be why Rachel knew the details of a family event. "And I knew they wouldn't appreciate having the fridge full of your cake—no offense."

"None taken," Sadie said, prying her attention away from the fascinating ovens and racks around her to remain focused on Rachel and this conversation. "I understand completely."

"So, anyway, it just sounded weird that you wanted someone else to pick up the cake so that you could store it there. When I put your niece—or this Jane woman, I guess—on the spot, she was a little too insistent about picking it up. I've had enough orders unravel due to people trying to 'help' a friend that I don't take chances anymore."

"Thank goodness for that," Sadie said, following Rachel as she walked toward the far side of the kitchen.

"I told her I'd need to talk to you about the change." She led Sadie around a wheeled cooling rack, and Sadie stopped when she saw the cake. It was two tiers, fourteen inches wide on the bottom and eight inches on the top, with a perfect basket-weave detail around the sides of both tiers in Rachel's famous pearly white frosting.

Sadie took a step closer. "It's gorgeous," she said, walking around the table where the cake sat. It still needed the border of flowers along the top edge of the layers, and, as Rachel had said, it was missing the frosting daisies in a variety of shades of white and cream that would take the place of the cake topper, but it was as beautiful as Sadie had imagined it would be. Sadie had always loved a good basket weave.

"I'm so glad you're happy with it." Rachel grinned with the kind of pride Sadie recognized from the times she'd been the creator behind something exquisite. After a few more seconds of pure admiration, Sadie's brain cycled back to why she was at the bakery in the first place.

"What did Jane say when you said you'd need to talk to me?" Sadie asked, looking away from the cake to Rachel.

"She hung up and I called you."

"I'm so glad you did."

"I can't believe any woman would be so horrible as to try to mess up another woman's wedding. Even for a stalker that's pretty low."

The bell from the front sounded. Rachel headed that way, and Sadie followed, casting one last look toward the fabulous cake. For an instant she could see it on the small table she'd requested on the northeast side of North Hampton reception hall with her and Pete holding a knife together as they cut the first piece.

Pete was waiting at the counter when they emerged through the swinging door. Sadie smiled at him and went through the half door to join him on the other side of the counter. "So?" she asked. "Did they trace the number?"

"The phone belonged to another person here in Garrison—Brian McCollum."

Sadie was surprised to know the name. "I know Brian. He's a friend of Breanna's from high school. They didn't date or anything, just hung out sometimes. It was *his* phone?" Did it mean anything that she knew the owner of the phone or was it just a coincidence? Sadie knew a lot of people in town.

"He works over at Pep Boys and said we could come over. He had his phone when he got to work this morning."

"I'm so glad he'll talk to us," Sadie said, excited by the chance to get more information and glad that Pete didn't seem to be deferring to Malloy and his team on this. She smiled at Rachel. "Thank you so much for your help."

"Oh, I didn't do anything but stick to my policy. You still want the cake delivered to North Hampton at noon tomorrow?"

"Yes," Sadie said with a nod. "Nicole said she would be there to receive it. I'll stay close to my phone today. If the caller should try to contact you again, please let me know."

"Of course," Rachel said, nodding quickly.

"Thanks for all your help."

"You're welcome."

They said good-bye again, and Pete held the door for Sadie as they exited the shop. "I can't believe I left without buying anything," she said once they were on the sidewalk, not sure if she were proud or disappointed in herself for such restraint. "I'm certain it's the first time I've left without being at least twenty dollars poorer. Rachel's an amazing baker."

"I do love her cheesecake," Pete said as he opened Sadie's door for her.

"Is it better than my cheesecake?"

Pete made an exaggerated look of pained hesitation.

"Never mind," Sadie said, putting up her hand dramatically as she sat in the passenger seat. "I don't think I can handle the rejection right now."

Pete chuckled and was closing the car door when he tensed, staring over the top of the car. Sadie immediately turned to see whatever had captured his attention.

Across the street, in front of the UPS store stood a golden-skinned woman dressed in a pale blue sundress with white sandals that sparkled in the morning sun. Her blonde braid hung over one shoulder. At first glance, Sadie didn't see anything that would warrant Pete's tension other than the fact that the woman was staring at them, but in the next moment she took in the woman's height, the thin figure, and sharp detail of the portion of her face showing around the large sunglasses. Sadie's heart skipped a beat.

It was *Jane*—looking very different from the gothic-punk styled Jane Sadie knew. *That* Jane always dressed in jeans and dark colors. She had spiked dark hair and wore bright lipstick and nail polish. This woman wasn't anything like that, but of course she wouldn't be. Jane was playing a game, and she would need to look as different from the real Jane as possible. But she couldn't change her height, and a spray tan and wig couldn't hide the angular lines of her body. A rush of heat and anger took Sadie off guard. "Jane," she hissed.

The woman lifted her hand, giving Sadie a little finger wave, patronizing and calm with a self-assurance that made Sadie want to scream.

Sadie got out of the car and slammed the passenger door shut, narrowing her eyes as she hurried around the front of the car. She stopped to look both ways for a break in traffic. Main Street was the busiest road in town, but she needed to get across it.

Jane turned to her left and started down the sidewalk. She held a small white purse—like a little girl's—by the handles and swung it back and forth as she casually walked away.

"Jane!" Sadie yelled. Jane didn't respond. There wasn't enough of a gap in traffic for Sadie to cross Main Street safely, but she stepped into the road anyway, holding her hands over her head to make sure the cars could see her in time to stop.

"Sadie!" Pete called from behind her, but she didn't stop.

Jane looked over her shoulder and then began walking faster.

There wasn't much foot traffic so early in the morning, and she was making a quick getaway.

The screech of brakes caused Sadie to run the last few steps to the turning lane. Pete yelled her name again, but Sadie was intent on crossing the remaining two lanes of traffic.

Jane disappeared around the corner of a breezeway that went between two buildings on the east side.

"Jane, stop!" Sadie screamed in frustration and ran across the next two lanes of traffic as soon as there was a big enough gap in traffic for her to do so. She was determined to catch up with her and confront her face to face. She'd yank that braid right off her head!

"You promised!" Pete yelled when Sadie stepped up on the curb where Jane had been standing a minute earlier. Sadie looked back across the street where Pete still stood beside his car. Why hadn't he followed her? He'd said she promised—what did that mean? A split second later, though, she remembered. She'd promised not to go anywhere alone. So why hadn't he followed?

"She's getting away," Sadie called back. The door to the bakery opened behind Pete, and Rachel ran onto the sidewalk, her eyes wide as she called Sadie's name and waved her over. Pete turned toward Rachel, and Sadie watched them talk. Rachel was obliviously distressed.

Sadie looked toward the breezeway where Jane had disappeared and battled whether or not to pursue her. She had promised Pete she wouldn't, and the alleyway that Jane had entered was only semi-public. What if Jane ambushed her?

She looked back at Pete who stepped into the street with his hands out, but not in pursuit of her, rather just to stop traffic. When he saw Sadie watching him, he motioned her toward him. She dropped her shoulders and gave him a pleading look, but he pointed to Rachel who had her hands covering her mouth. Something was definitely wrong.

After casting one more glance toward the alley, Sadie looked both ways, confirmed that all the cars were stopped for her, and hurried back across the street, mouthing thank yous to the drivers who looked back at her with varying degrees of annoyance. One of the drivers was a friend from an old book group Sadie had been a part of, and Sadie waved at her. Samantha waved back but looked confused.

Pete fell in beside Sadie when she reached him, and he put a hand on her elbow as though to keep her from running again. They stepped up to the curb together.

"I could have caught up with her," Sadie said.

"And then what?" Pete asked, looking at her. They stopped in front of Rachel and Sadie turned her attention to her friend.

"What happened?" Sadie asked her, noticing tears in Rachel's eyes.

Rachel shook her head as though she were in shock or something.

"What is it?" Sadie asked a second time, putting a hand on Rachel's arm. She was really upset.

"I'm so sorry," Rachel choked out after lowering her hands. "I don't know how it happened, how it could have . . ."

Triple Chocolate Cake

1 chocolate cake mix, any kind
1 (3.4-ounce) package instant chocolate pudding
1 cup sour cream
¾ cup vegetable oil
¾ cup water
1 (12-ounce) bag semisweet chocolate chips
4 eggs

Preheat oven to 325 degrees F.

Put all ingredients in a mixing bowl and mix for nine minutes. Pour into a very well-greased Bundt cake pan. Bake 1 hour. Let cool in pan for 1 hour before removing. Store in refrigerator.

Though this cake does not require frosting—it is very sweet and very rich—it can be dusted with powdered sugar or drizzled with ganache for presentation purposes.

Note: This recipe adapts well to two standard loaf pans or six mini-loaf pans.

Makes 12 to 18 servings, depending on pan used.

CHAPTER 9

What happened?" Sadie asked even as she feared that whatever had Rachel so upset must be about the cake. Had Rachel accidently knocked it off the table? The idea made Sadie sick to her stomach, more for Rachel's anguish than her own though.

"Your cake," Rachel said, her voice breaking. She looked from Sadie to Pete, and when Sadie glanced at him, she knew whatever had happened was more than an accident.

Rachel opened the door to the bakery. Pete put a hand at Sadie's back, and they hurried straight through to the back kitchen. They rounded the table of éclairs and then the wheeled cooling rack. Sadie skidded to a stop, and she let out a squeak of surprise when she saw the cake.

The beautiful white frosting was splattered with what looked like blood.

"It's food coloring," Rachel said, waving toward a bottle next to the cake. The deep red liquid—almost black—pooled around a large chef's knife plunged into the top of the cake where the flowers should be and dripped from the unfinished edges of the tiers, creating rivulets of color through the basket weave.

The horror of what it looked like—a bloody wedding cake—moved aside for the *actual* horror of her cake being ruined. Then even *that* moved aside as the exact fear she knew Jane had hoped this display would cause settled in around her. Was Jane sending a message about how far she would go to get her revenge against Sadie's rejection? Or was this just about creating a horrific image?

"I can make another one," Rachel said quickly. "I can't do this exact design—I wouldn't have time for the layers to age enough to hold the weave—but I have some layers of, um, a white cake, and I think there is some chocolate hazelnut in the freezer. I always keep a few extra things on hand. But it's not the yellow cake you'd ordered and not the exact sizes. I just—I can't believe anyone would do this. I'm so sorry."

"This isn't your fault," Sadie said, shocked, but not wanting to make Rachel feel any worse than she already did. Jane had been here. Minutes ago, maybe even when Sadie and Rachel had been in the back. And then what? She'd turned the cake into a monstrosity and run outside to wait across the street so Sadie would see her?

"I'm going to call Malloy," Pete said. He turned to Rachel. "You and Sadie go to the front. I'll wait here until the police come to secure the scene."

"The scene?" Rachel asked, wiping at her eyes. "Like, a crime scene?"

"I'm so sorry you got pulled into this," Sadie said, putting a hand on Rachel's arm and guiding her to the front, continuing her apologies and assuring her that everything would be okay. Rachel was in shock, to the point where Sadie wasn't sure she was even listening. Sadie led Rachel to a stool behind the counter and got her a bottle of water from the cooler.

A customer came in, and Rachel stood quickly as though she didn't know why the woman would be coming inside the shop. Or maybe she thought it was Jane.

Sadie stepped forward and acted the part of employee, boxing up a dozen sugar cookies and helping the woman choose a cake for her mother-in-law's birthday brunch. Sadie recommended the lemon poppy seed Bundt cake; it was her favorite snack cake, and Rachel's recipe was divine. She'd given the recipe to Sadie a few years ago after Sadie complimented it for the fiftieth time, it seemed.

Rachel seemed to recover in time to ring up the woman's purchases, which was a good thing since Sadie didn't know how to run the cash register. After the door closed behind the woman, Sadie pulled Rachel into a hug that was stiffer than Rachel deserved only because Sadie couldn't hide her tension completely. She pulled back with her hands on Rachel's shoulders and smiled.

"I'm so glad I got to see the cake before Jane ruined it. She can never destroy my memory of how fabulous it looked."

Rachel shook her head as though still unable to comprehend what had happened. "I can make you another one."

Sadie was touched by the offer—made for the second time—but hesitated to accept it as she pictured the cake again and shuddered. She remembered the scene of Mrs. Wapple's house when she'd gone in and found the red paint that looked like blood all over the floor. This was so similar. Too similar. Mrs. Wapple had been unconscious when Sadie found her. What if Jane had hurt Rachel like she'd hurt Mrs. Wapple?

She didn't, a voice said in her head.

But what if she had?

Were the people around her in danger because of Jane's

vendetta? If Jane was the one who'd withdrawn Shawn's money—and it was hard to imagine any other explanation—then she'd already started targeting people close to Sadie. What would she do next? Where would things go from here? The confidence Sadie had felt about going about her day as though nothing had happened was feeling pitted and weak. Had she been wrong about this? And yet, wasn't she drawing Jane out just as she said she wanted to?

The bell above the door jingled, and Detective Malloy came in. He wasn't nearly as good with his bland detective face as Pete was, which was why Sadie could see his satisfaction at being needed. It made her angry to think he would be anything but concerned about what had happened.

"Back here," Pete said from where he held the swinging door open.

Malloy nodded and headed in Pete's direction. After Malloy passed into the back of the shop, Pete looked at Rachel. "Did you have the back door propped open this morning like it is now?"

Rachel nodded, instantly sheepish. "It gets so hot when the ovens are going."

Pete smiled, likely to help assuage her regret. "I just wanted to make sure. We'll only be a little while longer."

While Malloy and Pete were in the back, Sadie and Rachel helped three more customers, and with each transaction, Rachel seemed to come back to herself a little more. One of the customers picked up a cheesecake, and Sadie shared Pete's compliments of it, which, after the customer left, led to a comparison between Sadie's recipe and Rachel's. Rachel's recipe didn't use cornstarch but that seemed to be the biggest distinction, which led to a discussion about what, exactly, cornstarch would do in cheesecake. The more they talked about baked goods, the more Rachel perked up. When Malloy and Pete were finished, Malloy took turns talking to Rachel and Sadie and then summarized his findings for all three of them.

Malloy suspected Jane had come in through the back door, found the food coloring, which wasn't difficult to locate, and used it and the knife to ruin the cake. Officially it was trespassing and destruction of property, but there was no proof Jane did it, just strong supposition. Malloy said he'd talk to the owners of the shops that shared the alleyway with Rachel's Bakery to see if anyone saw anything out of the ordinary. Then he told Rachel to crack a window instead of the door in the future.

A photographer was on his way to take photos of the cake and the door—Rachel was to steer clear of the back until that was finished—after which time the police would dispose of the cake, and Rachel could get back to business as usual.

Sadie felt it was hardly a comprehensive investigation, but she kept her thoughts to herself since she didn't want to complicate the situation. Plus Rachel seemed more relaxed with the police presence.

Malloy and Pete went outside to wait for the photographer while Sadie said good-bye to Rachel, who restated her offer to make another cake.

Sadie hesitated again, realizing that her knee-jerk reaction to what Jane had done was to call everything off: the wedding, the cake, everything. But she didn't trust herself to be thinking rationally right now. "If you can make something else by tomorrow, that would be wonderful, but if you don't have time—"

"I can make something else," Rachel assured her. She sounded relieved to have the chance to make things up to Sadie even though the cake disaster wasn't her fault.

"Don't let it interfere with any other orders," Sadie said. "And I'll pay for both cakes."

Sadie gave Rachel one more hug and was heading outside when she had an idea. She popped back in and discussed the possibility of a wedding cheesecake. Rachel loved the idea—she'd done them before, she said—and it would be easier to put together by tomorrow than a traditional frosted cake.

They discussed crusts and presentation for a few minutes, finally settling on a twelve-inch base, an eight-inch middle layer, and a four-inch top layer. A champagne-colored topping for each cake would add a hint of color, and the same flowers intended for Sadie's original cake would still be the topper, tinted to match the off-white color of the cheesecake layers.

Since Pete loved Rachel's cheesecake, he'd love the surprise, and this cake would be different enough from the one Jane had destroyed that they wouldn't be reminded of the first cake so much. Rachel promised that she could cook the tiers today while she worked on her other orders and have it ready by noon tomorrow. When Sadie finally left, Rachel was focused and positive.

Malloy cut off whatever he'd been saying to Pete when Sadie stepped onto the sidewalk in front of the bakery. They were either talking about something Malloy didn't want her to overhear, or they were talking about Sadie herself. Either way, she didn't want to talk to Malloy anyway. She passed them, heading for Pete's car still parked at the curb. She planned to get in the car and wait for Pete to finish, but he ended his conversation by telling Malloy he'd check in with him later.

Sadie scanned the other side of the street to make sure Jane hadn't come back. Pete used the key fob to unlock the doors, and she slipped into the passenger seat. What would have happened if she'd caught up with Jane in the breezeway? Would she have been able to take Jane down? Could this be over now? Or had Jane planned an attack Sadie couldn't counter?

She remembered what she'd told Pete that morning about coming out of hiding because she'd prefer an encounter over not having a life. Was she willing to put other people at risk so she didn't have to hide?

"You okay?" Pete said after he started the car. He checked the street for a break in traffic and pulled away from the curb.

"I don't want to do this anymore," Sadie said as Pete fell into line with the other cars on Main Street.

"Go to Pep Boys?"

Sadie shook her head. "No, I don't want to do any of this. I should have stayed at the hotel like Malloy wanted." She felt emotion rising and blinked back tears of surrender.

"Do you think that would have changed anything?"

Jane had already hacked Shawn's accounts by then and must have already had a plan in place for the cake. Being in the hotel wouldn't have changed those things, but Sadie felt foolish regarding her earlier certainty that she could handle whatever Jane had in mind. The burden of feeling responsible for other people sat heavy on her shoulders, in her chest, and in her head. Sadie wiped at her eyes discreetly as the frustration and regret she felt transformed into tears. Like crying would help anything right now.

Pete noticed her emotion and put on his blinker, pulling over to the side of the road and parking. He reached across the seats to smooth her hair behind her ear. She leaned into his touch automatically, eager for comfort even though she hated that she needed it so much.

"This isn't your fault," he said in a soft voice. It didn't surprise her that he knew why she was upset.

"There were only a few minutes between when Rachel and I left the back room and when Rachel discovered what Jane had done. She was probably right there when Rachel and I went into the back. She likely listened to every word and then destroyed the cake as soon as we left. Hours and hours of work. What if she'd hurt Rachel instead? What if Rachel had gone into the back alone while Jane was there?" Sadie let out a breath and stared through the windshield. "She's here because of me—we all know that. If I weren't here, Rachel wouldn't have had to face that today." Sadie didn't want to sound as though she were finding reasons to make other people's hardship—Shawn's and Rachel's—all about her, but she felt so accountable.

"You are not responsible for what's happening here," Pete said, scooting as close to her as possible across the seats and putting his hand on her arm. "This is *Jane.* It's always been Jane."

"But she's here to prove something to *me,* and people are getting caught in the cross fire. That cake . . . was so awful."

"And dramatic," Pete pointed out. "It was actually pretty silly—juvenile even. She wants you to feel scared, and she *hasn't* hurt anyone. More than that, you feeling responsible interferes with your ability to hold *her* accountable. Don't let her do that to you."

It made sense when he said it that way, but she still felt bad about everything.

"What we need to do," Pete said, "is find her. Anything that gets in our way of doing that works in her favor."

Like having an emotional breakdown on the side of the road? Sadie thought. She felt a pinch of resentment toward Pete for not letting her take a time out, but it lasted only a moment because he was absolutely right. Every person had only so much energy to expend at any given time. If Sadie focused her energy and attention on fear and regret and embarrassment, she would have less to funnel into finding Jane.

A common bit of wisdom she heard over and over as a child at church came to mind about how happy the devil was when God's children were sad. Sadie remembered being a young girl and taking that very seriously; when she was happy and doing the right things, the devil—the ultimate bad guy—was mad. When she was mean or unfair, the devil was happy. Sadie had no doubt that Jane would love knowing how overwhelmed Sadie felt right now. Just like little-girl Sadie not wanting to make the devil happy, grown-up Sadie did not want to expend energy that played into Jane's sense of satisfaction.

"You're right," Sadie said. "But how do we catch up with her? Everything she's done is so calculated."

"She'll make a mistake," Pete said with a shrug of forced casualness. "She probably already has. We just have to find it and take full advantage of it. She isn't smarter than all of us, Sadie. She isn't."

Sadie wasn't so sure, but Pete's point hit home. It had never been Sadie's idea to play this game of cat and mouse, it was Jane's. They had to find a way to outsmart her and turn things around.

"How do I protect the people I love in the meantime, Pete?"

"Find her as quickly as we can—whatever it takes."

Sadie was silent as she thought about that. What could they do that wasn't chasing her? "We need to get ahead of her somehow," she said, her eyebrows pulled together as she considered their options. "Do something she doesn't expect that puts her on the defensive."

"I agree," Pete said. "I just haven't figured out what that is yet."

Sadie started to shake her head to indicate that she hadn't figured it out either, then stopped as an idea presented itself. She met Pete's eyes. "She's been around town—last night to get that phone and then the ATMs as well. So she must be staying in Garrison, right?"

"Possibly," Pete said. "She could be staying out of town and coming in as needed. Though there aren't that many options within less than an hour's drive of Garrison."

"Could Malloy do a search of the hotels?" She frowned as soon as she said it. "But she wouldn't sign in under the name of Jane Seeley."

"No, but she would have to interact with desk clerks and staff," Pete said, looking thoughtful. "The more people we ask about her—even if they haven't seen her—the more people will be on the lookout. Garrison isn't a big town. She can't hide completely. Checking the hotels in Fort Collins and Sterling wouldn't be difficult to do either."

Sadie pondered a moment, her brain moving past hotel clerks to a larger group of people. "Our chances of finding her increase exponentially with every person in town who knows we're looking for her. What do you think about putting something on Facebook? Put the whole town on alert to look out for her?"

Pete nodded. "I've seen it done with missing persons cases several times, and it's had great results."

"Except, we don't have a picture of her," Sadie said, feeling her excitement dwindle. It had been one of their biggest hurdles in trying to determine Jane's true identity: no photos.

Pete was quiet for a few seconds, then looked at her quickly.

"What if we did a composite drawing instead? The art teacher at the high school, Ray Meyers, has done a few for us over the years when we couldn't get the guy from Denver up here. He's good and he's fast."

"A drawing?"

Pete nodded. "Not as good as a photo, and useless in regard to the facial-recognition software we've wanted a photo for in the past, but it's an image all the same. It could be spread around the Internet just like a photo could."

"It could work," Sadie said, feeling hopeful. "And a composite drawing gives the impression she's a criminal."

"Right," Pete said. "You and I know what Jane looks like; maybe we could do one drawing from our memory of her in Boston and another drawing of what she looked like this morning. We can include information about the cell phone thefts, breaking into the bakery, and that she hacked Shawn's accounts. I think people could really jump on board with it. We could canvass the city."

The plan was growing by the moment in Sadie's mind, then hit a red light. "Are we doing this with Malloy or on our own?"

Pete paused long enough that Sadie realized he wasn't entirely comfortable with his answer. "This is something we'd do on our own. Malloy won't love it, but if it works, he'll have a hard time arguing."

Repentance instead of permission; Sadie could be on board with that.

"We could also contact some media outlets," she said. She knew from experience how powerful they could be if they decided to help. "Maybe the editor I worked with at *The Denver Post* would be interested in doing a follow-up on the situation. They were all over what happened in Boston." Sadie hadn't loved that story—she hated having her personal life filleted and served to the masses—but it was worth the discomfort if it brought resolution. A media blitz was aggressive and uncomfortable, but it would make it hard for Jane to remain hidden in a small town like Garrison. "I can't think of a better way to get ahead of her," Sadie said after letting the plan build itself into a solid possibility.

"And she'll never expect it," Pete said, his eyes twinkling. He sat back in his seat and pulled out his phone. "I'll call Meyers and see if he can make time for the composite. In the meantime, are you still up to talking to Brian at Pep Boys? I'd like to do that before we work on the sketch."

Sadie nodded. They'd found a way to be in control of something, which restored her confidence in the planned interviews with the employees at Pep Boys—specifically Brian since Jane had stolen his phone.

There was no time to wallow in her regrets or fear; she couldn't risk expending that much energy. Pete had said Jane would make a mistake, that she may have done so already. The trick was to widen the scope of people who might know what the mistake was and to be ready to exploit that error as soon as they found it. In order to make that happen, they had to be at the top of their game from here on out.

Sadie's Yummy Cheesecake

Crust

1½ cups graham cracker crumbs
⅓ cup white sugar
⅓ cup brown sugar
½ cup butter, softened

Filling

4 (8-ounce) packages of cream cheese, room temperature
¾ cup whipping cream*, room temperature
1⅔ cups white sugar
1½ teaspoon vanilla
2 large eggs, room temperature
⅓ cup cornstarch

Preheat oven to 325 degrees F.

Set out the ingredients for the filling to allow them to come to room temperature.

Grease the bottom of a 9- or 10-inch spring form pan and wrap the bottom of the pan in tinfoil, which will protect the crust from the water bath later on.

Crust: In a large bowl, mix graham cracker crumbs and sugars. Add butter. Mix to a consistency like thick Play-Doh.

Press the crust mixture evenly into bottom of pan only (traditionally cheesecake does not have crust on the sides).

Bake for five minutes, or until the crumb mixture looks shiny. DO NOT OVERCOOK! Remove from oven, let cool a few minutes, and gently re-press crust.

Set crust aside to cool while you make the filling.

Filling: In a large bowl, mix the cream cheese and whipping cream until smooth. Add remaining ingredients and mix until the batter is smooth and creamy. Pour filling over crust until about one inch from the top of the pan. The cake will rise when cooking. Place cake pan in a water bath. (Use a jelly roll pan filled with about a half-inch of water. This helps to cook the cake evenly.)

Cook 1 to 1½ hours. Cheesecake is done when the top is golden brown and firm in center.

Let cool for 30 minutes, then refrigerate at least 3 hours; the longer the better. Serve plain or with your favorite toppings (nuts, cherries, apples, etc.).

Serves 16.

*Can substitute ½ cup half-and-half for whipping cream.

Note: Do not be tempted by Neufchâtel, light, or fat-free varieties. Outcome cannot be guaranteed if anything other than original cream cheese is used.

Chapter 10

Ray Meyers taught art at the high school during the school year and painted sets for the Fine Arts Center during the summer. That's where he was when Pete called: putting the finishing touches on the Billis Laundry set for the end-of-summer production of *South Pacific*.

Pete explained the situation and offered Ray two hundred dollars if he'd do the sketch this morning. Ray told them to come to the art center any time before 3:00, although he'd be going home for lunch around 1:00. While Pete talked to Ray, Sadie texted Shawn to check on how things were going at the bank. Shawn called her back just as Pete pulled into the Pep Boys parking lot.

"Go on in," Sadie said as she lifted the phone. "I'll join you as soon as I'm done talking to Shawn."

Pete nodded, then got out of the car.

"Hi," Sadie said into the phone. "How are things going?"

"Ugh," Shawn said with a growl. "What a disaster."

"What's happening?"

Shawn was eager to relay the details. "Apparently she used my account access card, not my debit card, which doesn't have the same protections. I'm going to have to go through my files when I get back to Michigan to verify it's not there."

"You think she stole the card from your apartment?"

"That's the only thing I can think of. I haven't seen that card for years, but I know I had it in that file box you gave me when I went away for school. The paper they mailed me with the PIN number is in the file too so she must have gotten into my apartment. With three roommates who can't remember to lock the door, it's not hard to imagine her being able to pull it off. Unreal."

"I'm so sorry," Sadie said. "I can't believe she planned so many details."

"Yeah, she knew exactly what she was doing," Shawn said, disgusted. "The bank ran a credit check and found a credit card with a balance of almost two thousand dollars. I need to file a fraud report with them, too. As it is, the bank manager froze my credit for now. I guess I need to contact some consumer protection group for help with long-term alerts and things in case she's filed for additional credit cards that haven't shown up in my file yet. Some people have things coming in for up to a year. Good thing I have so much time on my hands and I'm not in a point of transition in my life where stuff like this might interfere." He ended with a sarcastic snort.

"I'm so sorry, Shawn. I don't know what to say."

He was more inclined to talk than seek solace and continued, "The upside is I reacted fast and I have a solid history with both the bank and the credit bureaus, which will work in my favor. Also I've never had a credit card, which speaks to the fact that I wouldn't have applied for one now. It's a royal pain to have to deal with this, but it's going to work out. Some people have spent years trying to get their credit fixed and a criminal record erased after an identity theft. The bank manager and the police officer keep telling me how lucky I am so I'm going with that. How are things with you guys?"

Sadie told him about the bakery, then reprimanded him when he swore in response. After he apologized, she told him where she was right then—the Pep Boys parking lot—and why.

"I remember Brian," Shawn said. "Weird that Jane stole *his* phone."

"I know. But maybe it's not that surprising I know someone she targeted—I've lived here a long time—but it makes me feel twice as bad about it. I hope he has insurance on his phone."

"Hang on a minute," he said. His voice was muted for a few seconds, then he came back on the line. "I need to go sign some stuff, but I'll call you when I'm done. Oh, and tell Pete thanks for calling someone to come over. It saved us a lot of time to do the police report at the same time we filed the fraud."

"I'll let him know," Sadie said. "Good luck with everything. I'm so sorry this happened."

"Yeah, me too, but I'm more motivated than ever to nail Jane to the wall!"

Sadie ended the call and only then remembered she hadn't told Shawn about the Facebook idea. *It can wait*, she decided. She stepped out of the car, scanning the area in order to take in what was close by as she wasn't particularly familiar with this section of town—a block east of Main Street with retailers that she didn't frequent.

There was a Family Dollar store across the street and a thrift store next door with a building available for lease on the other side of Pep Boys. None of these businesses would have been open before ten, which cut down on the potential people who could have seen Jane coming or going. Hopefully the Pep Boys employees would remember a tan, blonde woman in a sundress since that likely wasn't their typical customer.

Sadie was a few steps away from the entrance when Pete came out, bringing her up short. She could tell from his expression that he'd learned something.

"They prop the back door open too," Pete said to her, waving her around the side of the building. They walked down a narrow strip of grass toward the back where a different parking lot opened up. There were four cars parked—employees, Sadie guessed. Pete led her to the back door where, sure enough, a wooden wedge held the door open a few inches.

"It locks automatically when it closes, but two of the guys working today smoke and so when their manager isn't here—like today—they prop the door open to make it easier to come in and out on their breaks. Brian thinks he put his cell phone on the desk in the office after he texted with his wife earlier this morning—"

"She's eight months pregnant with their first baby," Sadie cut in. "A boy. They're so excited. I ran into her at the library last week."

"Right," Pete said. "Anyway, the office is just inside the back door." He pulled the door open, waved to a young man Sadie didn't know, and then led her inside. Just ten feet inside was a doorway to a small office with a window that looked out into the back of the store, which was more of a warehouse, with twelve-foot metal shelves filled with boxes and car parts. It smelled like metal and oil and dirt, but Sadie was careful not to wrinkle her nose at it. It was an auto parts store after all.

"Brian has called his phone a dozen times since we informed

him of what happened to it. He's pretty ticked, especially when he found out it was you she's harassing."

They both looked into the office and then toward the back door and then around the warehouse. They'd only seen that one guy since coming in; it wasn't a stretch to imagine Jane slipping in and out without anyone the wiser, but it would still take a fair amount of luck to pull off. Sadie felt the same way toward "luck" as she did toward "coincidence"—they begged to be reconsidered to make sure it wasn't planning and manipulation that really brought them to fruition.

"So she wasn't a customer," Sadie said, realizing that she'd assumed Jane had come to the front of the store.

"No."

"And no one saw her back here?" Sadie questioned even though she knew the answer: a woman in the back of the shop would certainly get someone's attention.

Pete shook his head. "I talked to a couple of the employees, and Brian had already talked to the one who'd been helping a customer when I came in. No one remembers seeing a blonde in a sundress in the front of the shop, and they certainly didn't see her back here. They did say it's been pretty busy this morning and they've spent a lot of time up front."

"We need to include on the Facebook post that people need to lock their doors," Sadie said, looking at the back door Jane used to get inside. "She's obviously picking up phones all over town." The grocery store she'd lifted last night's phone from was a good three miles from here so Jane wasn't limiting her thefts to one part of town.

"I agree," Pete said. He took pictures of the back door and

the office with his phone. Sadie hurried to move out of the way. "Brian's compiling a customer list of who came in this morning so we can follow up with them. It's a time-consuming task to make the calls so I'll see if the department will do the legwork on it. Malloy will be thrilled." He gave Sadie a sarcastic smile, and she hoped they were coming together in their feelings toward Malloy's involvement.

"Hey."

Sadie looked past Pete to see Brian come from the front and head toward them. "I might have something for you. Hi, Mrs. Hoffmiller," he said, then immediately frowned. "I'm sure sorry about all this."

"I'm sorry you got pulled into it," Sadie replied. "Especially with Darcy so close to delivery. I hate that you don't have your phone if she needs you."

"We have a phone here at the shop too so I'm not out of reach."

"You found something?" Pete said.

"Right," Brian said, holding up a sticky note. "We were putting together the customer list and in the process I remembered when I had last texted Darcy—it was right after Anders Greenburg came in for a new feeler gauge." He consulted the paper in his hand. "That happened at 9:32."

"Rachel said the call to her bakery happened at 9:37," Sadie remembered.

"Which means Jane knew exactly what she was going to do with the phone when she took it," Pete added.

"Have the police found the tower the call pinged off of yet?" Sadie asked Pete. She hadn't ever gotten an update on his conversation with the officer who ran the trace.

"The one on Fourth," Pete said, pointing in the general direction. "Not surprising since it's the downtown tower. She could have called from anywhere between here and Rachel's or half a mile past." Rachel's was a few blocks south of Pep Boys. They both looked at Brian as they realized they had taken off on a tangent.

"Sorry," Sadie said sheepishly. "There's a lot going on right now."

"No worries," Brian said with a shrug. "The other thing we figured out was that there was a silver Civic parked on the side of the thrift shop around the same time." He pointed toward the front of the store, indicating where the thrift shop was in relation to Pep Boys. "Milo walks to work since he lives right around the corner, and he saw the car parked on the south side of the building. He thought it was odd since the thrift store doesn't open until ten, and no one, ever, goes in early to that place. The owners literally pull in at 9:59 and unlock the front doors on their way inside. But, well, it's a thrift store." He shrugged as though that explained everything. It obviously did for him. "Plus, the couple who runs it drive a '78 Cougar—all original parts, if you can believe it—and they park out front not around the side like the Civic was. Of course, Milo didn't think about it until all of this happened. He clocked in at 9:25, but he didn't see some lady walking around or anything."

"Does Milo remember any other details about the car?" Pete asked.

"Wyoming plates," Brian said. "He's guessing it was probably a '05 or '06—he's not sure. Silver metallic paint rather than flat silver, factory wheels, dark gray interior. The bottom corner of the driver's side door had a dent so the edge wasn't flush with the chassis. That's all he remembers."

Was there anything left to remember? That was an amazing

amount of detail, but then they worked at an automotive store. Picking up on those kinds of details about a car was probably a lot like Sadie identifying the spices in a recipe just by taste.

"No one else saw it?" Pete asked.

Brian shook his head. "Like I said, it was parked along the south side so none of us could see it from the lot or the store."

Pete shook Brian's hand. "This is great information, thank you."

"You bet," Brian said, smiling broadly. He had unfortunate teeth—the only thing that kept him from being a real heartthrob—but he was as nice a man as Sadie had ever met. "I'll have that customer list for you in a few more minutes," Brian added, pointing his thumb over his shoulder. "There's three who weren't in our system—most of our regulars are—but we have the card info for two of them. The other guy paid in cash, but he wasn't here until 9:40."

"Excellent," Pete said. He dug into his pocket and removed his wallet, extracting a business card left over from his years as a detective. "If you'll fax that list to this number," he said, pointing out the detail on the card, "I'll let them know it's on its way."

"And whoever calls will be sure to tell the customers that we're participating in an investigation, right? I don't want them thinking we just give up information willy-nilly."

"Absolutely," Pete reassured him.

Brian turned to Sadie. "I hope we find this lady that's bothering you, Mrs. Hoffmiller. Some people are just nuts."

Sadie agreed completely and yet his comment reminded her of something Pete had told her once—even crazy people have motives, and Sadie still had no idea what Jane's was. Hopefully this new information would give them a leg up on whatever Jane had planned. Sadie was more eager than ever to get the sketch of Jane posted online. Maybe they could make posters to put up around town too. And they had her car information. That had to make a difference.

Pete and Sadie said their good-byes and let themselves out the back door, removing the wedge in the process so that the door closed behind them. Pete immediately pulled out his phone, and before Sadie could ask who he was calling, he'd greeted Detective Malloy and started giving the information he had on the car. He suggested an "APB," which Sadie knew stood for All Points Bulletin and meant the car info would be shared with the entire Garrison police department and perhaps neighboring cities and counties as well. Apparently, Malloy agreed with Pete's suggestion, as there was no argument back and forth. Pete also told Malloy about the soon-to-be-faxed customer list and gave him the suspected time of the theft of Brian's phone.

Once inside the car, Sadie texted Shawn about the Facebook idea and the sketch, hoping he would help her and Pete with the social media since he was far more familiar with it than either of them. She worried he might still be overwhelmed by his financial situation, but he immediately responded with two words: "I'm in!"

His enthusiasm was appreciated. Assuming he was still busy at the bank, she didn't linger over the conversation and instead looked up the number for the *Garrison News Journal* on her phone. By the time Pete turned onto Second Street, Sadie was gushing thank yous to the editor who had been more than happy to put a notice on their website. The weekly paper for Garrison had already gone out that morning, but Lori said she'd post something online as soon as Sadie got her a copy of the sketch and they could finalize the text. She also offered to call the editor at *The Denver Post* to see if they could run something in tomorrow's paper. Sadie thanked her profusely for her generous help.

Sadie finished the call, thinking for a few moments. Jane knew the bakery Sadie was using for her cake and had entered from the back. She'd also snuck into Pep Boys, which had a back entrance hidden from the main parking lot. Such familiarity, and yet based on what Sadie knew of Jane, she had only been to Garrison one other time. How could she know the town so well in twenty-four hours?

"I think Jane's been in Garrison for a while," she said.

Pete turned into the Fine Arts Center parking lot. "What makes you think that?"

"She knows so much about the town. No way she arrived yesterday and coincidentally chose all the right places to get phones from. I remember Malloy saying that the grocery store didn't have cameras, right? Did Pep Boys?"

"Not in the back," Pete said.

"How would Jane know that?"

Pete parked the car and looked at Sadie. "Maybe when we get this sketch done, we should go back to the employees at Pep Boys and the grocery store. Maybe she *has* been here for a while, staking things out."

"And we can't assume it's a coincidence that she's back in time for the wedding. How does she even know that's happening? How did she know Rachel's Bakery was doing the cake?"

Pete furrowed his eyebrows together. "Those are really good questions." Neither of them had obvious answers, however.

They let themselves out of the car and Pete reached for her hand. He smiled at her when she looked up at him.

"We're on her trail," Pete said. "A few more quick steps and we'll pull ahead."

Sadie smiled and squeezed his hand, optimistic that he was right.

CHAPTER 11

It was almost an hour before they had the sketches right. At one point, when Mr. Meyers stepped out of the room to take a call from his wife, Sadie asked Pete if it always took this long. He assured her that things were moving really fast. Sketches based on verbal descriptions were extremely difficult to put together. Sadie felt better knowing that, but every hour was precious right now, and she'd never been good at waiting. Especially when there was so much to do. She hadn't done anything from her to-do list, and it was already 11:30 when they'd arrived at the Fine Arts Center.

Not surprisingly, Sadie had the best sense of what Jane looked like since she'd spent the most time with her and had reason to be more attentive to detail. Pete was still helpful, though. In the end they had two sketches: one of the old Jane and the other of the new Jane with the long blonde braid and the strappy sundress. Sadie hadn't expected the sketches to look as good as a photograph, but she had hoped for a bit more lifelike detail. She worried Jane wouldn't be as recognizable as they'd hoped when Pete first suggested this idea.

"Have you got a 400 DPI scanner for high-def res?" Mr. Meyer asked as he sprayed the paper with what looked like aerosol hair spray. To set the pencil, he said.

"Wh-what?" Sadie asked, not sure that what he'd said was all in English.

"You need a digital image, right?" he asked, fanning the paper slightly.

"There's a guy at the station who can convert it," Pete said.

Sadie frowned. Anything involving the police department would take ten times longer than it needed to—especially if Detective Malloy were involved. She was certain he would use any excuse to remind her who was in charge. Or at least who he thought *should* be in charge. What if he put the brakes on the Facebook page?

"I need to run home for lunch so I'll just scan it and e-mail it over to you guys. It'll be faster that way." Mr. Meyers got up from the stool he'd occupied while translating their descriptions. "I just need an e-mail address to send it to once it's digital."

Sadie told him her e-mail address, which Mr. Meyers put into his phone while Pete wrote out the check. She'd offered to pay but he'd refused. Sadie was certain that paying for a sketch of someone's stalker was the highest sign of love and devotion. They all shook hands, and she thanked Mr. Meyers again. Pete held the door for her as they left the building.

As soon as they were in the car, Sadie wondered out loud how things were going with Shawn and noted that Breanna's flight would be landing around 1:30. She'd texted her plans while Sadie had been at the bakery. That meant she and Liam would be in Denver in just under an hour and would then wait for Maggie; her plane landed at 3:40. Hopefully Sadie would know by then whether or not it was safe for the three of them to come to Garrison. She hoped the Facebook blitz would change the game.

Pete pulled out of the Fine Arts Center parking lot onto Main Street and headed toward Sadie's neighborhood. "Are you hungry?" he asked once she put the phone in her lap to await Shawn's response.

"I could eat." It had been awhile since those cheese blintzes.

"The Inn has their basil chicken as the special on Wednesdays. How does that sound?"

Basil chicken with a side of stuffing and a baked sweet potato was perhaps the only thing Sadie would agree to sit down and eat right now. But the idea of doing more waiting was borderline repulsive. "Could we get it to go and take it home? I think I'm too anxious to sit in a booth while they make up a plate, but if we call it in, it could be ready by the time we get there."

"Sure," Pete said. "Wanna call?"

Sadie looked up the number, and while she was putting in the order—for three meals in case Shawn would be home in time to eat with them—she heard a buzz indicating an incoming text message. Hopefully it was Shawn with an update. Sadie finished the call and hung up. "It'll be ready in about ten minutes," Sadie said to Pete.

She toggled to her text messages and then tensed when she saw that the new message was from an unknown caller.

> *Unknown:* They gave you back your phone, huh? Is that so you can better draw me out? So predictable. You have no idea what you're up against, Sadie. No idea at all.

Sadie felt her hand tighten and looked around as though expecting to see Jane watching them from the curb.

"What's wrong?" Pete asked when he saw her reaction.

Sadie read him the text message.

"You should block the number," Pete said. "The police can still run it, but then she can't get to you."

"I'm not blocking it. I want to know what she's thinking, and the best way to do that is to keep her talking."

Pete didn't argue, and Sadie stared at the screen of her phone, trying to come up with a response. She didn't want to wait so long that it sounded like she didn't know what to say. She thought of something, typed it out, and then hit send. It had been nearly a minute since Jane's text had come in.

Sadie: Maybe you're the one who doesn't know what she's up against.

Unknown: You wish. What time does Maggie arrive? I'd like to meet my replacement in person.

Heat rose in Sadie's neck and face. *Her replacement?* Jane may have manipulated Shawn into thinking they had a relationship when they didn't. But what Shawn felt for Maggie was nothing—*nothing*—like whatever he may have felt toward Jane. Sadie forced herself to take a calming breath, knowing that reacting in anger wouldn't help things. She took another breath to make sure she was thinking things through clearly.

"What did she say?" Pete asked.

"Just a minute," Sadie responded as she started typing again.

Sadie: What do you want, Jane?

Unknown: You don't know?

Sadie: I used to think you wanted us to be friends, but I was wrong about that. Now I have no idea.

Unknown: I never said I wanted to be friends.

But that had been her motivation in Boston, at least Sadie had thought it was.

Sadie: Maybe the two of us could just talk things out.

Unknown: We're waaaaay past that.

The response annoyed Sadie. She was the one Jane attacked with a chloroform-drenched rag. She was the one who ended up in the trunk of a car. What had she ever done to Jane other than not give her the attention she wanted? Why on earth did that dismissal—as Jane saw it—equate into this?

Sadie: Then what do you want?

Sadie waited for a response the rest of the drive to the Inn but nothing came. Jane wasn't going to tell her what she wanted. Did *Jane* even know? Had she become so wrapped up in this game she was playing that she'd lost sight of her goal? Sadie reminded herself again that she was thinking like a normal person; Jane was not normal.

Daryelle's Sweet Basil Rub for Chicken

2 tablespoons salt
2 teaspoons sugar
½ teaspoon granulated garlic
½ teaspoon granulated onion
½ teaspoon paprika
1 tablespoon lemon juice
1 teaspoon black pepper
2 tablespoons basil
½ cup extra virgin olive oil
1 whole chicken, rinsed, heart and neck removed

Move oven rack to the bottom third of the oven and preheat to 450 degrees F.

In a small bowl, mix salt, sugar, garlic, onion, paprika, and lemon juice. Add pepper, basil, and olive oil. Mix until well blended. Rub all over the outside and inside of chicken. Place chicken in 9x13-inch pan, breast side up. Bake uncovered for approximately 12 minutes per pound. Check doneness by pricking thighs to see if juices run clear.

Note: To use this rub for turkey, double the spices and cook turkey according to baking instructions.

Note: The drippings make excellent gravy.

Basil Chicken Stock

After removing as much meat as desired, put the chicken carcass in a large stockpot. Add a couple ribs of celery, a carrot, and a small onion, if desired. Add water until chicken is covered. Add a teaspoon of garlic salt. Cover pan and boil overnight on low heat.

The next morning, remove pan from heat and allow to cool. Strain out bones and vegetables. Stock can either be refrigerated for use within seven days, frozen (in zip-top bags or Tupperware) for up to two months, or home-bottled in a pressure canner according to processing directions.

Chapter 12

"What did she say?" Pete asked as he pulled into the parking lot of the Inn. It was a squat, brown building that most people assumed was a dive, but the food—prepared by two brothers from back East—was amazing.

"She hasn't responded since I asked her what she wants. Maybe she isn't telling me because she's getting it: our full attention. We're still chasing her."

"But we're on our way to doing a lot more than that," Pete said.

"And I guess we have another number to track," Sadie said out loud. "I'd still like to talk to the gal from the grocery store who had the first phone stolen."

"I'll talk to Malloy," Pete said, but it was obvious he still didn't want to cross into Malloy's investigation. "I'll be right back." He let himself out of the car.

Sadie re-sent her last message to Jane, wanting to keep the dialogue open. By the time Pete returned with two plastic bags of Styrofoam containers, Jane still hadn't responded. Sadie put her phone back into her purse and took the bags Pete handed to her and arranged them by her feet.

"If we give this newest number to the police, can we still be the ones to follow up on it? Like with Brian?"

"I'll ask him about it."

Sadie kept her voice even despite being annoyed by Pete's continued vagueness. He knew she didn't want to involve Malloy but wasn't approaching that topic directly. "If we can't have access to the owner of the phone by going through Malloy, I'd rather try my hand at tracking it down ourselves. Shawn's a whiz at that kind of stuff." Sadie was pretty good too, but she felt like she had too many other things to do.

"I'll talk to Malloy."

Sadie pressed her lips together to keep from saying something she'd regret.

Shawn finally replied to her earlier text and said he'd just gotten to the house. She texted back and forth with him until they pulled into the driveway behind Sadie's car. The smell of the chicken had triggered Sadie's hunger, and she was ready to eat all three meals herself by the time they were heading up the front steps.

"You need to keep the doors locked," Sadie said to her son as she let herself into the house. He was sitting at the computer so his back was to them. "All the time."

"I'd love for Jane to come in while I'm here," Shawn said. "If it wasn't so hot, I'd leave the door wide open as an invitation." He turned in his chair. "Ah, man, that smells great."

Sadie got out plates and flatware—she didn't mind getting takeout but she hated eating from Styrofoam containers—and transferred the meals to plates while Shawn and Pete talked about what happened with Pep Boys and the sketch. While they ate, Shawn told them that the police report had been filed and the bank had assigned his case to a bank fraud investigator based in Seattle. They'd call Shawn later that afternoon. They'd also given him a one thousand dollar line of credit to use until things were resolved. Pete and Sadie agreed it was generous of them in hopes Shawn would see the blessing. His current annoyance at the complication made that hard for him to do, however. Maybe he'd better recognize how fortunate he was when a bit more time had passed, or Jane was in jail.

Lunch was good, but she only ate about half of hers before she pushed the plate toward Shawn and stood up, eager to be moving ahead again.

While Pete and Shawn finished their lunch, Sadie gathered the shortbread ingredients. She was determined to contribute to the dinner she optimistically believed would still happen in her backyard six hours from now. Shortbread was easy to make, and since the dough needed to be chilled before she formed the actual cookies, it could be flexible with her increasingly complicated schedule. Plus, she needed to be busy, and the more she reviewed the morning's events, the more she needed something to do with her hands. Without an outlet, she felt sure her head would explode.

Shawn asked to see Jane's text conversation, and Sadie directed him to her phone, which was in her purse on the living room recliner.

"I still need to get the newest number to Malloy," Pete said once Shawn had the phone in hand and was scrolling through the conversation. Shawn read the number to Pete, who typed it into his phone before leaving the table and heading down the short hallway that led to the back door so that he could make the call to Malloy.

Sadie was beginning to realize that finding Jane through the cell phones wasn't going to happen. She was obviously stealing phones in order to remain undetected, and she was moving through them faster than the police could catch up. She wouldn't risk stealing the phones only to be reckless in how she used them. It felt like another dead end.

"How does she know about Maggie?" Shawn asked when he'd finished reading through the text exchange a second time.

"I don't know," Sadie said, shaking her head and giving him a sympathetic look.

Shawn read the texts again. "Gosh, I hate her."

Usually, Sadie challenged her kids when they said they hated anything—it was such a strong word. She kept her critique to herself though and creamed the butter and sugar together instead. Maybe hate was a gentle word to use after all Jane had put Shawn through. Between the emotional manipulation of him prior to Boston and the current circumstances, he had every right to be angry.

Shawn brought his dishes to the sink. "We need to get this Facebook thing going," he said with determination. "I'm starting to think it's the only way we're going to gain any momentum here."

"I agree," Sadie said, stopping the beaters in order to crack the eggs into the bowl. "Mr. Meyers was going to e-mail me the sketches he made. They might be in my in-box already."

"Sweet." Shawn went back to the computer in the living room. "You changed your e-mail password since the last time I logged in for you, what's the new one?"

Sadie gave him the new password so that he could log in while she mixed the eggs, vanilla, and extracts in the bowl.

"Is the photo there?" she asked after she added the dry ingredients.

"Sure is," Shawn said. He began clicking and moving things

around, and Sadie left him to his work as she continued mixing the dough. When she finished, she put all the dirty dishes in the sink. She scraped the dough onto a piece of plastic wrap, which she wrapped up tightly before putting in the fridge to chill.

"Are you sure you're okay with me taking over this Facebook thing?" Shawn asked.

"Are you kidding? It would take me twice as long and be half as good."

"Okay, I just wanted to make sure," Shawn said, busily tapping away at the computer. Not only would Shawn be better at it, but Sadie was now free to call the other vendors on her "Day Before the Wedding" to-do list.

She picked up her cell phone and started at the top of her list. She skipped Rachel since she already knew where things stood with her and got to work on the other vendors. The caterer, videographer, and reception hall all verified that everything was in place—thank goodness—and they didn't seem to find it strange when she asked that they be sure to communicate only with her.

She left a message for the hairdresser, and another message for the rental company handling the tablecloths, centerpieces, and archway. Sadie was relieved that Jane hadn't interfered with any of these plans and she finished making the calls faster than she'd expected she would. After hanging up the phone, she turned her attention to the dishes.

As was always the case when Sadie began the somewhat rhythmic and relaxing task, she soon found herself deep in thought—mostly about the few different questions that had come up through the course of the morning. Specifically, she thought about Shawn's most recent concern: How did Jane know about Maggie?

Sadie looked out the kitchen window that faced the cul-de-sac and scowled—as she often did—at the black walnut tree that blocked her view of most of the neighborhood. She couldn't see any of her neighbor's homes without leaning over the sink and craning her head around, and even then it wasn't a good view. And yet Jane had known Shawn arrived last night. She had to have seen it, right? Probably when Shawn came home. That meant that somehow she'd known Shawn had taken Sadie's car to the bachelor party. Maybe Jane had seen him leave and come back, but that meant Jane had been watching the house for hours.

Jane knew other things too, though—things that made Sadie feel as if she were being watched in a more specific way. The watched feeling reminded Sadie of the anxiety levels she'd experienced after Boston. Sadie had gone to Hawaii to both hide and recuperate, but even on an island in the Pacific Ocean, she'd felt as though she were under surveillance, like she wasn't safe. Just remembering that time made Sadie shiver. She'd come such a long way since then but she could feel the familiar tingles that had haunted her back then. And Jane *was* here now. She could, literally, be right around any number of corners.

Sadie scanned the street in front of her house, searching for somewhere Jane could position herself that would give her a vantage point into Sadie's house. There was a large picture window in the living room, but it would be difficult to see past the black walnut tree in order to get a good view from almost everywhere except from the empty building lot directly across the street. Until last year it had been full of some trash trees and overgrown shrubbery, but since the owner was actively trying to sell it he'd cleared the lot, leaving it empty.

Pete came into the living room and asked Shawn how things were going. Sadie waited for them to finish their conversation before interrupting.

"How does Jane know so much about what is going on?" she asked, bringing her questions to the forefront.

Pete shrugged. "Like you said earlier, she may have been in town for a while. By the way, Malloy put two officers on the hotel detail. They're contacting everyone from Sterling to Fort Collins and up into Laramie as well. Since Brian said the car had Wyoming plates, they're expanding their search into the southern counties."

"That's great," Sadie said. "Having been in town for awhile might be how she knows so much about the stores and the town and where to steal phones, but how did she know *when* I was picking up my cake? She gave Rachel the right delivery information even though I'd changed it last week. And she knew Shawn came home last night and that Maggie's arriving today. That she knows about Maggie at all is strange."

"She must be watching the house or something," Shawn said with a casual tone.

"But watching the house doesn't explain how she knew about the cake delivery being changed or Maggie's flight. How could she *watch* that?" Pete asked thoughtfully.

"I don't know," Shawn said, distracted. He lifted a hand and waved her over. "But check this out. What do you think?"

Sadie didn't like leaving the topic of discussion but did as he requested, looking over his shoulder in order to read the update he hadn't yet posted on a Facebook page he'd made called "Garrison Stalker"—a little dramatic but catchy.

Sadie read through it. "You should specify cell phones, not just phones. And I think you have a comma splice in the second sentence."

Shawn made the changes, and Sadie read it again, start to finish:

> GARRISON RESIDENTS: Please be on the lookout for this woman. The sketch to the right is how she appeared two years ago; the one on the left is what she looked like this morning in downtown Garrison, but she is known for wearing a variety of disguises. She is harassing Sadie Hoffmiller, a citizen of Garrison, and she is suspected of stealing several cell phones from various residents and hacking financial accounts. There is an APB out for her car: a mid-2000 silver Honda Civic with Wyoming plates. If you've seen her or her car, please contact Shawn Hoffmiller. Please share this status so we can spread the word and put a stop to this public menace!

Beneath the words were the side-by-side sketches of Jane.

"Once I post it here, I'll share it on my wall and tag people like Uncle Jack, Breanna, and a couple other Garrison friends I know will share it as soon as they see it. Tagging them just sends them an extra alert."

"Great idea," Sadie said. "It looks really good."

Pete read it and also gave his approval.

Shawn took a breath and then hit the "Post" button. Immediately, his words and Jane's picture appeared on the top of the Facebook page. They all sat and stared at it as though they could watch it be shared on other walls. He navigated to his personal page. "I still need to fill in some details on the page, then I'll put it on Twitter and Instagram too."

"I need to send the photo to Lori at the *Garrison News Journal.* She was going to send me a quick write-up for me to approve. Can you check and see if she's sent it already?"

Shawn clicked over to Sadie's e-mail folder that was still open. "I don't see anything from her, but do you want me to forward the photo and direct her to the page? That might have information that would help her."

"That would be great. Her e-mail is in my contacts. Lori Hunsaker at the *Garrison News Journal.*"

"When did you tell me about the changed delivery time for the cake?" Pete asked, drawing Sadie's attention back to him. "Was it last Saturday?"

"I think so," Sadie said. It was after she'd had the final fitting of her dress because it was during the fitting that she'd thought it would be better to have the cake delivered at noon rather than 1:00, which would have been only an hour before the ceremony. The fitting had been Saturday morning, and Pete had come over for dinner that night, which was probably when she talked to him about it.

"What else does she know that's surprised us?" Pete asked.

"We still don't know how she learned about the wedding," Sadie said. "She knew I had my phone back, which means she knew the police had taken it in the first place. And she knew we were going to go about our regular routines and draw her out—those are the exact words she used. Didn't you use those words this morning?"

Pete nodded and his expression turned to consternation. He gestured for Sadie to join him in the kitchen. Shawn kept working on the computer. "Well, she might have assumed the police would take your phone since she'd texted you on it, but that doesn't explain how she knew you had it back unless she saw you with it."

"I put my phone in my purse at the station and then plugged it in . . . in the kitchen." She looked at her charge cord. Jane could have seen her plug it in through the kitchen window, but she'd have to have an amazing view—maybe a telescope, maybe in a tree? Sadie shook her head at the ridiculous thought. "With Anne's situation all those years ago, Detective Madsen had cozied up to Jack's daughter in order to learn as much information about him and his family as possible. Could Jane have some kind of mole connected to us who is relaying her information like Trina had unwittingly done?"

"Who other than the two of us knew that the police had your phone?"

"The police." Sadie had never gotten over the lingering distrust Detective Madsen had inspired. Police were people, after all, with motivations and opportunity just like anyone else. They were also far more educated on procedure than the average person, which made getting away with their crimes easier to do.

"Who at the police department knew about Maggie or your delivery plans being changed with the cake?" Pete asked.

Sadie paused, then shook her head. "No one. In fact, no one but you and I knew *all* of that information. Even Shawn didn't know about the cake, and you didn't know what time Shawn came home last night." She frowned. "But *she* knows all those details. How?"

As soon as she said it she looked around her kitchen again, noting that everything she'd just mentioned were things she'd discussed *here*. The cake, the phone, Maggie, Shawn leaving for the bachelor party, his return when he'd thought he was being so amusing.

She glanced at Pete and put a finger to her lips as she hurried to the computer desk and pulled a paper from the printer tray and a pen from the cup holder. In Boston, Mrs. Wapple had been tormented by a neighbor with an audio device that made the already unstable woman agitated and confused. Was it so far-fetched to think a reverse situation could be involved here?

Sadie placed the paper on the kitchen counter and wrote a single sentence. She showed it to Pete. Shawn seemed to notice their silence and turned to look at them. After Pete had read the sentence, Sadie moved the paper close enough for Shawn to read it too.

What if my kitchen is bugged?

Chapter 13

For a lot of people the idea that their house had been bugged would be a ridiculous consideration, but Sadie, Pete, and Shawn had faced enough ridiculous situations to know that it wasn't so far-fetched. Instead, Sadie was kicking herself for not having thought about it sooner.

Shawn stood from his seat in front of the computer and exchanged a look with Pete that seemed to say "Now what?"

"I think that shortbread dough is ready for me to roll out," Sadie said, a bit louder than she usually would. She cleared her throat; it was imperative that she act normal since, if she were right, Jane could be listening right now. She didn't want Jane to know their suspicions. "I'm probably being silly. It's all just getting to me you know?"

She didn't head toward the refrigerator, though. She stayed right where she was and raised her eyebrows at Pete and Shawn. Surely they understood what she was doing. She was surprised at how violated the idea of an electronic bug in her kitchen made her feel. There was no safer place for Sadie than her home, and a good portion of her life took place in the kitchen. It was her happy place, her safe haven. To think that Jane had intruded on that was both frightening and infuriating.

"Right," Shawn said after another moment, also too loud.

Sadie made a face and shook her head. He shrugged as though to say "What?" She scribbled on the paper.

Act normal.

Shawn nodded. Pete was already walking around the kitchen, looking around cautiously. Sadie scribbled another note and held it up for him.

Would the police have checked for a bug when they inspected the house last night?

Pete shook his head and mouthed the words "Not automatically."

"So, what can I help you with?" Shawn asked, then clapped and rubbed his hands together.

"Um," Sadie said, thinking fast about the items on her to-do list that she could give Shawn to do as they played out this charade. "I need to polish Grandma's silver platter, could you help me with that?"

Shawn scowled; he hated that kind of thing. He preferred the more active tasks like carrying heavy objects and fixing stuff. Sadie wasn't really going to have him polish anything; he was far too inattentive to detail to be trusted with a task like that.

Pete took the paper out of her hand and picked up the pen. He wrote something down on the opposite side and turned it toward her. Shawn read it too.

DO YOU HAVE A PORTABLE RADIO?

Sadie was confused. Did he want the radio because music would cover up their conversation? Shawn, however, seemed instantly excited about the question and grabbed the paper.

RF Transmitter?

Pete nodded.

Sadie looked back and forth between them. *What's an RF transmitter?*

"Don't you keep that silver platter in the garage?" Shawn said, already heading toward the back door.

"No," Sadie said. The platter had always been kept above the fridge; only an idiot would store silver in a detached garage. Shawn gave her a play-along look over his shoulder. "I mean, yes?" She hadn't meant to make it sound like a question.

Shawn smiled as though to say "that's better" and a few seconds later the back door opened and shut again.

"And now I have you all to myself," Pete said, putting an arm around Sadie's waist and pulling her close.

"This is not the time, Pete," Sadie said, pushing at his arms. She was so not in the mood for stealing kisses right now, but his lips were already at her ear.

"A portable radio will pick up the relay if the bug is a radio frequency transmitter," he whispered. "That's the easiest kind of listening device a civilian can buy."

Even though he wasn't saying anything the least bit seductive, Sadie shivered all the same. She put her arms around his neck and nuzzled until she could whisper in *his* ear. "I changed the cake delivery time almost a week ago," she said quietly. "Could she have bugged my house that long ago?"

"Are you sure you didn't mention it another time since?"

"Who else would I tell but you? But how could she have access to the house? I'm so diligent about setting the alarm."

Pete was thoughtful for a moment before nuzzling her ear again. "The only thing I can think of is the open house two weeks ago. The realtor said two dozen people came and went. Maybe Jane was one of them."

The back door opened, and Pete and Sadie pulled apart, but not fast enough for Shawn, who rolled his eyes with unnecessary drama.

"Found it," he said. "Where's the polishing stuff?" He started turning the hand crank on the radio. It made a whirring sound, which caused Shawn to stop and head down the hallway. Without saying as much, the men had tapped into Sadie's assumption that the bug was in the kitchen. It's where Sadie spent 85 percent of her time and where 100 percent of the information she feared was overheard had been shared.

Sadie hurried to close the kitchen blinds, just in case, then banged some cupboards as though looking for the tarnish remover. She removed the platter from the cabinet above the refrigerator and set it on the counter.

Shawn came back in, the white noise of the radio turned to a low volume. Pete pointed toward the ceiling and then the floor, then made a swishing motion with his hand. Shawn followed Pete's instructions perfectly and lifted the radio high above his head—almost touching the ceiling—then low, just barely above the floor. He moved forward a few inches at a time, lifting and lowering as he went.

Pete began a visual inspection of the nooks and crannies in the room, then motioned Sadie toward the fridge.

"How are the cookies coming?" he asked, making a talking motion with his hand.

She nodded to tell him she understood his silent instruction even though she realized that if Jane were listening she would have to know something was up due to the sudden awkwardness of their conversation. Still, it was better than not talking at all.

"So," she said, removing the plastic-wrapped dough from the fridge. She pulled open a drawer to get her rolling pin, the one without handles that she'd used for nearly two decades. Nothing stuck to that baby after so many years of oil being absorbed into the wood. "Did you know that shortbread was originally made with only flour, butter, and sugar?" She unwrapped the dough and sprinkled some flour on the counter before shaping the dough into a disk. "It was three parts, two parts, one part, respectively, mixed only until combined and then shaped and baked. Short meant crumbly—in Scotland of course, which is where the recipe originated—and so it was *short*-bread, meaning crumbly bread, though I don't know why it's bread and not biscuit, since that's what a cookie is called in the UK."

She rolled the dough out in every direction, expanding the circle a little at a time, all the while watching Shawn and Pete make slow progress around the kitchen. She was about to go into the difference between shortbread and shortcake—leavening agents and liquid ratios mostly—when Shawn suddenly paused.

He crouched down and held the radio close to the floor at the end of the island. The white noise of the radio was cutting out, as though something were interfering with the signal. Shawn looked at Pete, who instantly went to his knees, making Sadie cringe; his bursitis did not like it when he put weight on his left knee.

Pete put his head low to the ground and looked under the edge of the island, that four-inch gap between the cabinet and the floor. He motioned to Shawn, who quickly joined him.

After a few seconds they popped up in unison and waved Sadie over. She quickly wiped her hands on the front of her pants even though she knew she'd regret it later, and joined them. She attempted a more ladylike position, but there was no way to avoid it entirely if she wanted to peer at the underside of the cabinet lip. Once she was in the right position, she could just barely make out a black box about half an inch thick and the size of a credit card attached to the underside of the cabinet overhang.

Shawn cleared his throat and a little green light lit up, then went black. "I don't really care about the history of shortbread," he said, "I just want to eat it." The green light turned on again.

Voice activated? Her house was bugged with a voice-activated device! Sadie scrambled to her feet and wrote another sentence on the paper, her handwriting choppy and her emotions churning.

She was in my house!!!

Pete pointed toward his phone and then pointed at the back door. He was going to call Malloy and it annoyed her. *She* wanted to talk about this. To rant and rave and find a way to use this latest discovery to *their* advantage. "I'm going to call Malloy and check on things. I wonder if they ever figured out whose phone she used to call the bakery this morning."

For an instant Sadie was confused. They already knew Jane had stolen Brian's phone from Pep Boys and used it to call Rachel. But a moment later she realized that Pete was trying not to give away additional information.

Shawn headed back to the computer. "I need to look something up."

"Okay," Sadie said to Pete. "Ask Malloy about that weird letter too, see if they've figured something out. I'm sure it's got to be involved in this."

Pete looked confused this time, and Sadie grabbed the pen and wrote another note:

Might as well mislead her.

Pete nodded but didn't seem all that supportive of her idea. He let himself out the back door, and Sadie returned to rolling out the dough with harsh, angry motions. She pictured Jane in her house, looking around, *touching* things.

Sadie kept her personal files in a locked cabinet, which might be why she hadn't suffered the same financial losses that Shawn had, but there were so many other things Jane could have interfered with if she had access to the house. Her feelings of vulnerability increased tenfold.

"Uh, Mom?"

Sadie looked at Shawn, who waved her over to the computer. She complied, bracing herself. She didn't like the tone in his voice. When she stood behind him she scanned the e-mail program on the screen. It was not *her* e-mail though, it was Shawn's. When she looked back to his in-box, she saw that his most recently received e-mail was from her e-mail address and titled "What I'm planning to do on my honeymoon."

Sadie's stomach dropped as she remembered telling Shawn her e-mail password so he could access the picture Ray Meyers had e-mailed. That meant Jane had overheard it too. How many times had Sadie heard never to say those things out loud or write them down? She kept all her passwords in a locked program on her phone, but she hadn't thought twice of saying her password out loud in her own house.

What have I done?

Sadie hit Shawn on the arm and indicated for him to get out of the chair. He didn't argue and even walked into the kitchen, which seemed to confirm that he had the same fear she did of what was contained in this e-mail. She clicked on the message and felt her cheeks flame as a pornographic picture came up on the screen. She closed the e-mail immediately before realizing that Shawn might not be the only person Jane sent this to. She took a breath and opened the e-mail again, looking only at the "to" field. She clicked the button to show all the recipients and felt the room spin as she realized that this image had been sent to every single person on her contact list. Hundreds of people. Friends, family, church members, customer service representatives.

"How bad is it?" Shawn asked from the kitchen.

"Really bad," Sadie said, closing and deleting the message. She swallowed and logged out of Shawn's in-box. She needed to change her password as quickly as possible to keep Jane from sending anything else. Her face and neck were on fire with humiliation as she thought of more and more people who could even now be pulling up that horrible picture on their computers.

When she typed in her password on the log-in page, a pop-up informed her that the password she'd used was inaccurate. Panicked, she typed it in again, and once again she got an error message. *Jane must have changed it*, she realized. There had to be something she could do to fix this. Her phone rang in the kitchen, and she swiveled in her chair to see Shawn pick up her phone, look at the screen, and then answer the call.

"Hey, Uncle Jack." He paused, then met Sadie's eyes. "You got it, too?"

The back door opened and Pete came in, walking fast. He held his phone out to Sadie. "What the heck is this?"

Lemon-Almond Shortbread

1½ cups butter, room temperature
1 cup sugar, plus a little extra for sprinkling
1 teaspoon vanilla extract
¼ teaspoon almond extract
Zest from ½ a lemon
¼ teaspoon sea salt
3½ cups all-purpose flour

In a large bowl, cream butter and sugar together. Add the vanilla, almond extract, and lemon zest. Mix well. Add salt, then gradually add flour while mixing on medium-low speed. The dough mixture will be dry but should stick together when pressed. (If it's too dry, add a teaspoon of milk.) Continue to beat until ingredients are well combined. Form dough into a ball, flatten, and cover with plastic wrap. Chill for 20 minutes.

Preheat oven to 350 degrees F. Remove chilled dough and roll out on a lightly floured surface until it's ½-inch thick. You can either cut it into fingers, circles, or use shaped cookie cutters. (A pizza cutter makes cutting dough a breeze.)

Place cookies on an ungreased baking sheet, 1-inch apart. Sprinkle cookies with sugar, then bake for 15 to 20 minutes until the edges just begin to brown. Let the cookies cool on baking sheet for 5 to 10 minutes before moving to cooling rack.

Makes about 30 finger shortbread cookies.

Note: Letting cookies overbake gives them a crispy texture and nutty flavor.

CHAPTER 14

Malloy said he would send someone over to track the bug in Sadie's kitchen and search the rest of the house, but in the meantime, he wanted Pete to come down to the police station. Malloy wasn't happy that the Facebook post had gone up without his knowing about it.

Normally, Sadie would have been annoyed with Malloy's attitude and the fact that he wanted Pete to come in instead of her—it was such an overt rejection of Sadie's position in this case—but she was far too overwhelmed by Jane's latest trick to care. She wished Pete luck and gave him carte blanche for whatever agreements he wanted to make with Malloy, then she tried to change her password only to learn that the "Password Update" capabilities on her e-mail account—limited to four a day—had been maxed out. She couldn't make any additional changes until tomorrow.

Since Shawn was talking to Jack on Sadie's phone, she used Shawn's phone to call the hosting company, which led her through automated messages for ten minutes before she got an actual person on the phone. By then she was frantic—two more e-mails had been sent, as reported to Shawn by Jack and a dozen of Sadie's friends who'd texted or called. She hoped they knew her character well enough to know she wouldn't have sent such obscenities.

"I can freeze your account while we investigate the situation," the woman on the phone said after Sadie explained what was happening. "But it will disable all access."

"That's fine," Sadie said. "Freeze it. Cancel it all together if you have to, but I can't keep it accessible. This woman is spamming all my contacts with pornography!"

Sadie nearly lost her mind when the woman put her on hold in order to discuss the situation with her supervisor. Pat Benatar's song "Hit Me with Your Best Shot" was playing as the hold music. Sadie was not amused.

"Are the new e-mails as bad as the first one?" Sadie asked Shawn, still manning her phone.

"They're pretty bad," Shawn said. "You don't want the details."

No, Sadie didn't want the details, and she didn't want to know how Shawn knew the details either. Had she ever been so humiliated in her whole life?

The woman she'd been talking to with the e-mail company came back onto the line. "Okay, Mrs. Hoffmiller, your account has been frozen for seventy-two hours in order for us to complete the review. I'll need you to go to the following website to file an official report so we can best resolve your concern."

Concern was not nearly a strong enough word in Sadie's opinion, but she thanked the woman all the same, hung up, and then went to the website so she could get the report filed and the review started. She was keenly aware that Jane's bug was still in the house. Jane was surely enjoying every minute of this and yet there was no time to plan a better course.

Shawn's phone rang, and he crossed the room to pick it up from the desk. He looked at the screen. "My fraud investigator, I think," he said. "I'll take it outside." He headed out the back door.

It took a few minutes for Sadie to fill out the computer form, and though she wanted an instant response, all she got was a pop-up informing her that she would be notified when they had a chance to review her case. They'd contact her through the phone number she'd provided on the form, not her e-mail, right?

Sadie kept thinking of specific people in her contact list, like her aunt Judy in Edmonton who set up her own e-mail for the first time a few months ago and loved instant access to her nieces and nephews but typed in all caps. And then there was Sister Nelson from church who talked often about her husband's pornography problem and how porn seemed to be everywhere these days, interfering with her husband's ability to feel God's light and healing power. Fabulous.

Sadie stood up from the computer and saw the cookie dough drying out on the counter. It was a small aside to consider that Jane may have managed to ruin the cookies too, but it was also reflective of how intricate Jane's interference had become. Sadie returned to the kitchen and lifted a corner of the dough to see if it seemed salvageable. She couldn't be certain, but regardless, the dough needed to be chilled again. She gathered it back into a ball and wrapped it in plastic before returning it to the fridge.

Every moment had a surreal quality about it, creating a feeling of distracted focus that Sadie struggled to break free of. She felt more foolish than ever for having thought that drawing Jane out would be easy and painless. It had been hours, they'd been all over town, and yet Jane was still finding new ways to twist the knife. It was a relief when her feelings of detachment and disbelief hardened into anger.

Sadie welcomed the anger while she finished cleaning the kitchen with sharp motions. She absolutely hated that despite their goal to get ahead of Jane they were once again cleaning up behind her. Through Sadie's on-again, off-again therapy, she'd learned ways to cope with her anger using visualization exercises and release techniques. She tried to still her mind enough to start those processes, but another wave of rage would take her off guard and push her back to the starting line. Over and over she would start and rage and start and rage again. It didn't help that three more people texted her to tell her about the e-mails. That her anger was so much more powerful than her ability to overcome it made her angrier still.

"Want some good news?"

Sadie spun around at the sound of Shawn's voice, a wooden spoon gripped tightly in one hand. She must have been scowling because Shawn stopped and lifted his eyebrows. "You okay?"

"I'm furious," she said, but she relaxed her grip on the poor spoon and proceeded to the drawer where she put it away.

"Furious is good," Shawn said coming the rest of the way into the kitchen.

"Furious is weak," Sadie corrected. "It puts Jane in control of how I feel, and I hate that. Anger blinds a person, and I can't afford to be blind right now. I need to outsmart her; I need to get ahead."

They'd been trying to get ahead all day and instead of making progress, Sadie had said her e-mail log-in information out loud in a bugged room! Jane couldn't have known Sadie would do such an idiotic thing, yet she'd taken full advantage of it when it happened. Jane knew that Sadie's kitchen was her ultimate sanctuary, and she had found a way to invade it. Infuriating!

Her eyes went to the counter where the bug was still listening to their conversation, and she clenched her jaw. She wanted to rip the bug out and bash it with a hammer, but Malloy was going to track it so it had to remain active. Had she said anything else that Jane could use against her? She would know the police were checking local hotels, and she would know about the Facebook blitz and the sketches. Sadie wasn't sure how Jane could use that information to her advantage, but if there was a way, she would certainly find it.

"Well, maybe just live in the anger for a minute," Shawn said, drawing Sadie's attention back to him. "Let yourself be as mad as you need to be instead of trying to push it away."

Sadie didn't comment, but she did consider the option even though it went against everything she had learned about coping with negative emotions. She believed that a person's mood gave off an energy that attracted similar energies back. If she were happy, she would attract happy energy back. If she were depressed, she would pull depressive energy back, making it worse. Anger would do the same thing, and she didn't want to attract any more of that kind of energy.

At the same time, she *wanted* to be mad right now. She had every reason to feel the way she did, so maybe she *should* embrace the rage and stop trying to fight it. Being mad didn't help them move forward, though, and they were as stuck as they'd ever been.

Another text message came through from a friend on the library council asking Sadie if her e-mail had been hacked. Sadie responded, then sent a text to every person on her contact list, explaining she'd been hacked and not to open an e-mail from her. There were plenty of people on her e-mail contact who wouldn't get the text message, but sending that one simple text made her feel better, like she'd remedied something a tiny amount.

She looked at Shawn and remembered what he'd said when he came in. "You said you had good news? I'm desperately in need of some of that."

"The Facebook page got off to a slow start, but it's picking up speed. We're up to sixty-eight shares," Shawn said, holding up his phone so Sadie could see proof of his claims. He put the phone in his pocket and moved to the computer where he opened Facebook on a bigger screen. "Seventy-one . . . uh, seventy-four. Sweet!"

Seventy-four people had reposted the information and sketch of Jane. That was good. Any number of people could have seen those updates. It was the only thing that Sadie's team had done that wasn't cleaning up something Jane had thrown at them. Sadie felt some of her angry energy shift just a little.

"That's great," she said. "I'd actually worried that posting it in the middle of the day might not go as well with people being at work and things."

"Being at work doesn't keep people off Facebook," Shawn said. "If anything, they use it more than ever when they need a break from The Man."

Sadie kept her sympathy for all those employers to herself while she finished putting away the rest of the dishes.

"Eighty-six shares," Shawn said. "Holy cow, I can't believe how fast it's spreading. Ninety."

His phone rang and he pulled it out of his pocket, not looking to see who was calling before putting it to his ear. "This is Shawn," he said. He paused. "Yeah, how you doin'? . . . Oh, yeah? . . . You're kidding!"

Sadie stopped with the silverware drawer open and tuned into

Shawn's side of the conversation. He leaned back in his chair, and Sadie hoped it didn't give out on him entirely.

"That is awesome, yeah." He leaned forward and grabbed a pen from the cup holder by the screen and pulled a piece of paper from the printer. "No. . . . Totally won't blow your cover. . . . Got it. . . . Thanks. Go Yankees!" He laughed and hung up before turning toward Sadie.

"Go Yankees?" she said, trying to put those words into context with the rest of the conversation.

Shawn opened his mouth but didn't speak as his eyes darted to the portion of the island where they'd found the bug. He nodded toward the back door, and Sadie followed him outside. They walked under the shade of a red maple tree—it was hot outside—and then both cast furtive glances to make sure no one was close enough to overhear. Shawn tilted his head toward Sadie, and she moved in closer.

"Mack's a die-hard Yankees fan," Shawn said quietly with a shrug. "Goes to show there's no accounting for some people's taste in sports teams." He gave an exaggerated roll of his eyes and then held up the paper he'd brought outside with him. "But I'll root for the Yankees if it leads me to Jane's address."

A tremor ran through Sadie's body, and she took a step back. "What?"

"Mack's buddy is hot for this girl who moved into the top apartment in his four-plex over on Stanicker. Mack met her the other night when he stopped by to pick up some tools. Swears it's her even though she had shoulder-length brown hair when he met her."

"Oh my gosh," Sadie said, grabbing the paper so she could read the address for herself. Stanicker Street wasn't exactly downtown Garrison, but it was still in the central part of town. A lot of the older homes in the area had been converted into upstairs-downstairs apartments or other types of multi-family dwellings, though many had fallen into disrepair once they didn't have a dedicated homeowner to keep them up. It was a shame, really, since the homes had at one time been so stately and unique.

"We should tell . . ." She didn't finish the sentence because Shawn pulled the paper from her hand—nearly giving her a paper cut in the process—and held her eyes in a way she couldn't misinterpret. "You think we should check this out ourselves?" she said instead of what she was planning to say.

"Don't you?" Shawn asked.

It took only an instant for Sadie's mind to go that direction. "The police have to get approvals before they can go," she said, justifying why they *shouldn't* share the information.

Shawn nodded quickly. "And we both know Malloy isn't hip on *anything* that's our idea. If Jane's at this apartment, we call the police once I've tackled her to the floor. If she's not there, *we* can get inside. The cops will need a warrant."

Sadie felt a rush of energy at the potential progress this meant to their side of the investigation. To intrude on Jane's space just as she'd intruded on Sadie's was like a hot fudge sundae in a waffle cone! But then that rush of eager anticipation hit a speed bump. "What about Pete?"

Shawn made an uncomfortable face. "Isn't he talking to Malloy right now?"

Sadie didn't have to ponder the reason for Shawn's discomfort since she suddenly felt it just as strongly. "Which means he might not have his phone with him."

"If he did have his phone, telling him would be telling Malloy.

Pete wouldn't be able to keep it from him if Malloy's right there," Shawn added.

"So, basically telling Pete would put him on the spot. If he tells Malloy, he goes against us. If he doesn't, he's working against his buddies at the department."

Shawn nodded. "Exactly. It's a heck of a position to put Pete in."

Sadie hated keeping things from Pete, but it's not like she wouldn't tell him at all. Just not this minute, and only because he was with Malloy. Instead, she'd wait until she and Shawn either had Jane in hand or they were in a stronger position through whatever they might learn in her apartment if she weren't home. Sadie felt certain that by the end of this visit, they would have one or the other and perhaps both if they had a little luck on their side.

"We need to go right now," Sadie said, the decision made but her mind not completely settled about it, "before I second-guess this."

Shawn consulted his phone and then grinned at his mother. "A hundred and seventeen shares," he said, obviously impressed. "And over three hundred likes."

People were looking for Jane around town, and the police were checking with all the hotels in a 150-mile radius. Pete was having a tête-à-tête with Malloy, and Shawn had procured Jane's address. They were in the most powerful position they'd been in so far, and in the wake of the anger and frustration she'd felt, Sadie was ready to take full advantage of it.

Besides there was supposed to be a barbeque in her backyard four hours from now. Time was of the essence. "Do you want to drive or should I?"

CHAPTER 15

Sadie played copilot while Shawn drove, but it wasn't hard to find the address for the faded blue two-story home that, according to Mack, was made up of four smaller apartments. Sadie had noticed the house before; there weren't many blue houses around.

"So, there's two apartments on the main floor," Shawn said as he slowed down in front of the house but made no move to pull over. "Mack's buddy lives in the basement apartment, and Jane—who he thinks calls herself Beth—moved into the top floor just a couple of weeks ago."

"And Mack met her when he was visiting his friend in the basement?"

Shawn nodded and sped up again now that they had identified the house. There was no silver Honda parked anywhere in the vicinity. Shawn drove a block south before he pulled into the back parking lot of the senior center and parked next to one of the Meals on Wheels vans.

They locked their doors behind them and headed toward the uneven sidewalk that ran in front of Jane's apartment, discussing their plan. Shawn would go to the door first in case Jane was home.

Sadie kept to herself her concern about Shawn wanting to be the person to throw Jane to the ground. While she didn't support violence, she had a hard time coming up with reasons why Shawn shouldn't have a chance to work through the frustrations Jane had caused. If Sadie thought she could adequately restrain Jane physically, she'd probably vie for the chance to do it herself.

If Jane wasn't home, Sadie would be the front man. She would pick the lock to get inside and take a good look around in hopes of finding something of value. It had been more than a year since Sadie had picked a lock, and doing it again felt a little bit like ending her days of sobriety, as it had been a habit she'd consciously tried to break. Too bad they didn't give out tokens of success for overcoming things like that. And yet she'd felt a giddy sense of familiarity as she'd pulled the case of tools from the desk drawer where she stored them and slid them into her purse before leaving home. She wore the purse across her chest so she could be hands-free if necessary. There was something empowering about knowing that whatever lock Jane had on her door would not keep Sadie out.

"Where's the entrance to the upstairs apartment?" Sadie asked, taking in the two front doors off the bungalow-style porch surrounded by a badly peeling white railing. Sadie didn't want to accidentally break into someone else's apartment.

"Mack said there are some stairs around back." Shawn indicated a driveway on the far side of house. The entrance to the basement apartment ran alongside the house, and a teal minivan was parked in the driveway.

Sadie kept close to the side of the house in hopes of staying out of view of the neighbors on the main floor. She and Shawn rounded the back corner of the house, and she immediately saw a long stairway heading straight to the second floor. At the top was a simple door cut into what Sadie assumed had originally been a window when this house had only one family living in it.

Sadie stayed at the bottom of the stairs with 911 on speed dial. She watched Shawn go up the stairs and braced herself for what could be a dramatic few minutes.

At the top of the stairs, Shawn knocked on the door and then put his ear against it, listening for any movement on the other side. Sadie was frozen just like Shawn for ten seconds until he pulled back. He knocked again, paused again, and then tried the knob. It didn't move in his hand. He looked at Sadie and shook his head, obviously disappointed. He headed back down the steps and Sadie, in turn, started up them. They met at the halfway point.

"I'll play lookout for you," Shawn said, his expression showing his reluctance to step out of the center ring. "I'll call your phone with any alerts so make sure you answer it."

Sadie nodded, then stepped ahead of him and continued up the narrow stairs. Where was Jane if she wasn't here? She'd hacked Sadie's e-mail less than an hour ago—where had she done it from? Could she have hacked it from here and then left in order to execute the next devious plan on her list? What that might be reminded Sadie of everything Jane had already done and the resulting fresh wave of anger helped solidify her motivation.

At the top of the stairs, Sadie pulled out her pick set and got to work. Picking a lock wasn't as much like riding a bike as one might think; Sadie felt as though she were all thumbs, and the heat from the sun at her back made her increasingly uncomfortable. She finally got the lock on the doorknob undone but then let out a breath of frustration. The dead bolt was engaged as well.

Dead bolts were already the hardest type of lock to pick, but this one was particularly tricky since it was old. The pins were either rusted or just stiff. Sadie doubted the landlord changed locks between tenants, which not only was an unsafe practice, but it also created great difficulty for her attempts to break in. She wished she'd thought to grab her WD-40 from home. It wasn't the best product to use in a lock—it got sticky as it dried and would probably ruin the lock entirely given a few weeks to pick up dirt, dust, and metal shavings from inside the casing—but it would work for the immediate situation. Sadie didn't keep liquid graphite on hand like she should.

Finally, with sweat dripping from her hairline and down her back, she got the last pin to pull back and the lock opened. She looked at Shawn as she turned the knob, surprised he hadn't come up to help her. Not that he knew anything about picking locks, but simply because of the time it took her and the increasing anxiety that each second cost them both. He nodded and waved her inside.

Sadie pushed the door open on well-oiled hinges—not a squeak or a grind to be heard—and then shut it quickly. She blinked in order to help her eyes adjust to the darkened interior. The miniblinds had been twisted closed, muting the daylight that filtered in, but also hiding her from anyone who might see her or notice the lights on.

She flipped the light switch next to the door and took in the apartment. Calling this a second-floor apartment was generous. It was more an attic space since both walls sloped with the roofline. The room was long and narrow. At the end was a small kitchenette and two doorways, both of which were open enough to show a bathroom and a small bedroom.

Sadie scanned the room and guessed it had been listed as a furnished apartment due to the old and utilitarian furniture: a brown couch, '70s era coffee table with narrow legs and a parquet design on top, two end tables, and a halogen light in one corner. There was a small butcher-block table closer to the kitchen area with two chairs pulled up against it.

She walked toward the doorways on the other end while scanning every inch of surface area within the small space. At first glance, everything seemed bare—as though Jane had moved out already—but then Sadie saw a plastic file box under the table and, as she got closer to the kitchen, a stack of newspapers on the far side of the two-burner stove.

Her heart rate increased with both the numbing fear of being in Jane's space and the anticipation of what information she might be able to find. She pulled the cotton garden gloves she'd thought to bring from her purse and put them on before she opened the fridge to reveal a few dozen yogurt containers, a carton of orange juice, and a few packs of Camel cigarettes. Jane hadn't given up smoking, apparently—that would be something they could put on the Facebook page. There was no mustard or butter or salad dressing—things that would make the apartment seem a bit more lived in.

Sadie's phone vibrated in her pocket and made her jump. She pulled it out, noting it was Shawn before quickly answering his call. "Is she back?" She felt a rush of anxiety while turning toward the door.

"No," Shawn said. "I just want to know what's up there."

Sadie turned back to the kitchen, relieved. "So far a file box and some newspapers, but I haven't checked out her bedroom yet. The place barely looks lived in."

"Which makes sense if she's only been here a couple of weeks," Shawn said.

"And isn't planning to stay long," Sadie added. She headed to the bedroom and flipped on the light. The unmade queen-sized bed was pushed up underneath the sloped ceiling on the right side. There was a dresser on one end with some papers on top, which Sadie moved toward. She knew better than to touch anything. It could interfere with a police investigation, and there was the added risk of Jane noticing if something were out of place. Sadie wanted to learn what she could without Jane knowing she'd been there.

"You're in the bedroom now?" Shawn asked.

"Yeah," Sadie replied. She turned her head so she could read the paper on top of the stack, which turned out to be a copy of Sadie's property listing with the county. A sense of vulnerability shot down her spine. Why would Jane want this?

She explained what she'd found to Shawn and after a brief debate with herself about not touching anything, moved the paper aside. The next sheet was a printed copy of an article Jane had written in *The Denver Post* about Sadie almost three years ago, calling her a magnet for murder and implying an inappropriate relationship between Sadie and Eric. The humiliating article had been followed up with a TV interview where Eric had reflected a far more serious relationship between the two of them than had really existed and raised questions regarding Sadie's moral code. The whole situation had been so embarrassing—yet Jane hadn't seemed to fully understand what Sadie was so mad about. Did Jane keep the article because she loved the reminder of the damage she'd done with it?

Sadie's uneasiness turned into a full-fledged case of the creeps as she moved on to an article about Shawn's birth mother, Lorraina, being life-flighted from a cruise ship to a hospital in Anchorage. Another article was from a press outlet in London, reporting on

Breanna and Liam's upcoming wedding. The wedding had actually taken place in Alaska on the fly, but most of England didn't know that and Breanna and Liam were still planning a large celebration in October. Did Jane know Breanna was already married? Sadie's motherly instincts rose at the inclusion of her kids in Jane's stalking.

Beneath the article was a photocopy of one of Pete and Sadie's wedding invitations. Sadie could hardly believe it. She'd only mailed fifty invitations out. Where would Jane have found one? Someone on her guest list had either willingly shared information with Jane or had been unfairly targeted because of their connection to Sadie. Her mind spun with possibilities, and she had to consciously calm herself from the rising anxiety.

"What am I looking for?" she asked Shawn as she turned to get a three-hundred-and-sixty degree view of the room. "I'm losing my focus."

"Uh, well, we want to know what her intentions are here and who she really is," Shawn reminded her.

"Right," Sadie said. The stack of papers were the only things in plain sight, and she finished glancing through them, not finding anything that explained who Jane really was. Since Sadie was in the bedroom, she started pulling open drawers and rifling through socks, underwear, and T-shirts, looking for anything that might be a type of identification. There was a red T-shirt that said "Tigers Earn Their Stripes, 2003." Could it be a high school shirt? She told Shawn about it.

"So we just have to find a high school somewhere in the country with a tiger mascot and red as one of their school colors? I'm sure there are only about five hundred of them."

Sadie frowned and put the shirt back.

"She's not going to leave anything that might lead to her real identity just lying around," Sadie said to herself as much as to Shawn. "She could have bought that shirt at a thrift shop for all I know." Still, it was the only item that advertised any kind of personalization.

"Right," Shawn confirmed. "So look between mattresses, underneath things, behind drawers. Places she'd hide something."

She finished rifling through the drawer—carefully so as not to make it obvious things had been rifled with—and closed the last one. "What if nothing's here?"

"At least we'll know that," Shawn said. "Dang, I want to be up there helping."

"You need to stand watch."

"I know, but I still wish I were up there."

Sadie, however, was glad he wasn't. She couldn't possibly keep her anxiety in check if he weren't making sure Jane didn't walk in on her. Though she'd broken in to plenty of places over the years, she'd had enough bad experiences with it that she'd lost the thrill of victory that came with her earlier snooping. "I need both hands to move faster and displace less, I need to go."

"Okay, I'll let you know if I see anything. Though if you hear me beating someone up down here, you might want to hurry."

Sadie barely registered what he'd said until after she'd already ended the call. Then she started looking beyond the obvious places. She pulled all the drawers out of the dresser, looking around the floor inside the dresser where it would be easy to hide things. She found nothing.

In the closet were three boxes. Two of them were indoor plant lights. Why on earth would Jane need those? The other was filled with a variety of wigs, not including the blonde one Sadie had seen earlier. She reached to the bottom and moved things carefully, not wanting to disrupt any organizational efforts Jane might have in place, but it seemed to simply be wigs—seven or eight of them in different styles and colors.

After putting everything back in the closet, Sadie checked under the bed, behind the dresser, and between the mattress and box spring—nothing. She returned to the living room, moved furniture, pulled off cushions. She even checked the edges of the carpet to see if anything pulled back. Nothing.

She made sure to put things back as perfectly as possible even though she knew that every time she touched anything she was taking a huge risk. Her stomach hurt from the tension. When she moved into the kitchen, she had to pause to stretch her arms over her head and take a few deep breaths in hopes of calming herself down both physically and mentally.

A bit more centered, she continued on, opening the fridge again and taking a picture of the contents. Did the limited food on hand mean Jane was eating out a lot? If so, maybe people would have recognized her at restaurants, right? Plus, there were only about twenty eating establishments in the entire city. How hard would it be to canvas those places with a copy of the sketches? She filed that idea away for later and began checking all the cupboards and drawers, most of which were empty save for a few dishes and utensils.

In the cupboard next to the sink was a jar of instant coffee and a jar of creamy peanut butter. She moved the two jars apart to see what was behind them and then moved them back when the rest of the cupboard was empty. She turned the peanut butter in an attempt to get it in the exact same position it had been before she touched it. She wished she'd taken a "before" picture.

Only the bathroom was left and, once again, Sadie turned up nothing other than some Paul Mitchell shampoo and the same brand of deodorant and perfume Sadie wore—creepy. She was feeling discouraged when she found herself staring at the toilet. In San Francisco, she'd removed the back of the toilet and used it to free herself from her bindings. She knew the back of a toilet was an often-overlooked compartment, somewhere people might store or hide things they didn't want anyone else to find.

Sadie carefully lifted the lid off the back. She looked into the stained interior and frowned—it was empty. Then she looked at the underside of the lid. Velcroed to the top of the lid were three prescription bottles. Clever.

Carefully, she put the lid on the bathroom counter, upside down so the bottles faced her, and got close enough to read the information. Between the three of them she was able to get a full name.

"Valerie Smith," Sadie read out loud. Was it Jane's real name or another alias? It sounded like an alias. Either way, the name might have a history they could access that would give them information they simply didn't have right now.

All three prescriptions had been filled at a Walmart in Omaha, Nebraska, within the last two months. One of them—for something called rabeprazole—had been filled less than three weeks ago. Sadie pulled out her phone and took half a dozen pictures at different angles, feeling high on the success of this discovery but increasingly anxious about how long she'd been in the apartment. They were lucky Jane hadn't come back, but that relief only reminded Sadie that Jane had to be gone so long for a reason that certainly wouldn't work out in Sadie's best interests.

Sadie's phone rang, making her jump, and she looked to see that it was Shawn before answering it. "Is she back?"

"No," Shawn said, "but you've been up there for twelve minutes and I'm getting freaked out. I also found something regarding the guy in the basement apartment I want to show you."

"Okay, I'm almost done. I found something good."

She ended the call and replaced the toilet lid, looking around to make sure she hadn't missed any other similarly clever hiding places. She quickly checked under the sink and behind the miniblinds before heading toward the door, scanning the apartment one last time on her way.

Her eyes landed on the file box under the table, and she hurried toward it, kneeling down so that she could assess it before she touched it. There was a small padlock on the front, the kind used on luggage, which made the contents of the box all the more intriguing. What treasures did it hold? She'd have to break the lock somehow to find out, which would certainly put Jane on alert.

Sadie vacillated for the space of two seconds, and then shook her head. She didn't want Jane to know anyone had been there and that meant Sadie couldn't take anything but pictures. And the pictures she had were good ones that she hoped would be beneficial to the investigation.

Assured she'd done what she could, Sadie exited the apartment, and only as she turned the thumb lock on the inside of the knob did she realize that she couldn't relock the dead bolt from the outside without a key.

"Biscuits," she said under her breath. Why hadn't she thought of that before? But she knew why. Sometimes her brain protected her from information that she didn't really want to think about at the time. If she hadn't picked the dead bolt, she wouldn't have gotten inside, and she'd *needed* to get inside.

But now she was in a pickle. Jane would know the dead bolt had been opened, so she would know someone had been inside. After pondering on the situation for half a second longer, Sadie realized there was nothing to be done for it and hurried back inside. In for a penny, in for a pound.

She grabbed the file box from under the table and was almost back to the door when she remembered the newspapers in the kitchen and the articles from the bedroom. She went back for them, her stomach a bundle of nerves. Would Jane retaliate when she realized her apartment had been searched? The idea left Sadie's heart thudding in her chest and her head buzzing. Then again, all this information might help them locate her and put an end to this.

Sadie made sure the thumb lock was turned, though it seemed superfluous, and then hurried down the stairs, the loot held close to her chest.

"I didn't know you were gonna take stuff," Shawn said, alarmed, as she descended the steep staircase as quickly as she dared. "Are you sure that's a good idea?"

"I wasn't planning to take anything either, and, no, it's a really bad idea!" When she reached the bottom, Shawn took the loose articles from the top of the file box. "I couldn't relock the dead bolt, which means she'll know someone was here anyway so we might as well take what we can. Let's get out of here. What did you find?"

"At the bottom of the stairs." He nodded in the direction of the basement apartment entrance as they hurried up the driveway, but Sadie didn't look, her heart was racing. "There's a spot set up for smoking—a couple of chairs and an overturned bucket. On that bucket was a mug they've been using for an ashtray."

"Okay," Sadie said impatiently.

"From Pep Boys," Shawn said.

Sadie looked at him with her eyebrows raised.

"So I called Mack and he said that his buddy used to work there. He quit about four months ago to take a job with the Chevy Dealer in Sterling."

"That's how she knew her way around Pep Boys," Sadie said.

"I guess," Shawn said with a shrug as they took quick jog-steps to make up for how much time Sadie had spent in the apartment.

"I'll have Pete get Malloy to bring this guy in for an interview. You have his name?"

"Yeah, Mack texted it to me."

"Great," Sadie said, the euphoria of accomplishment almost replacing her anxiety. They were nearly to the sidewalk when a police car came to a quick stop in front of the driveway. They both froze, then looked at each other as though to say "Are they here for us?"

"Stop right there!" an officer yelled as he stepped out of his car. He hadn't pulled his gun but had his hand on his hip holster as he faced them.

Sadie knew 90 percent of the Garrison police force so she recognized him but didn't know his name.

"We received a report of a possible break-in at this address. I'll need to see some ID and hear a pretty good explanation for why you're in such a hurry to get out of here."

CHAPTER 16

For the second time in one day, Sadie was at the Garrison police department explaining herself to Malloy who fixed her with that condescending stare she hated. She assumed Pete was in the building somewhere, but she didn't know if he was aware of what had happened. At least she was no longer on the sidewalk where the neighbors had come out to see what was going on. Jane could have driven by at any time and seen them standing outside of her apartment, which is why Sadie offered to drive to the police station with the officer and have Shawn follow in her car. She'd rather talk about what happened in private.

"You should have given us the address," Malloy said. "And let us follow up on it."

"I know," Sadie said, trying to sound humble in hopes it would diffuse Malloy's anger. It was easier to be humble since things had unraveled. If she and Shawn had gotten away with it, she would probably have been a bit more defensive. "But I worried that the red tape you guys would have to go through to get a warrant would slow things down."

"Instead, you broke the law by breaking and entering. Not to mention theft."

"But it was Jane's apartment," Sadie said, "and—"

"We do not know if that apartment was this Jane woman's apartment."

"It was absolutely her apartment," Sadie said, trying not to sound condescending. "She had all those articles about me and my family. She had a copy of my wedding invitation."

"We have no *verification* that it's her apartment," Malloy said. "I understand *you're* convinced, but the police department needs facts, not assumptions. Which is why we have to get a warrant before we just randomly break into apartments. Do you realize our chance of apprehending her when she returned is lost now? If a neighbor hasn't already told her about you being there, she'll learn as soon as she returns."

"The neighbors!" Sadie said, leaning forward in her chair. "Have you guys talked to the neighbors? They can verify it's her apartment and identify her. If one of them *did* call her to tell her about the break-in, then they would have her actual phone number rather than the stolen phones she keeps calling us from. The documents I took from the apartment ought to prove it's her apartment as well."

"The documents you took illegally, you mean?" Malloy countered angrily. "You say you understand police procedure, but we can't use those documents when they were obtained illegally. You're hurting this case, Sadie, not helping it, and you're putting all of us in a very awkward position."

Sadie let out a breath and looked at the floor. "I was trying to help." This time her humility was perfectly sincere. "I was trying to figure out who she was—who she *really* is." She thought of the pictures on her phone of the prescription bottles. If she told Malloy about them, would she get in even more trouble? Would he be able to follow up even though she'd obtained that information illegally too? She didn't dare take the risk, and she didn't want to give him more reasons to distrust her either. If only that tenant hadn't called the police. People were such busybodies. "Even if the file box is inadmissible in court, can't you look through it to get other information?"

"No, I can't look through it!" Malloy said, his neck getting red. "It was obtained *illegally*! We can't go through illegally obtained evidence."

"Just like you couldn't go into that apartment without a warrant, but I could," Sadie countered. She really wanted him to understand her motivations, but he clenched his jaw even tighter. "So, maybe *I* can look through the papers and see what might be in there? That file box could have—"

"You stole them!" Malloy said loudly enough that Sadie pulled back in her seat. "You burglarized someone's apartment. I can't give you back the items you stole. Do you have any idea how complicated you have made things? You could very well end up on the wrong side of this situation and be the one facing jail, Sadie."

"Well, it's not like she's going to file charges," Sadie said. "And she's certainly not going to *show* herself in order to file a police report—then you'd get her for the phones and the cake and everything else." And if Jane didn't go back to her apartment, she was limited in regard to the disguises she could use from here on out. Maybe she had some items in her car, but Sadie felt confident that the majority of Jane's costume supplies had been stored in her apartment. Along with those weird lights.

"We don't know it was her texting you any more than we know

she's the one who defaced your cake or stole those phones or even rented that apartment," Malloy countered. "The only person we know who broke the law is you, Sadie."

"The apartment!" Sadie said as another idea struck her. "Have you contacted the landlord to see the rental agreement? And this guy who lives in the basement apartment—he's sweet on her and used to work at Pep Boys. If they were close enough that she pegged his former employer as a good place to get a phone from, then he's got to know something."

Malloy clenched his jaw and his face reddened, informing Sadie that she had pushed him further than she should have. He leaned forward and pointed a finger at her, his words tight and angry. "You are hurting this case, Sadie. My men are having to clean up the messes you keep making, and now I have the district attorney's office involved. I have to come up with—"

Malloy's phone cut him off, and they both looked to it for salvation. He picked it up before it rang a second time and turned away from her in his chair.

"What," he said brusquely before listening for several seconds. The look on his face changed from anger to surprise. "Are you sure? . . . I want a full scan run on the number that called in that tip ASAP. . . . No, I'll handle it myself. . . . Send Beacon with me. . . . Yes. . . . Yes." He hung up the phone and met Sadie's eyes. "We're done for now."

Done? Hadn't he just told her she'd broken the law? Wasn't he about to tell her she was under arrest? What was it about the phone call that took priority over Malloy's chance to put Sadie behind bars, which she had no doubt was exactly where he wanted her to be?

"What was the call about?" Sadie asked, figuring she didn't have anything to lose by asking. Clearly a tip had come in from a number that Malloy wanted tracked, just like they'd done with the numbers Jane had texted from.

"None of your business," Malloy said, standing up from his chair. "Go home and stop playing Cagney and Lacey while we try to figure out what to do about all of this. There are serious things happening, and every time you get yourself involved you make it worse."

Sadie pulled back. Is that really what he thought of her? That she only made things worse? "I found her apartment," she reminded him, no longer feeling guilty that she hadn't told him about the pictures of the prescriptions. "And Garrison is on the lookout for her because of our Facebook page."

Malloy glared at her, then walked to the door and pulled it open. "Go home," he said sharply, then paused and let out an exasperated breath. "Actually, you can't go home. I have a team preparing to go to your house to follow up on the listening device—which would have been done an hour ago if you hadn't pulled this latest stunt. I need you to go somewhere else until we've cleared the house." He said the last part with a touch of smugness Sadie did not appreciate in the slightest.

"And where am I supposed to go?" Sadie asked, putting her hands on her hips.

Malloy matched her pose and gave her a sarcastic smile. "Maybe you could go back to the hotel where I wanted you to stay in the first place."

Sadie glared at him. She wasn't going to the hotel. She could go to Pete's, but other than the air mattress he'd been sleeping on and a few boxes he'd been planning to move today, his house was empty.

Still, it would be better to go to his house if for no other reason than the fact that Malloy wanted her to go to the hotel.

"Or," Malloy continued, "if you're going to continue being difficult, I can put you in a cell. That might be the best option for everyone. I assure you I have plenty of legal cause to do so."

Sadie didn't respond, she just stood and let herself out of his office before he got too excited about that idea. Shawn had been taken somewhere else when Malloy had directed her to his office upon their arrival, but he was outside the door when she stepped into the hall. They exchanged a look that communicated how irritated they both were at this turn of events and then headed toward the front doors of the police station in silence, Sadie looking for Pete on their way.

She was increasingly anxious about his reaction to all of this. It was the day before their wedding, and she'd broken in to Jane's apartment without telling him. Again, if it had worked out well, it would be an annoyance, but it hadn't worked out well, and she had no doubt Malloy would make a point of using this against her. It put Pete in a precarious position and she felt bad for that.

The back portion of the police station where the business took place was separated from the public areas by a glass and metal door that an officer in the reception area buzzed people through via a button located at her desk. When Sadie and Shawn reached the yellow line painted on the floor with the words "Wait for Dept. Approval" painted above it, they did exactly what the instructions said, and stopped and waited to be buzzed through.

"Malloy hates me," Sadie said in a pouty voice. "And everything I do makes him hate me more. He won't even listen to *why* we did what we did."

Shawn nodded. "They made me put the department's number instead of mine on the Facebook page. I had to promise that if anyone calls me about the page, I'll forward them to the police department." He let out a heavy breath. "The guy I talked to said they can't use any of the stuff we took from the apartment because we stole it. Maybe we *should* have had them follow up with the address."

Sadie felt a twinge of guilt. If Shawn had been confident about what they'd done, Sadie could be confident too. When he questioned it, on the other hand, it made her question it as well. If she'd just left everything in the apartment, they could have told the police and had them get the warrant to retrieve it legally. She hated that she'd made such a mess of things. She hated even more that important information would be ignored because she'd taken it in the first place. Who knew what they could learn from the file box?

They were quiet for several seconds until Sadie wondered why they hadn't been buzzed through. She looked around for the officer who usually manned the desk and saw the young woman standing at another desk on the other side of the room, chatting with another officer—a dispatcher, Sadie thought. Sadie was irritated at the dereliction of duty until she realized that whatever tip Malloy had been talking about would have been called in, probably to the dispatcher. Malloy had wanted to handle the tip himself, which meant there was something unique about it. Unique enough that the front desk officer was distracted from her job? Unique enough to be jawed about with her coworker?

It took mere milliseconds for Sadie to determine that the connection was entirely probable.

Sadie gave Shawn a "wait here" look and then casually walked toward the two women, positioning herself so she was blocked from the woman sitting at the desk by the woman standing in front of it. She walked as quickly as possible without making enough noise to be overheard. She could be all but silent when she wanted to. As she came up behind the woman standing there, she caught the tail end of what the woman at the desk was saying.

" . . . I guess Beacon's going with him. I triple-checked it just to be sure it was Cunningham's address, that's why . . . uh, excuse me, ma'am?"

The woman's head moved to the side and she made eye contact with Sadie, who was a couple of feet behind the woman standing. Her cover blown, Sadie pasted an innocent expression on her face and stepped casually to the side as though she hadn't been using the standing officer as a shield.

"We just need to be buzzed through," she said, though her heart was racing. Something had happened at Pete's address? She forced a smile and pointed her thumb toward Shawn still standing at the yellow line.

The woman who should have been at the desk glanced toward Shawn. "I'll be right there." She waved Sadie away.

When Sadie reached Shawn, she gave him the slightest shake of her head, and he responded with an even slighter nod, agreeing to wait for her to explain until she could do so without being overheard.

The desk officer returned a few seconds later and buzzed them through. Once on the other side of the glass dividing wall, they collected the personal items they'd had to surrender upon arrival. Sadie slung her purse over her shoulder while Shawn slid his wallet into his back pocket. They pushed through the front glass doors into the bright summer day together. Only when they'd reached the parking lot did Shawn ask his question. "What happened? You're scowling."

"We need to go to Pete's," Sadie said, already bracing herself for the reprimand Malloy would give her when she arrived. "Someone called in a tip that has to do with his house. We haven't heard anything about Jane's antics in over an hour. I'm worried Pete's her newest target. You drive while I text him. I hope he's got his phone."

Chapter 17

Shawn and Sadie pulled up in front of Pete's house just as Malloy was stepping out of the unmarked police car. He'd only beaten them there by a matter of seconds. When Malloy saw her, he scowled and said something to the officer who'd come with him, Beacon.

Sadie held Malloy's eyes while Shawn shifted into park, then she unbuckled her seat belt, took a deep breath, and stepped out of the car to meet Malloy on the sidewalk. Shawn said something about a text from Maggie—her flight had landed early—and so he stayed in the car.

Beacon headed toward the gate that led to the backyard of Pete's house. Sadie itched to follow him, but she had two hundred and forty pounds of obnoxious police detective in her way.

"I told you to go to the hotel," Malloy said.

"You told me I couldn't go home. Where else do you think I would go?" She raised her eyebrows as though daring him to argue with her logic. She'd thought of it on the drive over and was quite proud with herself. "What are *you* doing here?"

When he didn't answer right away, she pretended to put the

details together on her own. "Does this have anything to do with the tip you received when I was in your office?"

The slight tightening of Malloy's jaw told her she was on the right track, and she could almost hear his brain racing to come up with a different explanation. She spoke again before he could come up with anything. "What was the tip about?"

Sadie looked past him at the house that would be Pete's for only another week. The day after she and Pete would return from their honeymoon, the new owners would close on the house and Pete would hand over his keys. Beacon let himself into the backyard and closed the gate behind him. Did the tip have something to do with the backyard, then? She looked at Malloy again. "Did you tell Pete there was a tip regarding his home?"

Sadie knew he hadn't told Pete because when *she* texted Pete, he'd known nothing about it. He'd been talking to the owners of another one of the stolen phones but cut the interview short, calling Sadie for more details and saying he was on his way to meet them. She explained what had happened, but left out the part about her and Shawn having been caught with armloads of Jane's stuff outside her apartment. Pete had enough to worry about right now.

"It's not typical for us to call the subject of a tip prior to substantiating it," Malloy said. His voice was as tight as his expression.

"Even when he's a good friend?"

"*Especially* if he's a good friend," Malloy spat back. "Do you have any idea the number of conflicts I'm up against with this investigation? It's a very complicated situation that is becoming more complicated thanks to you and your constant meddling!"

"I'm not the one who called in a tip about Pete's house," Sadie reminded him, trying to remain calm. "I'm not the enemy here."

His face reddened slightly. "I don't know how to make it more clear to you that *we* are handling this and *you* are not!"

"And I don't know how to make it more clear to you that this is *my* situation, and I'm not going to sit by idly and hope that you get things figured out when I've already seen the progress we've made without you!"

She thought Malloy's eyes might pop out of his head as rage filled his face. "I can have you arrested!" he yelled, pulling himself up to his full height.

Sadie was not cowed. She'd had it with this man. "For what? Being unlikable?"

"For breaking and entering that woman's apartment!"

Oh, yeah, that, Sadie thought, somewhat diffused.

Malloy continued, "And for interfering with a police investigation!"

The sound of tires squealing into the driveway interrupted them. Pete jumped out at almost the same moment his car came to a stop. He looked at Sadie as he strode toward them, the sides of his jacket flaring out as he did so.

"What's going on?" he asked Malloy. "What are you doing here?"

Malloy let out a breath and looked at Sadie with narrowed eyes. He might not *know* what she'd told Pete or how she knew the tip had been about his house, but he knew Sadie was the reason Pete was here. "An anonymous tip was called in," he said finally. "Beacon and I came to check it out."

"What kind of tip?" Pete asked.

"You know I can't tell you that," Malloy said irritably. "I have to follow procedure."

"Beacon went into the backyard," Sadie said, causing both men to look at her. From the look on Malloy's face she knew that she had to give him some credit for not slapping handcuffs on her right then.

Pete turned toward the back gate without another word. Sadie followed; she didn't want to be left alone with Malloy. Pete pushed opened the back gate with one hand.

Beacon was walking through the flowerbeds on the west side of the yard. Pete's late wife had been an avid gardener, and though she'd passed away nearly six years ago, she was still reflected in the array of flowers and shrubs in the yard. These days, Pete paid a landscaping company to keep up the yard; he didn't have the green thumb she'd had.

"Beacon!" Pete yelled, taking purposeful steps toward the younger man. "What are you doing?"

"Cunningham!"

Sadie came up short at the sound of Malloy's voice behind her. She stepped aside to allow Malloy to catch up to Pete on his own but still stayed close enough to overhear what was happening. Malloy grabbed Pete's arm, and Pete spun toward him while simultaneously pulling his arm away. His expression was thunderous as he glared at Malloy, who was a few inches shorter than Pete. "What is going on here?" he yelled, genuinely angry.

Malloy had either overcome his procedural hesitation or he knew it was impossible to stick to. "We got a tip about marijuana plants in your yard."

Pete froze for the count of a breath. "What?"

Beacon cleared his throat and everyone looked at him. "Eight so far, five flowering females."

"What!" Sadie and Pete said at the same time.

"Interspersed with the landscaping." Beacon waved toward a

shrub at his feet, and Pete moved toward him quickly, coming up short as he looked at whatever Beacon was pointing at. His head moved slightly and he stepped a few feet to the left, then his eyes moved again and he took a few more steps in the same direction. He then stopped and looked to a few more specific points.

From where Sadie stood at the edge of the patio she couldn't see anything other than flowers and shrubbery planted so close together that she couldn't tell where one plant ended and another began. She certainly couldn't pick out the pointy leaves of a marijuana plant. But Pete's expression confirmed what Beacon had said—there were marijuana plants growing in the flowerbeds.

Sadie instantly remembered the indoor grow lights she'd seen in Jane's apartment. She gasped and opened her mouth to tell them about it, but Pete started talking before she had a chance.

"You know I didn't plant these," Pete said to Malloy. "The very idea that I would is ridiculous. And an outdoor female plant wouldn't flower until fall. Obviously they've been transplanted."

"You know I have to follow up on a tip like this," Malloy said, regret in his voice. "I had hoped it was leading us on another wild-goose chase and there would be nothing here." He turned to Beacon. "Have you inspected the entire yard?"

"Only this side," he said, waving to the west side.

Sadie scanned the rest of the yard. If Beacon had found eight plants in just one half of the yard, how many more could be in the other half? Sadie didn't know what the importance was of some being flowering or female but Pete obviously did. Her stomach sank. Even though she wanted to argue that Jane was obviously behind this, Malloy couldn't ignore this many marijuana plants. Six per adult were allowed under Amendment 64 in Colorado, but they had to be in a secure area, not a backyard. From Pete's silence she knew he was thinking the same thing, except he knew so much more about the law enforcement's responsibility regarding such a situation.

Sadie heard the hinge of the gate and looked over her shoulder to see Shawn entering the backyard. He joined her on the patio, observing the scene silently like she was. She leaned toward him and whispered what the tip had been. Shawn's eyebrows went up, but he said nothing. Pete was still standing in a flowerbed, then he took slow steps back onto the lawn where he stopped in front of Malloy.

"The landscape company I use for maintaining all this"—he waved his arm to include the entire yard—"was here a week ago. You can call Robert at Redman's Landscaping, and he can verify that there were no marijuana plants here at that time. Surely there is someone who can determine how long ago these were transplanted. I had no idea these were here, and if I had known, I'd have alerted you to it." He spoke with a professional calmness that made Sadie's heart ache. Couldn't Jane have left him alone? First Shawn's bank account, then Sadie's e-mail, and now Pete's home. Would this affect the sale? Would Pete be arrested?

"I don't doubt any of that," Malloy said to Pete with a softness that reminded Sadie that Malloy's investigation had been anything but easy. "And I'm sure we will find adequate proof that there's a conspiracy here, but my belief in your integrity can only change the course before us so much." He glanced toward Sadie, and she was taken aback by the genuine concern on his face—the first she'd seen all day. He looked back at Pete. "I have tried to handle this situation to the best of my ability, but I can't ignore this. I have a responsibility to my position and have already brought in the DA for Sadie's burglary charge."

Pete looked at Sadie, and she gave him a penitent look. She would explain it to him but right now she had another detail she needed to share. "There were grow lights in Jane's apartment," she said. "In the bedroom closet."

"You can search the apartment yourself now that you have probable cause to believe she was involved in this, can't you?" Shawn added.

"They have a point," Pete said to Malloy.

"I'll have to talk to the task force about that," Malloy said. "This is out of my hands. I can't be the one making decisions on how we move forward without clearance from higher-ups. All this has sufficiently painted me into a corner."

"You have to call the task force?" Pete asked, his shoulders slumped.

"You know I do. These are federal charges." He let out a heavy breath, and Sadie felt a teeny tiny bit of sympathy for him. "As lousy as all this is—and it's lousy—the fact that all three of you have been targeted shows a pattern. I only hope the DA sees it that way. This whole thing is so unprecedented I can't begin to guess how we'll proceed."

Pete let out a breath. "What do you need from me?"

"I need to call the task force, and you need to come to the station and give a statement. Do we have your permission to search the house?"

"Absolutely not," Pete said, though his tone was casual and Malloy didn't seem surprised. "I'm calling an attorney and will talk to you after I've consulted with him."

Pete had told Sadie before that no one should ever consent to a search or talk to the police without an attorney present. It seemed odd to Sadie that Pete would be so certain of this—especially since it complicated his job when he was the investigating officer and the suspects asked for these same things—but she felt she understood a bit better now that she was watching the situation unfold. What if Jane had placed other things in the house in order to frame Pete? An attorney would protect Pete's rights and hopefully get things cleared up quicker. She chose not to think of the expense of an attorney or the impact a federal investigation against Pete would make on their immediate future.

"I think I should take Sadie in too," Malloy said. "I don't want them to suspect preferential treatment."

Pete shook his head. "I think my situation oversteps hers," he said. "I'd like her left out of this as long as possible."

Malloy vacillated, but then nodded. "I'll do what I can."

"Thank you," Pete said, and Sadie felt herself soften toward Malloy even more. This situation *was* so incredibly complicated. She didn't wish to be in Malloy's shoes as he tried to figure out how to handle it.

"Make whatever calls you need to make," Pete said. "Can I talk to Shawn and Sadie while you do so?"

"For a minute," Malloy said.

Pete nodded, then crossed to Sadie. He put a hand on her upper arm and guided her a few yards away from Malloy so he couldn't overhear. Shawn followed, and when they came to a stop, Pete looked between both of them before focusing his attention on Sadie. "It's going to be okay," he said.

His calmness annoyed her. "You don't have to patronize me. This is bad."

"It *is* bad, but it will also be okay. We have enough information against Jane that they'll be able to prove this was a frame. It will just be ugly for a little while. There's a lot of procedural stuff they need to untangle."

"How long is a little while? We're supposed to get married tomorrow. We're supposed to have our kids together for a barbeque in three hours at a house I'm not allowed to go back to and *your* house is a crime scene." She realized how angry she sounded and shook her head by way of apology before she spoke again. "I'm sorry, I just can't believe this is happening."

Pete didn't reply to anything she'd said, but instead asked, "What did you get from the apartment?"

Sadie hesitated, realizing that she'd mentioned finding the lights but hadn't told him anything else.

Pete interpreted her hesitation correctly and explained, "I called the station to ask about the tip, but of course they wouldn't tell me. But they *did* say you were brought in for taking items from an apartment on Stanicker. I can only assume you got a lead and found Jane's apartment."

He wasn't mad? Sadie didn't waste time celebrating that fact and told him about the lights first—since that was directly tied to his situation—and then explained what she'd taken from the apartment.

"But the police took it all, and Malloy says they can't use it because we obtained it illegally," Shawn added. "Is that true?"

"Maybe." Pete glanced at Shawn before looking at Sadie again. "Did you learn anything important before the police confiscated the items?"

It took Sadie a moment to shift gears. "I found information from prescription bottles—a name and a pharmacy. I didn't tell Malloy.

The bottles were Velcroed under the toilet lid, so I left them there but took pictures."

"Excellent." He looked at Shawn. "Can you track the name on the prescription?"

"Absolutely," Shawn said with a sharp nod.

"Good," Pete said. "Dig as deep as you can on your own as quickly as possible. Update the Facebook page and—"

"They made me take my name off it," Shawn said. "Any leads will go to the police now."

"But they didn't make you take it down, and you're still the owner of the page, right? The police didn't take your log-in info?"

Shawn shook his head.

"Good, then keep working it. Keep the pressure on Jane even if the tips are relayed to the police department. The more people who know who she is and the fewer places she has to hide, the stronger we get." He turned to Sadie. "And don't cancel the barbeque."

Sadie pulled her eyebrows together. "Don't cancel it? Malloy told me I can't go home until the bug is cleared."

"We don't want to have it there. Call my kids and tell them what's going on. I've sent them a couple of updates throughout the day so they know things have been crazy. You said Liam had offered to hire a security company, right? Ask him to call Allen Security out of Denver. He'll need to call right away for them to get here in time. Tell him to ask for Troy."

"I think we should cancel it," Sadie said. "After all this I—"

"Cunningham," Malloy said from the other side of the yard. "We'd better get to the station."

Pete's hand on Sadie's arm tightened, the only evidence of his tension, but he kept talking. "She's going after all of us so there's no point in hiding. If she thinks we're going on as though everything's normal, she's likely to become more and more daring with what she does. You've cut her off from her apartment, which is going to make her mad, and we've taken away her anonymity around town. Those two things might make her desperate enough to act rashly. I know it doesn't feel like it, but we're gaining ground here, we can't let up now."

"Cunningham," Malloy said again.

Pete held Sadie's gaze. "I'll call you as soon as I can, hopefully before the barbeque, but we can't let her think she's winning." He leaned forward and lowered his voice even more. "Don't go through Malloy anymore, things are too complicated for him."

"Cunningham," Malloy said a third time, louder.

Pete straightened. "I'm coming," he said in a normal tone. He moved his hand from Sadie's arm to the back of her neck and leaned in, kissing her fast and hard. When he pulled back, he looked into her eyes and Sadie felt emotion rise in her throat. "It's going to be okay," he said again, but his smile was too false to be taken at face value. He looked at Shawn. "You're not to let her out of your sight, okay?"

"Okay," Shawn said.

Pete looked back at Sadie and held her eyes long enough for Malloy to call his name again. "I love you," he said in barely more than a whisper. He turned and headed toward Malloy. "Let's go," he said in his official voice. "The sooner we get started on this, the sooner it'll be over."

CHAPTER 18

Sadie was usually good about snapping into action and focusing on the job at hand, regardless of the job that needed doing. But she was silent and introspective for the drive home from Pete's house, and Shawn didn't push her. They weren't going to stay there—as much as it galled her, she agreed the hotel was likely the best place for them to go—but she needed her overnight bag. And she wanted to make sure the house was locked up so that Malloy would be forced to call her when his crew showed up. She wanted to be there when they went inside the house.

"We could have the family dinner at Farley Park," Sadie said once they were closer to home. "They have those charcoal pits Pete's kids can use in place of the grill." She didn't want to say out loud how much she did not want to do this dinner. She was already so wound up and stressed, trying to make nice with people at a party felt beyond her. But Pete wanted it, and she understood its purpose.

"That's a good idea," Shawn said. "Can you reserve the pavilion this close to game time?"

"I hope so." When she'd reserved it in the past for different community or church events she'd been involved in, she'd always had weeks' worth of lead time. "I'll grab the Garrison phone book at the house and call Lynette at parks and rec." Sadie glanced at the clock on the dashboard: 3:50.

Shawn nodded his agreement. Sadie pulled out her phone and called Breanna. She should have landed a couple of hours ago. Why hadn't she checked in before now?

"Hey, Mom," Breanna said when she answered. Was there a hesitation in her voice or was Sadie's paranoia on overdrive? Or both? Could Jane have interfered with Breanna the same way she'd created problems for Sadie, Shawn, and Pete today?

"Hi. Is everything okay? You didn't call when you landed." There was a pause and Sadie tensed. "Breanna?"

"I didn't call because I didn't want you to tell me to stay in Denver."

"What?"

"We picked up our rental car and hit the road." She took a breath and then spoke quickly. "I know you didn't want us to come, but Liam and I talked about it the whole flight and we want to help. Neither of us felt okay about waiting in Denver. Maggie said she was fine getting her own car since she'd reserved one anyway and that she'd come as soon as she landed. We love you, Mom. We don't want you to face this alone."

Sadie didn't know what to say. She didn't want to discount Breanna's feelings, but having both her children here added stress all the same. But they were already on their way, and in truth, she couldn't wait to see them. "How close are you?"

"We're just coming up on the Jackson exit," Breanna said.

"So you're an hour out?" Liam had to have been speeding to make that kind of time but Sadie chose not to reprimand him.

"Yeah. Don't be mad, okay?"

"I'm not mad," Sadie said, her voice soft and a bit choked up. "I was going to tell you to come, so I'm relieved you're almost here."

She could feel the relief in Breanna's voice when she said she was glad to hear that. Then Breanna asked what had happened since they talked last, and Sadie's heaviness returned. She told Breanna about the failed break-in of Jane's apartment and the marijuana plants at Pete's—again it was an unbelievable story to tell. It felt even more unbelievable to tell her that Pete insisted they hold the barbeque anyway. She felt sure someone was going to validate her own concerns and argue against the party, but Breanna seemed to find it completely reasonable to continue on as normal.

"We'd like to take Liam up on his offer to hire a security company." Sadie felt silly asking him to do it, she wasn't impoverished and could probably afford it, but Pete had told her to ask Liam, and she couldn't deny that it would be a relief not to have to coordinate it herself. She relayed the details to her daughter.

"That's great," Breanna said. "Allen Security?"

"Yes. But they're out of Denver, and the barbeque is in less than three hours so I don't know if they can do it. Maybe Pete knows someone out of Fort Collins or—"

"We'll call Allen first and talk to them about it," Breanna cut in. "Is the barbeque still at 7:30? Will you text me the address for Farley Park when we finish this call? I know how to get there, but the security company will need the physical address."

"Yes, it's still at 7:30," Sadie confirmed. "And I'll text you the address. Thank you for doing this."

"No problem," Breanna said. "We'll let you know the progress we make, and we'll see you soon."

Sadie hung up feeling a little better and answered Shawn's questions as they finished the drive. As soon as Shawn turned into Peregrine Circle, Sadie noticed an unfamiliar vehicle parked in the driveway and felt herself tense up. It was red, so it probably wasn't an unmarked police vehicle, but Sadie couldn't think of anyone else who should be at her house. An instant later she saw a large sign planted in her front yard with balloons tied to the upper corners. Sadie squinted and read the bright blue words on the sign:

HONK! I'M GETTING MARRIED!

"What on earth?" Sadie said under her breath as Shawn slowed at the curb.

"Is that Gayle?" Shawn asked, pointing out the passenger window.

On the driveway stood Gayle, Sadie's best friend who had moved to Kauai over a year ago to help Sadie out after an emotional crisis, had fallen in love with Sadie's former therapist, and had gotten married on the North Shore six months ago. Life really was stranger than fiction sometimes—no one would ever believe that kind of thing in a novel.

"Gayle!" Sadie said and threw open her door. She jumped out and hurried toward her friend who could not have arrived at a better moment. Gayle met her halfway and they embraced tightly. "You said you couldn't make it," Sadie said as they pulled back from one another.

She glanced past Gayle's shoulder to see Dr. McKay, her old therapist, stepping out of what must be a rental car. He wore a colorful Hawaiian shirt and khaki shorts—the standard outfit he'd worn during each of Sadie's sessions with him in Kauai. Not for the first time,

Sadie wondered if he owned any other type of clothing. When she and Pete had gone to Kauai for the wedding in January, he'd told them to call him Bill, but Sadie hadn't been able to make the transition yet.

"I wanted it to be a surprise," Gayle said, smiling proudly. Her hair was as red and curly as ever, and she'd stopped wearing the colored contacts she used to wear every day. Her brown eyes lit up every time she looked at her new husband, which more than made up for whatever she might have lost giving up the colored lenses. "And I've been needing to come home and take care of the house now that my kids have picked it over, I'm sure. Most important, of course, is that I'm here because *you're getting married!*" She ended her words with a squeal, a sound closely followed by the honk of a car horn.

Sadie jumped and looked around; the honk had come from the main road that ran to the east side of her house. She caught sight of a red VW bug before it disappeared from sight.

"Everyone wants to celebrate with you!" Gayle said, clapping her hands together.

Sadie was confused until Gayle waved toward the sign and Sadie read it again. Even then it took a second for it to download—Gayle had put the sign in the yard so people would . . . honk? Another car honked its horn.

Sadie waved at the driver politely but felt her neck heat up all the same. This kind of thing wasn't really her style even though the sentiment was sweet.

"You can't take it down," Gayle said, putting her hand on Sadie's arm and giving it a little shake. "Promise me you won't."

Whatever embarrassment Sadie felt was quickly overshadowed by the fact that Gayle had come all this way to be a part of Pete and

Sadie's day, and she'd found a way to put her own little stamp on things. Sadie shook her head, unable to hold back a smile. "You must lie awake at night trying to think of things to be obnoxious about."

Gayle's smile didn't falter; in fact, she might have smiled a bit bigger. "Nah, it comes to me pretty easily. Besides, I didn't get to help with anything else for the wedding, so this is my contribution."

Shawn joined them on the sidewalk, prompting Gayle to give him a quick hug too. After Shawn and Dr. McKay had been introduced to one another, Gayle said she and her new husband would be spending about three weeks in Garrison. She'd been living in Kauai for over a year and had resident status, but she wanted to sell the house in Garrison and make the relocation permanent in everyone's minds. Apparently, her kids kept thinking she was going to come back.

"I promised them I'd cover the flights for their families to come see me once a year and that settled them down a little. Plus between Skype and Facebook, it's easy to keep in touch. I plan to come twice a year for extended visits too, of course. It's good for them to stand on their own two feet a bit more; I've always babied my girls."

Sadie had often felt that Gayle overcompensated for her divorce by involving herself in the lives of her daughters and their families too much, but she had never said so before and certainly wasn't going to now.

"And I'm so excited to be at your wedding," Gayle said, smiling broadly. Gayle had promised to be at their wedding when Sadie told her about Pete's proposal, but a week later said she couldn't make it. Sadie had understood—it was such a distance to travel—so having her here now was surreal.

At least until Sadie remembered all that had happened today. She felt her smile fall.

"What's wrong?" Gayle asked, concerned. "I can still come, can't I? It wasn't one of those RSVP or there won't be a seat, was it?"

"No," Sadie said, putting her hand on Gayle's arm. "I mean, yes, you can still come. It's just that things are kind of complicated."

"Complicated how?" Gayle asked, pulling back slightly. "Don't tell me you called it off."

"No, but—"

"Jane's back," Shawn cut in.

Gayle gasped. Dr. McKay, standing behind his new wife, lifted his eyebrows. As Sadie's former therapist, he knew about Jane too.

"She's back?" Gayle said, her expression one of pure fear. "I thought she was gone for good."

"So did I," Sadie said. She quickly updated Gayle on what had happened since last night—it sounded like a made-for-TV drama—and Gayle's expression showed increasing outrage the more she heard.

"I'm taking down that sign," Gayle said after someone laid on their horn for five full seconds while they drove by.

"No, the sign is fine," Sadie said. *Annoying, but fine.* "It supports what we wanted to do, which is to appear as though we're still going on with everything in hopes Jane makes a mistake." Sadie explained that they were going to have the dinner tonight as planned, though with a security team in place. Which reminded her that she still needed to reserve the pavilion. She glanced at her watch and felt the urgency. It was after 4:00.

Gayle wrinkled her nose. "Farley Park?"

"They have that covered pavilion and the fire pits. They're not the nicest park in town, but they're the only one with both features."

"And if the wind's wrong, it smells like Rosen's dairy farm," Gayle added.

"Excellent point," Shawn said with a nod. "I knew there was a reason I didn't love the idea, and now I remember why. Remember that church picnic? I think three different kids puked up their cheeseburgers."

"Thank you, Shawn," Sadie said, giving him a look she hoped reminded him that he'd been taught manners at some point in his life and ought to use them.

"Why don't you use my backyard?" Gayle said. "It's only a few blocks from here."

Sadie pictured the long narrow yard Gayle had behind her house. She had lilac trees along the fence and a covered back porch that had three picnic tables and a built-in grill. Before the divorce, her husband had renovated it, which gave Gayle particular satisfaction when he didn't get the house in the settlement. There was also a swing set the younger kids would love. It was perfect and fully fenced, making it more secure than the park could ever be.

Sadie didn't want to pursue the offer, it was so intrusive on Gayle, but she couldn't ignore how well it would work. "Really?"

Gayle nodded. "We haven't stopped in to see it yet, but Amber's husband has been keeping up the yard for me. I know the kids have used it a few times for family dinners and stuff. I would love for you to use it."

"I've got some tables I borrowed from the church around back. I bet Pete's son-in-law could bring his truck over and pick them up." Miles had offered the truck to help Pete move so Sadie hoped he was equally available for this task. "You're sure it's not an imposition?"

"Not one bit," Gayle said, and Sadie knew she meant it. Gayle loved to help people, which was one of the reasons why Sadie loved her so much. She hugged her friend again. "Thank you so much," she said mid-squeeze. "You're a lifesaver."

"I do it for the adulation alone," Gayle said with a grin, then looked at the house. "You said you can't stay here. Where are you going to stay tonight?"

"We were at the Carmichael last night so I think we'll just take our things back there. I can't imagine they're booked on a Wednesday night. Breanna and Liam will need a room, too, I guess. And maybe Pete now that his house is a crime scene." She made a mental note to call on that soon. There was so much to do.

"I'm sure the police will clear everything before we have to worry about staying overnight, don't you think?" Shawn said. "I really hate their beds. They're rock hard."

"I'm sorry, sweetie," she said, frowning, "but even if they clear the house, I don't think it's safe for us to stay here. Knowing Jane's been inside makes me nervous."

"Of course you'll stay with us," Gayle said as though it were obvious. "I've got two guest rooms—one with a queen and one with a full—and a couch bed in the basement that I'm told is quite comfy."

"Oh, I couldn't," Sadie said. She was dominating Gayle's life as it was, using the backyard for the dinner. Gayle had just gotten into town, and it didn't sound like she'd even seen her kids yet.

"Of course you could," Gayle said, waving off Sadie's objection. "I know you were excited to have your kids staying with you at the house, and you can all fit at my place. I won't stand for anything else. Bill and I can help load up whatever things you need for the wedding right now, and we can store it at my place so you don't have to worry about it one bit tomorrow."

Sadie felt such relief to have someone she trusted making these decisions so easy for her. "Oh, Gayle, you have no idea how heaven-sent you are right now."

"We better get going, though," Shawn said, turning toward the front door. "Heaven-sent or not, we've got a lot left to do, and it's hotter than Hades out here."

Sadie had been so wrapped up in the moment that she hadn't noted the temperature, but she suddenly felt the heat and was eager to follow Shawn across the lawn and up the front steps. Gayle and Dr. McKay followed, Gayle chattering on about how strange it was to be back in Garrison after over a year but that she already missed Kauai. Her skin stayed soft thanks to the humidity, and she could feel the dry air of the Rocky Mountains making up for lost time.

Sadie smiled at Gayle's commentary while Shawn used his key to open the door. She heard it open and stepped in after him, only to walk into his back when he stopped short. She looked to the side of him to see what it was that had stopped him as the alarm started beeping to announce that a door had been opened.

The living room carpet was covered in birdseed and mangled pieces of tulle and ribbon from the favors she'd set beside the door last night. The monogrammed napkins she'd ordered weeks ago were also torn and scattered across the floor. Sadie's chest hitched slightly, but as quickly as she felt the shock, she got angry. She was so tired of being manipulated by Jane's games! Favors and napkins—what a silly thing to have wasted her time on. As though Sadie cared when she compared such antics to Shawn's bank account or Pete's pot plants. Knowing Jane had been in the house again bothered her more than anything. There had been no realtor's open house today that would have given her access.

She pushed past Shawn in order to turn off the alarm, which

was beeping faster as it counted down to the end of the thirty-second delay. But as soon as she stepped into the house, she forgot about the alarm. She forgot about everything.

Her wedding dress—the dress she was supposed to wear when she promised herself to Pete—had been a two-piece, ivory-colored skirt and jacket set. But it now consisted of at least a dozen pieces laid out on the floor directly inside the door, as though the different pieces were a puzzle that could just be snapped back together.

Sadie stared at the dress, heard Gayle gasp from behind her, and waited for the frustration to fill her up as it had been doing all day today. *Of course* Jane had found some way to access the house—despite the alarm system Sadie had bought specifically to keep her out. *Of course* she'd found Sadie's dress and shredded it before making it into a display Sadie would see when she came home next. *Of course* she hadn't moved her attention from Sadie entirely and had found one more way to dig in her claws and make Sadie hurt.

"Oh, Sadie," Gayle said from behind her.

The beeping of the alarm was still speeding up, a warning that the time to disarm it was running out. Sadie decided to let it go. The alarm would alert the monitoring company, who would call her. She could verify that the alarm was valid, and the company would notify the police. Not having to make the call herself would keep her from having to deal with Malloy.

She surveyed the living room for another moment, then stepped around the dress and headed for the kitchen.

"Let me grab my phone charger," she said, as though that was the only thing she had on her mind.

On the way to the kitchen, she noted her laptop on the floor by the computer desk, the screen cracked and several of the keys pried from the keyboard. She stared at it for a few seconds before continuing into the kitchen, the beeping from the alarm becoming more and more insistent. "Shawn, where's your laptop?"

"In my room," he said, watching her carefully from the doorway.

It took everything she had to remain calm and not show the lurching she felt inside. She could break down later, when this was all over and she was alone.

"Go see if it's okay." She reached the part of the island where the bug had been planted and then got on her hands and knees so she could peer into the space. It was gone, but its absence didn't make her feel any less vulnerable. She stood and continued into the kitchen where she unplugged the charger. For a moment, she considered retrieving the cookie dough from the fridge, but then realized she wasn't going to be making cookies today.

Shawn reappeared, a bag in each hand, one of which was her overnight case. "My laptop's fine," he said, lifting his bag slightly as though indicating his computer was in it. "I grabbed your bag too. The rest of the house looks okay, but we probably don't want to mess with anything, right?"

"Right," Sadie said. Malloy might get mad at her for taking the bags—*her* house was a crime scene now—but she was going to take her things with her anyway. "I think that's it," she said, turning toward Gayle and Bill.

"You have everything you'll need?" Gayle asked. The warning beep of the alarm changed to a sharp wail, and she startled, but Sadie didn't react.

"That's everything," Sadie shouted above the sound of the alarm.

"Hair stuff? Makeup? Spanx?" Gayle reiterated, equally loud. The alarm cut off, leaving a heavy silence in its wake. Gayle paused, cleared her throat and then continued in a normal tone of voice. "You don't want to have to come back."

It was a good point, and Sadie nodded before heading to her room. She grabbed her secondary overnight bag and started throwing anything she might need before the wedding inside. Would they really go through with it? What would she wear?

She returned to the living room and attempted to ignore the sympathetic expressions of Shawn, Gayle, and Dr. McKay who stood in the threshold of the front door. Their sympathy weakened her resolve to be emotionless.

"Let's go," she said loudly, not pausing on her way to the front door, her feet crunching the birdseed as she made her exit. Sadie grabbed the doorknob on her way out and gave one more quick look at the dress and the mess and the symbol of just how much Jane hated her. She wouldn't bother locking up, that way Malloy and his crew could get in without having to contact her. They wouldn't be looking for the bug now, though. What was the point of locking the police out when Jane had full access?

How do I stop this? she asked herself as she followed Shawn to the car. How was it possible that after all they had done, Jane continued to stay one step ahead of them?

Chapter 19

The alarm company called Sadie's phone before they'd pulled out of Peregrine Circle, at least three minutes after the alarm had gone off. She'd have to reconsider her continued patronage to this particular monitoring service when this was all over. Luckily, no one was in mortal danger so Sadie explained the situation, and the nice young man on the phone assured her they would alert the police on her behalf. After that call, Sadie texted Breanna with Gayle's address instead of Farley Park and a promise to explain later.

Once they arrived at Gayle's, Shawn took up a position in the dining room, which was missing a table and chairs, but there was a sideboard he could sit at with the only remaining barstool from the kitchen.

Gayle hadn't been kidding when she said her kids had picked over her house. There were empty spaces all over the once meticulously decorated home. She kept looking toward certain walls or corners and frowning, but whether it was because she was mad at what was missing, worrying about Sadie's situation, or trying to remember what had been there, Sadie didn't know. And she didn't ask.

The numbness she'd felt following the sight of her mangled dress hadn't lifted yet. She was tired and overwhelmed and beginning to feel fatalistic, as though they would never get ahead of Jane, which made continuing to plan the barbeque less than enjoyable.

Bill said he would work on the backyard, and Gayle thanked him with such a sappy kiss that Sadie found herself jealous. They had such freedom, such ease and confidence in their relationship. How Sadie wanted that too. Right now she wondered if it could happen. It felt unobtainable, and when the numbness faded enough to let in the underlying anger and self-pity, she had to blink back tears. What would Jane do next?

"Three hundred and sixty-eight shares," Shawn called from the dining room. Sadie was in the kitchen, trying to make a new to-do list. Her thoughts were so scattered and disjointed she needed to be reminded of what she had left to do.

Shawn continued. "Eleven hundred likes, and I've gotten a couple of text messages about her having gotten coffee at Café Café a few times over the last two weeks. Looks like changing the contact information on the Facebook page doesn't change it for those updates that were already shared."

"Excellent," Sadie said, careful not to let her discouragement show in her tone of voice. "You've done a great job with that, Shawn. Thank you."

"No prob," he said. "I'm gonna get going on the profile. I already looked up one of those meds. The rabeprazole is for ulcers; maybe she's so miserable she gives them to herself as well as to the people around her." His keys tapped out a rhythm on his computer.

Sadie had hoped he'd make some quick progress and thanked him again for his overall wonderfulness before returning to her list, which was uncomfortably short. Basically, she needed to call all the barbeque guests about the change in plans. Why was she so hesitant to do it?

She tapped her pen on the paper and admitted she was avoiding the call to Pete's kids. She knew Jared the best; she and Pete had watched his kids when he and his wife had traveled to Texas to find an apartment after he matched with his residency after medical school.

It was during that babysitting trip that Sadie had come to realize just how warped Jane's attentions really were. Both Jared and his wife, Heather, had been so kind about the situation and seemed the least concerned about Pete and Sadie getting married.

But Pete's oldest daughter, Brooke, had been the one planning this dinner and the most hesitant toward Sadie over the years. Not rude, necessarily, and they'd made a lot of progress in recent months, but Brooke was the one Sadie always felt driven to impress. His other daughter, Michelle, was more easygoing and quiet but the least likely to take control of a situation.

Sadie consulted her lists—one of which had the phone numbers of all family members—and took a breath before making the unavoidable call.

Brooke answered on the second ring and took things better than expected. She offered to call her side of the family about the situation and the updated address for the barbeque. She was worried about Pete, which put her and Sadie on more equal ground than usual. Sadie was worried about him, too.

"We'll be to Gayle's by 6:30, and I'll have Jared and Miles pick up the tables and chairs from your garage," Brooke said. "We should have plenty of time to get it all done."

"That's great," Sadie said, grateful for Brooke's willingness to take some of the burden off Sadie's shoulders. "Thanks."

They ended the call, and Sadie put a check mark next to every name on the list associated with Pete's side, glad she wouldn't have to call people she hadn't met yet. Most of the people on Sadie's side already knew what was going on, but she texted Jack and his daughters and left a voice mail for her cousin Sandra, who was coming up from Boulder. By the time she finished, she'd received text confirmations from Jack and his girls that they would see her at the barbeque. That informing the guests had been so easy was both good and bad: good that it didn't increase complications, but bad because Sadie suddenly had nothing to do.

If her laptop hadn't been destroyed, she could be helping Shawn with the profile. She very much wanted to be part of uncovering Jane's history, but she couldn't very well kick him off his own computer. Especially since background checks were Shawn's specialty. Instead, she began straightening the cluttered kitchen, likely the result of Gayle's daughters rifling through Gayle's cupboards and drawers in search of those items they wanted for themselves.

There was a sense of calmness about restoring order to the kitchen—vases in this cupboard, bowls nested inside one another. She hoped that organizing Gayle's kitchen might organize her own thoughts, but she kept picturing her dress lying in pieces on the floor, then imagined Jane cutting it apart and envisioning Sadie's reaction to the destruction. Her chest got hot with rising anger and increased trepidation. What was next? Having been unable to anticipate what Jane had done so far left Sadie increasingly anxious about what might come next. Were the people around her still at risk or had Jane had her fun? Sadie didn't dare think that.

The sliding glass door opened, and Gayle stepped inside, making her way to the kitchen. "What if I made a big batch of lemon water for the dinner tonight? My contribution."

"You're giving us a venue," Sadie said, lining up the glasses in the cupboard from tallest to shortest, front to back. "No one's giving more than that. . . . But I do love your lemon water recipe." Gayle's father had been plagued with kidney stones for years until his physician gave him the recipe, which he claimed would cure the stones. Gayle's mom had started making it for Sunday dinner every week, and the man never had another kidney stone in his life. *That* was science. Delicious science.

Gayle had always made lemon water for different functions she was a part of, especially in the summer, and knew the equations by heart. Sadie had it written out in her Little Black Recipe Book, which she'd left at home. "Are you sure you don't mind?" Sadie asked.

"Not at all," Gayle said, reminding Sadie, again, of how much she truly liked to help people. She headed for the back door. "Let me just make sure the kids didn't run off with my five-gallon drink cooler. Will you check on the state of my sugar and see if I have citric acid and lemon extract in my cupboard? They last forever, and I always keep them on hand, but we better make sure they haven't been appropriated to one of my girls' kitchens."

By the time she returned, Sadie had the citric acid, lemon extract, and sugar set out and ready to go. Gayle would mix it with water and let it sit until right before it was ready to be served, then add a ton of ice and mix it again.

"How's the sugar?" Gayle asked, unscrewing the lid of the green cooler and smelling the inside. It must not have been bad because she shrugged and wrestled it into the sink so she could add water.

"Sugar's fine," Sadie said. It was flour that couldn't be unattended for a year and still be usable. Like Sadie, Gayle kept her baking items in airtight containers in her pantry.

"That's one thing I can't get used to in Hawaii," Gayle said loudly to be heard over the running water. "Bugs get into everything. I opened my sugar one day to find it riddled with ants. About lost my mind when Bill told me to just sift them out. I can't imagine I'll ever be able to do that, but apparently the locals are pretty kick back about that stuff." She shivered dramatically at the memory. Sadie shivered too. Ants in the sugar was normal? Yikes.

Sadie continued straightening the kitchen while Gayle measured out the ant-free sugar and lemon extract. They worked in friendly silence for a moment until Gayle cleared her throat. "So, what are you going to do about the dress?" she asked.

Sadie began stacking a variety of papers on the counter that Gayle would need to go through later. *The dress.* She let out a heavy sigh. "Honestly, Gayle, I'm not sure the wedding will even happen." She hated saying it out loud but was having a harder and harder time believing anything different. She faced Gayle, hating the pity she saw in her friend's expression as she put the cap back on the lemon extract.

Sadie continued, "With everything that's happening, I just don't know how it can work or if I even want it to. Who wants their wedding to take place amid this kind of stress and complication?"

"I'm so sorry," Gayle commiserated, exchanging the extract for the bottle of citric acid. "But I hate to see you give up on it."

"I'm not giving up on marrying Pete," Sadie clarified. "I'm just finding it hard to imagine the wedding will happen the way we've planned it. What better stage for Jane to play her final card than at my wedding? And what if she does something horrible? All my favorite people will be in one room."

"But she hasn't done anything to hurt anyone," Gayle said. "She's being sneaky and distracting and mean, but no one has been hurt."

"Can I trust that she won't do something hurtful? Can I believe that the reason she hasn't hurt anyone yet isn't simply to lull us into a false sense of security?"

Gayle considered that and measured out the citric acid. "Maybe you and Pete should just get married secretly, not have the public wedding at all."

"We've thought about it, but neither of us can imagine getting married without our children there. And everyone's come to town for this, and we've paid for everything already. I'd hate for all that money and effort and time to go to waste." She smiled at Gayle's confused expression. "I realize that completely contradicts what I just said about not wanting to have a wedding amid all this drama, but it's all just so . . . complicated. If it were up to me I'd have canceled this dinner, but Pete wants to keep it, and so we're going through with it. I have all the same fears about it as I have about the wedding."

A knock sounded at the door. Gayle turned off the water and moved to answer it. Sadie stayed in the kitchen until she heard Breanna's voice. Her breath caught and her eyes filled with tears before she hurried into the living room. She swept her girl into a mama bear hug, gushing about how glad she was that they were here.

Shawn joined them—whining a little about not having gotten the same welcome when he'd arrived yesterday—and then welcomed his sister with a hug that lifted her off the floor. Sadie hugged Liam, who then gave his report on Allen Security while Gayle and Shawn returned to their respective tasks.

"Their team is on their way and should get here at 6:00, in time to scout the neighborhood and get settled in. Troy shared his condolences that things are intense for Pete right now and promised to send his best guys."

"That is such a relief," Sadie said. "Thank you so much for doing that."

"I'm happy to," Liam said. "Truly."

"You said you'd have an update for me?" Breanna said, drawing Sadie's attention toward her. "Did something happen other than Gayle volunteering her house?"

Sadie told them about the dress, watching Bre's eyes go wide at the story. "How did she get in—twice?"

"I have no idea," Sadie said, shaking her head. "Pete and I bounced around the theory that she could have come as part of the open house the realtor held two weeks ago and planted the bug then. We'd spent the day in Fort Collins at his granddaughter's birthday party. It's the only time I can think the house would have been open. But today she got in without triggering the alarm. I don't know how."

"She could have disabled one of the sensors on a window or door, then used it to enter," Liam suggested. "In high school my buddy did that with the sensor on his window. He found instructions online about how to do it without having it show up in the alarm system status." He smiled. "I assure you I told him not to do such things."

Sadie smiled. "I'll suggest the police look into that. We took everything I'll need for the wedding tomorrow. I'm waiting to get an update from Pete. He's been at the station for going on two hours, and I'm hoping they've made some progress."

Sadie explained who was working on what right now, and Liam

and Bre volunteered to go to the house, talk with the investigative team there, and pull the tables out of the garage to make it easier for Miles to load up.

"Could you also go to Rachel's Bakery and pick up a couple dozen of her sugar cookies? I wasn't able to make anything for the barbeque and at least Rachel's won't taste store-bought."

Breanna laughed, told her to call if she needed anything else, and then gave Sadie a quick hug before they left. Sadie watched them go, wishing she had given them additional warnings to be extra careful. She retrieved her phone and texted it. Breanna replied with a smiley face.

On her way back to the kitchen, she stopped beside the sideboard that was functioning as Shawn's office. "How are things going?" she asked. She'd heard him on the phone when she'd been talking to Bre and Liam and was curious as to who he was talking to.

Without looking up from his laptop, Shawn pulled a Post-it Note off the sideboard and handed it to Sadie. Two names and two numbers were written there. One for Barry Smith and another for Professor Natalie Pruitt. From the area codes, Sadie thought Smith lived in Indiana and Pruitt was in Iowa, but she couldn't be sure.

"The top number is Jane's dad," Shawn explained. "The second one is Valerie's last obsession."

Sadie's eyes snapped up from the note to look at Shawn, who was still intent on whatever he was scrolling through on the computer. "Valerie? That's her real name, then?"

"Yep," Shawn said as though it wasn't a huge deal. He nodded to the paper Sadie was still holding. "The number for her dad is a cell number. I haven't tried it so I don't know if it's current. As for the professor, she teaches at the University of Iowa and filed trespassing charges against Valerie about four years ago—right before 'Jane Seeley' showed up in Denver."

Sadie's mouth hung open in shock. "How on earth can you know so much information? You haven't been looking for even a full hour yet."

Shawn settled more comfortably on his barstool, looking rather pleased by her question. "Well, I started looking for her in Nebraska, since that's where the prescriptions were filled—nothing on the public databases—and then branched out to border states. Found her name pretty quickly in Iowa's database, matched up the physical description, and found the link to her dad through that. He's had a couple DUIs, and the same address is listed on the protective order against her. I then followed the lead on Pruitt since she's the one who requested the restraining order."

"That's amazing," Sadie said, looking at the names again.

"You continue to underestimate me," he said, already turning back to the computer. "Anyway, I'm trying to get some leads on a possible juvie record, but those are hard to crack so I've got a buddy working on something behind the scenes for that part. It's gonna cost us, but if he gets us what we can't get otherwise, it'll be worth it."

Sadie always got a little uncomfortable when Shawn talked about his sources to underground information and preferred to know as little as possible about it. "You think I should call these numbers?"

"Yes," Shawn said, eyes on the screen again. "The dad might be iffy—he doesn't sound like a stellar citizen—but the lady professor seems legit and she doesn't have any kind of criminal record; I checked just in case. The two of you share a stalker, that's got to count for something."

Lemon Water

6 cups water
1 cup white sugar
1 teaspoon lemon extract
1 teaspoon citric acid*
1½ to 2 cups ice (depending on the size of your pitcher)

Mix the first four ingredients until sugar is dissolved, about a minute. Before serving, add ice and stir.

Makes 2 quarts.

*Citric acid can usually be found in the pharmacy section or canning section of your local supermarket. Specialty kitchen markets and online resources are your best bet if your local store doesn't carry it.

Note: If you leave out the citric acid, reduce sugar to ½ cup. It won't be as good, though. You've been warned.

Chapter 20

Gayle came in through the sliding glass door, coming to the kitchen sink to wash her hands. "The lemon water is ready. I took the racks out of my freezer and put the cooler in there to try to chill things a bit before dinner starts. Don't let me forget it's in there though. How are things going?"

"Things are going good," Sadie said, looking at the sticky note in one hand and her phone in the other. "Breanna's taking care of the security component of the barbeque, and Shawn found Jane's real identity. I have the number for her father and for another woman she stalked."

"Serious?" Gayle said, turning off the faucet and shaking the water from her hands before looking around for a dishtowel. Sadie pulled open the drawer next to the stove, and Gayle grabbed a freshly folded dishtowel, drying her hands. "That's fabulous. Bill got the grill working and trimmed up the grass. What time are the tables coming?"

"Around 6:30," Sadie said, distracted. She was still looking at the note, wondering what she could expect from the two people listed there. Would Jane's father be cooperative or hostile toward Sadie's questions?

"Do Bill and I need to help set up the tables?"

"No," Sadie said, putting the note and her phone on the counter and turning her attention to Gayle. "We'll have lots of hands."

"I only ask because I wanted to run an idea past you. Do you have a minute to talk?"

"Absolutely," Sadie said. Though she was eager to get information from Jane's dad and the other stalking victim, making the phone calls made her nervous too. She was so much better in person than she was on the phone. Maybe a few minutes of prep would get her feeling more confident about the calls.

"I've been thinking about what you said—about the wedding and everything—and I totally understand you want your wedding to be beautiful and special."

Sadie nodded.

"But you don't have to have it be *perfect* for it to be all those things," Gayle continued. "The wedding isn't as important as the commitment you and Pete will be making, and no one who loves you will hold it against you if you guys run to the courthouse first thing in the morning and then jump a plane for Costa Rica."

"Thanks, Gayle," Sadie said, meaning it. "I know you're right—the marriage is more important than the actual ceremony."

"Right," Gayle said. "And when you *do* get married—whenever and wherever that might be—you'll need a dress."

Sadie felt her expression fall as the memory of her cut-up dress came to mind. She'd bought the dress in Denver, had it tailored and everything. It was classy and slenderizing—despite it being white, which notoriously made Sadie look thicker than she really was—but it also hadn't necessarily looked bridal, which Sadie had liked since she wasn't a young bride. She'd felt beautiful in that dress, and now it lay in pieces on the floor of Sadie's living room.

"*If* you get married tomorrow," Gayle cut into Sadie's thoughts, "what are you going to wear?"

Gayle's concern made Sadie smile. It was so like Gayle to skip past the fear of bodily harm and psychological manipulation to focus on wardrobe. "I haven't thought much about it."

"I know you haven't," Gayle said. "What's more, I know you won't. You have too many other things on your mind far more important than a dress, which is why I was thinking that Bill and I should head down to Loveland tonight and get you some dresses."

Sadie pulled her eyebrows together. "Dresses? As in, more than one? And in Loveland?" Loveland was more than an hour away, but still the closest shopping mecca in this part of the state.

"You won't be there to try anything on, and there's no time to tailor anything anyway, so we'd just get a variety in order to make sure you ended up with something fabulous. I'll return whatever you don't like next week while you're frolicking on the beach with your beloved. The Promenade in Loveland has several stores where I know I could find some nice things on the rack. I'll try for white but might have to be creative. You'd look great in lavender or even a pale pink, and since it's a second wedding there are no hard and fast rules about color and style. Didn't you say Pete's suit is gray? Blue or pink or even a nice sea-foam green would look lovely with his suit. Bill could help me find a tie that would coordinate if we go with a colored dress. I'm sure there's a Men's Wearhouse down there." She finished, smiling with excited eyes.

"You'd do all of that?" Sadie asked, and even though a dress felt like the last thing she ought to be worrying about, she really didn't have anything else to wear other than Sunday dresses. Well, she had a velvet black formal dress and a sparkly navy blue one, but no one got married in black velvet or sparkly blue.

"You're going to get married sometime," Gayle said. "And you don't want me underfoot while you're with your family tonight."

"I would love to have you at the barbeque," Sadie said.

Gayle shook her head. "It's a family party."

Sadie abandoned that argument in favor of a new one. "What about your girls? You haven't even seen them yet." Surely after coming all this way, Gayle was eager to spend time with her family.

"We're going to Amber's for dessert around 9:30, after she's put her kids to bed—though I'm not sure they're ever really in bed before midnight. She's going to make those fabulous Rice Krispies treats—the ones with brown butter, so good—and Stacy's coming over too so we can all talk." She frowned. "I know my girls think my marriage to Bill is some sort of midlife crisis; I've been meaning to talk to them for a while and hope they'll understand that this is my life now. Getting some retail therapy will help me from getting too anxious about it. I really want to do this, Sadie. Please let me."

Sadie hesitated, but she didn't doubt the sincerity of Gayle's offer. "Really? I feel like I'm taking such advantage of you."

"Nonsense," Gayle said with a wave of her hand. "I've offered. And you have to admit, I have picked out some great stuff for you in the past."

Gayle did have a great eye, better than Sadie's. Sadie could easily think of half a dozen of her favorite articles of clothing that Gayle had insisted she buy even though Sadie hadn't been sure. In each case, after she'd worn them once or twice, she came to understand Gayle's insistence. "You're what, a size twelve?" Gayle asked.

"Closer to a fourteen," Sadie said, frowning slightly.

"Okay, so a big twelve or a small fourteen. I'll get half a dozen or so and whichever one you choose will be my wedding gift to you guys."

Sadie felt herself tearing up and blinked quickly to try to keep the emotion down. "I don't know what to say except that I'm so glad you're here." Her voice broke with the last few words, and Gayle made a tsking sound even though Sadie could tell she was touched.

Gayle put out her arms, and Sadie fell into another one of her friend's affirming hugs. In the moments of the embrace, Sadie reflected on their years of friendship, Gayle's first marriage crumbling, her children growing up and leaving home. They had always been there for each other so having her here, now, when Sadie needed that mothering kind of support no one else could offer, felt right. There was no doubt in Sadie's mind that Gayle's presence was nothing short of a blessing.

They pulled away and smiled at each other. "Thank you," Sadie said, trying to hold back her emotion. "I shouldn't let you do so much for me, but I appreciate it more than I could ever say."

Gayle let out a contented sigh. "It's not very often anyone gets the chance to play fairy godmother for someone else. This is my chance to pay back all the kindness and support you've given me for so long. There were so many times in my life where you were exactly that for me, it's only fair I get a chance to do the same."

Rice Krispies Treats with Brown Butter

½ cup unsalted butter
1 (10-ounce) bag mini-marshmallows*
¼ teaspoon coarse sea salt or kosher salt
6 cups Rice Krispies

In a large, non-dark bottomed pan, melt butter over medium to medium-high heat. (The hotter the pan, the faster it will brown and possibly scorch, so watch carefully if you choose the higher heat.) Stir frequently. Butter will foam, turn clear, and start to brown.

Once butter has browned, remove from heat and add marshmallows. Stir until marshmallows have melted. Add salt, mix. Add cereal, mix. Spread mixture into a buttered 9x13 pan. Coat hands in butter or nonstick cooking spray and press the treats firmly into pan. Let cool before serving.

Makes approximately 20 squares, depending on how you cut them.

*Because you are using the residual heat to melt the marshmallows, you must use mini-marshmallows. Full-sized marshmallows take too long to melt and need continual heat, which might burn your butter.

Note: Can use a 7-ounce jar of marshmallow cream in place of the mini-marshmallows.

Chapter 21

Gayle and Bill left for Loveland within ten minutes of Sadie proclaiming Gayle the best fairy godmother ever. Shawn continued his work on Jane's profile, and Sadie was left with the two phone numbers written on a Post-it Note. She wanted to make the calls before Breanna and Liam returned and so gathered together all her courage and confidence. She started with the top number on the list and, with each ring, her anxiety built a little bit higher. The gruff "Hello" didn't help to relieve Sadie's increasing nerves.

She cleared her throat. "Hi," she said. "I'm looking for Barry Smith."

"Yeah," he responded, just as gruffly.

Sadie took a breath. "Hello, Mr. Smith. My name is . . ." She hesitated. Did she want to tell him her real name? "Diane Hoffman," she improvised quickly. "I'm calling to ask you some questions about your daughter, Valerie."

Silence.

Sadie suddenly wondered why she hadn't thought this out before making the call. What questions should she ask? What questions shouldn't she ask? Where did she start and how would she be interpreted? "Um, maybe you could tell me when you last saw your daughter."

"Why are you calling me?"

"Because I . . . think your daughter might be in trouble."

"What kind of trouble?"

"I think . . . she's stalking a friend of mine."

"Then it's your friend who's in trouble."

Sadie opened her mouth when the silence changed from him being quiet on the other end of the line to there being nothing there at all.

"Hello?" she asked to make sure he wasn't there. No answer.

Was it a bad connection? Sadie hung up and considered whether to call back or not. The fact that she didn't want to was what convinced her to do it—she couldn't let fear rule her. She called the number again and braced herself. On the second ring, Mr. Smith answered.

"Not my problem," he said as gruff as ever. He hung up again.

This time her hesitation to call back was permanent. Perhaps it would be better if the police followed up with him.

Her eyes moved to the second number on the Post-it Note and her stomach tightened again. Would she get the same reaction from this woman? It seemed that she'd been a victim, just like Sadie, but would she be just as unwilling to talk as Jane's father was?

Sadie inhaled, committed to maintain her power regardless of this woman's reaction toward her, and blew it out in one quick breath as she dialed the number. The call went to voice mail after four rings.

"Leave a message," a woman's voice said, followed by a beep.

No name introducing herself? No greeting at all?

Sadie had only an instant to wonder how to address this woman before realizing that she should call her Professor Pruitt. She left as detailed a message as she could in the short period of time afforded her, then hung up with a new kind of anxiety. What if she didn't get to talk to Professor Pruitt? What if the professor didn't check her messages in time and Sadie didn't get the insight this woman could give her?

She was trying to determine if calling again might help her situation when her phone rang. The caller ID showed that the call was from the same number she'd just dialed. Professor Pruitt must have listened to the message immediately. Thank goodness!

"This is Sadie," she said into the phone.

"This is Natalie Pruitt."

Sadie waited for her to expand. When she didn't, Sadie spoke instead, "Thank you so much for calling me back. If you listened to the message then you understand my situation."

"Where do you live?"

"Colorado, a little city in the northern region called Garrison."

"How do I know you're who you say you are?"

This woman's history with Jane gave her reason to be suspect. "I don't know how to prove to you who I am," Sadie said, thinking fast, "but we have a Facebook page about what we're dealing with and an article on a local news site." She actually didn't know if Lori had posted the write-up yet; with her e-mail frozen and her laptop destroyed, she hadn't been able to follow up on Shawn's contact with her. She made a mental note to give Lori a call after she finished talking to the professor.

"What are the links?"

It took Sadie a minute to give the professor the information, after which she said she would call Sadie back if everything checked out. Sadie thanked her, hung up, and then waited nervously. It was eight minutes before her phone rang again, showing the professor's number. Sadie had managed to finish cleaning the kitchen and reorganize two drawers while she waited.

"Hello?" Sadie asked. "Professor Pruitt, did you read the information?"

"I did," she said, her voice softer than it had been during the first conversation, which gave Sadie hope that they were on the same team. "I'm very sorry that you're having to deal with her. I wouldn't wish it on anyone."

"Neither would I," Sadie said. "I'm sorry that you have had to deal with her as well."

"What do you know about my situation?" the professor asked, her voice tight again. "And how do you know it?"

Sadie relayed Shawn's background check that revealed the restraining order and told her about the call to Jane's father.

"He's useless," the professor confirmed. "I tried to get his help, too, but he wouldn't involve himself."

"He seemed to believe me, though," Sadie said. "When I told him what Jane was up to, he didn't try to defend her or anything."

"Jane?"

"I'm sorry, I mean Valerie. She was using a different name when I met her."

"I see," the professor said. "Her father knows what she is and claims to have washed his hands of her a long time ago—before I met her."

"He isn't a part of her life? What about her mother?"

"Her mother?" Professor Pruitt repeated. "She didn't tell you about her mother? I thought she used that on everyone."

Everyone? Who was everyone? "I don't know anything about her real life," Sadie said.

The professor was quiet for several seconds, then said with an air of caution, "Valerie drastically changed my life. I don't know you, and I don't speak of her lightly. If not for the precarious situation you find yourself in, I would probably insist that we talk face to face about this."

"I understand." Did she ever. "If not for my precarious situation, I would try for that as well. Seeing as I don't have time to come to you, I would very much appreciate any insight you can share with me."

"Are you a teacher?"

"Well, actually, yes. I mean, I was." Sadie was surprised to hear this question. "But not when I met Jane. I was retired by then."

"Three of the rest of us are teachers. The fourth was a neighbor."

A cold shiver ran down her spine. "Us?" she repeated.

"Five, including you. It's not a club any of us wanted to be a part of, but Valerie's particular attention put us there anyway."

Sadie was too surprised to respond.

"Ms. Hoffmiller?"

"I'm sorry," Sadie said, shaking herself. "I hadn't considered that she had a pattern. Well I thought so when I learned about your restraining order, I guess. But five women? Teachers? I-I don't know what to make of that."

"What you can make of it is that Valerie Smith is scary. My husband is a psychology professor, and we have spent a great deal of time trying to make sense of Valerie. What we have concluded is that she's a sociopath who targets motherly type women, usually teachers, and tries to create a version of a perfect mother-daughter relationship. Yet even while she longs for that connection, she is incapable of sustaining it."

It was a lot of information to take in at once, especially since Sadie was still trying to catch up to the idea of *five* women experiencing Jane the way she had. "I had no idea."

Professor Pruitt went on to tell Sadie of her history with Valerie. She had been Valerie's mentor at the University of Iowa and learned about her history before she became a target. Valerie's mother had been sixteen years old when Valerie was born—a girl unprepared to be a mother. She would leave Valerie alone for long periods of time, or drop her off with family or friends for days on end. Drugs, alcohol, and men had taken their toll until Valerie's mother overdosed when Valerie was seven years old. At that point Valerie was transferred to the care of her father, who was almost as broken as her mother had been.

"Valerie described him as an empty man," the professor said. "He provided for her, but only just. She did not feel that he wanted her—that anyone ever had—which of course is part of why I, and the others, were so sympathetic toward her when we learned of her history. She came across to each of us as very bright with a lot of potential and capability, if she only had someone to help her." She let out a humorless laugh, and her voice dropped when she spoke again. "She knew exactly how to play us, and every one of us fell for it."

"Teachers," Sadie said. It made more sense now. "Nurturers seeing a student in need of a little extra love." She'd had several students just like that over the years.

"Exactly," Professor Pruitt said. She went on to tell Sadie of

Valerie's sixth-grade teacher, who ended up moving to another city after years of Valerie coming to her school and home, breaking windows and pulling up flowerbeds when the teacher would not respond to her.

The next teacher was a junior high home economics teacher, who ended up with a vandalized office and slashed tires after she reported Valerie's obsessive behavior to the principal.

When Valerie's father moved out of state a few months before the end of her senior year of high school, she moved in with a neighbor. The neighbor felt sorry for Valerie having to finish high school in a new place and agreed to let her stay, only to have Valerie attempt a complete takeover of her life. Only when the woman's adult children intervened—nearly six months after Valerie graduated—did Valerie move to Iowa, where she took one of Professor Pruitt's classes and found her newest target.

"Over the next two years, she took every class I offered each semester," Professor Pruitt explained. "After things went bad, I came to realize that she probably did poorly in my classes to justify retaking them. I took her on as a student assistant in my office, and we became friends until it started getting weird the same way it had with the others: spending too much time at the school, pushing into my personal life, coming up with excuses when she crossed a line.

"When the semester ended, I didn't rehire her as my assistant, and she was very upset. She took all my classes again and would ask questions incessantly, stay after class, or wait for me in the parking lot. I reported it to my department head, and Valerie was told to keep her distance. That's when she started sending letters to the university alleging inappropriate behavior on my part. I also endured the smashed windows, flat tires, and calls made to my home phone number over and over and over again. She would fill up the voice mail on my office phone almost every weekend, playing the radio until the message time ran out."

"That's when you filed a restraining order against her?"

"On the advice of the campus police, yes. She didn't show up for the court date so the order was automatically granted, and it seemed to work. I've only seen her a handful of times since then—across a parking lot, or at my son's soccer game. She showed up at a university social last fall. Campus security took her outside and let her know in no uncertain terms that if they saw her again, she would be arrested. I haven't seen her since, but I'm always looking over my shoulder."

"You'll never be free of me," Sadie said out loud.

"Yes, that's exactly what she said the last time I saw her. How did you know that?"

"Because she said the same thing to me two years ago," Sadie said. "I'm terrified about how far she'll go now that she's back."

"Maybe she's just showing up, like she did with me," the professor said. "I think she takes great satisfaction in knowing I'm afraid of her. My husband thinks she comes back when she's feeling a loss of control in her regular life and needs a reminder of the power she still has over me. I don't handle it well when she shows up; she knows it upsets me."

"I want to hope she's just here to upset me too," Sadie said. "But she's targeting my son and my fiancé. She's broken into my house twice and attempted to interfere with my wedding in more ways than one."

"I wish I knew what to tell you," the professor said. "In talking to the other women—my husband thought it would be therapeutic for me and it was—it doesn't seem that her behavior escalated much between each of us. We all had the same type of treatment from her, though she became a little more sophisticated as she grew older, which is to be expected."

"She never physically injured any of you?"

"No," the professor said. "But she threatened to."

Sadie thought about Boston and told the professor about Mrs. Wapple, her sister, and Sadie's own experience in the trunk of the car. When she finished the professor was quiet for several beats.

"She never did anything like that with the rest of us," she said, a note of fear in her voice. "But then she was Valerie Smith with us, not Jane Seeley. Your situation has many new factors none of us faced, and I don't know how to process that. My husband would say it's a bad sign, though, that she's targeting you differently. It puts you in a more precarious situation."

They were both quiet for several seconds. Sadie tried to think of what else to ask but sensed she had what she needed to know. "I can't tell you how much I appreciate your help, Professor. You've given me so much insight. Can I call if any other questions come up?"

"Certainly," the professor said. "I don't answer my phone anymore. Valerie gave me an obsessive need to screen my calls, even if I know the number. Leave a message, and I'll call you back, though. And good luck with your wedding. For your sake I hope she disappears the way she eventually did for the rest of us."

Sadie thanked her and ended the call. She took a few minutes to write out her thoughts about what she'd learned, uncomfortably surprised to feel sympathy for Jane. She was still angry and embarrassed and frustrated, but she felt she better understood Jane's motivations, which gave her the chance to better preempt whatever might be coming next. At her core, Jane wanted a mother. How could Sadie not be sympathetic toward that?

She went into the dining room and discussed things with Shawn, who found it interesting but held tight to his belief that Jane was bent on hurting people.

Sadie's phone chimed with a text message, and she hurried to retrieve it from the kitchen counter, realizing en route that she hadn't heard from Jane in a few hours. Not since the media blitz had begun. Was this incoming text from her? Sadie braced herself, but the text was from her nephew, Ji, sharing his regrets that they wouldn't be able to attend—up until that morning he'd thought it was a possibility. He wished her luck and said he would look forward to seeing her when she and Pete came to San Francisco.

While Sadie was disappointed, she wasn't surprised Ji couldn't come and was even a little relieved that there were fewer people she would have to worry about. She thanked Ji via text message, then sent Pete a text even though she knew he wouldn't have his phone with him at the police station. The longer she went without talking to him, the more anxious she became imagining what might be happening. She imagined him being thrown in jail with real criminals, having to surrender his weapon, or post bond. Surely he would know she was worried and update her as soon as he could.

Breanna and Liam returned home after talking to the police who were doing a diagnostic on the alarm system. Miles showed up with a truck, and they helped load the tables for the party. Liam followed the truck to help unload, while Breanna helped her mom with more decorative aspects. Maggie was on her way. She'd called Shawn to confirm which exit to take off the main interstate.

Sadie continued with preparations and pushed away her fears

in order to try to keep a brave face as Pete's children arrived to get started with the cooking. Breanna was here. Shawn was here. Gayle was here. All these people who loved her were here to help her, to protect her, to make this work. Pete had said that everything would be okay; Sadie put great effort into believing that.

Chapter 22

The time between setup and the arrival of guests seemed to take place at warp speed. Shawn finished the profile he'd created for Valerie Smith using the forms he and Sadie had used when they ran Hoffmiller Investigations. The profile wasn't complete, but the amount of information he'd received coupled with the background Sadie had learned from Professor Pruitt was impressive for such a short period of time. Sadie gave a quick review of the form, complimented him again on his detail and speed, then thanked him when he offered to call the station and ask them how he should send over the information. When he was done, Sadie sent him to the store to get two bags of ice for the lemon water.

Maggie pulled up at 6:05, and Sadie ran down the front walk to welcome the sweet girl she'd first met just two months ago. Breanna and Liam said hello to her, and they were still in the front yard when Shawn arrived and quickly whisked Maggie away to the backyard under the guise of helping with the tablecloths, but more likely it was to have her to himself—their relationship had become serious over the last two months and yet they'd been thousands of miles apart.

Within minutes an unmarked SUV was in the driveway with four members of Allen Security. Sadie didn't catch all the details of the arrangement Liam had made with them, but she was grateful not to be in charge of it. Two of the men stayed out front, the other two took positions in the backyard and inside the house. After consulting with Liam and making sure they weren't expected to be inconspicuous, they put magnetic signs on the sides and back of their vehicle, advertising their company, which would, hopefully, help to keep Jane away.

Pete's children started cooking at 6:30—it smelled wonderful—and guests began arriving at 7:15. Still no word from Pete.

Sadie pasted a polite smile on her face as she welcomed the guests. She knew many of them, but there were a few unfamiliar faces she hated receiving without Pete's introduction. Pete's brother—who looked nothing like him—had come up from New Mexico along with Caro and Rex—who Sadie knew and loved. Well, she loved Caro and tolerated Rex but now wasn't the time for splitting hairs.

Lynn, Pete's late wife's sister, had come down from Wyoming, and Sadie was mildly uncomfortable until Lynn wrapped her arms around Sadie and told her how happy she was for her and Pete. It was impossible to doubt Lynn's sincerity. She pulled back and looked around. "Where's Pete?"

"He's still at the police station," Sadie said, keeping her polite smile in place even though her stomach sunk every time she had to say those words out loud. "We're expecting him back any time." It was a lie, but at least it was a consistent one; she'd given it half a dozen times already. She was relieved that no one seemed to be asking her a million questions. Maybe Brooke asked them not to, if so Sadie needed to thank Pete's daughter for the foresight.

"Hi, Aunt Sadie."

Sadie turned away from Lynn, who moved toward Brooke near the grill, and looked down into the sweet face of her nephew Trevor. He was tall for a seven-year-old and cute as a button. He had his dad's eyes—Sadie's brother Jack—but the shape of his face and color of his hair reminded Sadie of his mother, Anne. Sadie had counted her as a friend despite uncovering the deception that had been Anne's motivation for her part of their relationship.

After Anne's death, Jack had stepped up to be the dad he hadn't expected to be when he'd had an affair with a woman twenty-five years his junior. It had been a difficult, embarrassing, and yet ultimately rewarding experience for Jack in the years since. It was still difficult for his wife and daughters, however. It would probably always be that way—Sadie couldn't blame them for the difficulty of such a thing.

For her part, Sadie had just tried to love everybody, and in Trevor's case, that was easy to do. He was young enough to still have that sweetness about him, but old enough that she could see the young man he would be growing into over the next few years. She pulled him into a hug against her side. "How is my favorite boy?" she asked, ruffling his hair as she released him.

"I thought I was your favorite boy."

She turned to look at Shawn standing behind her and Maggie standing behind him, holding his hand somewhat shyly. "You're my favorite *son*," Sadie amended. He frowned dramatically and she chuckled. "Okay, you're my favorite man."

"What about Pete?" Trevor asked, his eyebrows pulled together. "Isn't he your favorite man?"

"Yeah, Mom, which of us is your favorite man?" Shawn said, lifting his eyebrows and cocking his head to the side.

"Uh . . . "

Jack stepped forward and put an arm around Sadie's shoulder, jostling her in his version of a hug. "Not only am I her favorite man, I've been her favorite for the longest." He smirked at Trevor and Shawn, then leaned in and kissed Sadie on the temple. "How are things, Sissy?" he asked in a sincere voice that everyone—except maybe Trevor—picked up on.

Jack's wife, Carrie, gave Sadie a quick smile and left to mingle with the other guests. Sadie and Carrie didn't have much of a relationship, but it seemed to suit them both fine.

"Hey, Trev, let's go check out the tree house," Shawn said, waving his cousin toward the far corner of the yard. Sadie wouldn't get within ten feet of that thing, it had to be infested with spiders and bugs, but Trevor was a seven-year-old kid and Shawn still liked bugs. Plus she knew that Shawn distracting his young cousin was mostly to give her and Jack a chance to talk.

Once they were alone, Sadie met Jack's eyes. "Things are pretty awful," she answered with all honesty. She waved toward the guests. "I feel like I've invited them all into a firing range or something. I'm on pins and needles waiting for something to happen."

"Yikes," Jack said. "Is it that serious?"

"I don't know," Sadie said, realizing she'd only sent him a couple of text messages by way of explanation. "Which means it might as well be that bad." She looked down and leaned onto her baby brother's shoulder. "Oh, Jack, I don't know what to do." She went on to tell him the things he didn't already know about the day. He listened silently.

"I'm so sorry," he commiserated when she finished. "Maybe it doesn't make you feel any better, but I know you'll figure it out."

Sadie let out a heavy breath. "Thanks for the support," she said sarcastically.

"I'm not just saying that," Jack said, giving her a strong look. "I look at what you've done these last few years, Sadie, and even when I think of how awful this woman is I can't help but think that she doesn't know who she's messing with."

Feeling repentant for the assumption that Jack had been being flip, she lowered her head. "I wish I felt that kind of confidence. This is different from those other things, Jack. With all the cases I've worked, I've had clues I've followed, and I've been the one a step ahead. This time, I feel like a puppet. We've tried all day to get ahead and every time we think we've made some progress, she manages to catch us off guard again."

"I don't think this situation is all that different than the other ones," Jack said. "The circumstances are, since she's come for you, but it's not as though you had an outline for those other situations. You didn't know exactly what to do or how to do it. You improvised, followed your gut, and made judgment calls with mere seconds to make those choices. And they worked." Jack touched her chin and made her look at him. He was a handsome man with a narrow face and their father's searching eyes. "Maybe you can borrow some of our confidence in you for a little while if you can't find your own. Every person here believes, without a doubt, that you're going to find what you need in that head and heart of yours and you're going to come out on top of this."

Sadie gave him a hug—a full hug; of everyone here, Jack *had* known and loved Sadie the longest. And he believed in her. That was powerful stuff. She'd been trying to get over her fear all day, sometimes she'd pulled ahead of it, but it overtook her again every time. Was that because she gave into it? Could she make a decision to not give into her fear anymore?

"Thank you, Jack," she said, smiling at him and realizing how much she'd missed him these last few years. Ever since Anne and Trevor came into his life, he'd faded out of Sadie's. She wanted to fix that and vowed that after the wedding, she would look at her life and prioritize her time and make the important things work.

Trevor came running back to them and grabbed Jack's hand, pulling him toward the tree house. Sadie smiled by way of giving him permission to go. Carrie melted out of the crowd and followed after them. Sadie was glad that Carrie had found room in her heart for Jack's son. Sadie couldn't imagine what it would be like to do so but admired her sister-in-law for growing into such a hard thing. Maybe Sadie would find room for a better relationship with her sister-in-law too.

Sadie had kept her phone in her pocket even though it made her hips look wider, because she didn't want to miss Pete's call. When she felt the vibration of a text message, she moved a few steps further from the mingling crowd. When she saw that the text was from an unknown number she paused, then moved slowly to open the text.

Unknown: How's your day been, Sadie? Everything going just as you'd expected the day before the BIG day?

Sadie inhaled, held it, and exhaled while thinking of how to respond. She wanted to communicate how angry and overwhelmed she was, or tell Jane all about the details she'd learned about Jane's other victims. She wanted to call her names and tell her how miserable she was making everything, but what if that was exactly what Jane wanted? After a few seconds of considering that, she decided not to say anything at all. When Pete got back she would discuss the options with him, but right now she was trying to keep herself together through this family dinner and Jane was not on the guest list. Jack had confidence in Sadie's ability to handle this situation and that made it easier to trust her own instincts. Sadie put her phone away without answering Jane's latest vie for attention. It felt good not to react.

When Jack came back from the tree house, Sadie asked him to help her put Gayle's drink cooler on the edge of the table. She hoped five gallons would be enough lemon water. Once people realized how good it was, it would be guzzled, she knew it. She had already arranged the cookies Bre had picked up from Rachel's Bakery on a plate and set it down beside a Jell-O salad with only a pinch of regret that the cookies weren't her own recipe.

"I think we're about ready for a welcome speech," Brooke said from Sadie's left. "Are you ready?"

Pete was the one who was supposed to take this task, but Sadie nodded. Brooke put two fingers in her mouth and whistled loudly. Everyone stopped talking to one another and turned to look at Sadie who stepped forward. She thanked them all for coming and for being patient with the last minute change of venue. "I'm hoping that Pete will be here at any time and wish I had an update for everyone, but I haven't heard from him." She had to look away from the sympathetic expressions. "I know that he would share my thanks for your patience today. It has been . . . extreme." The crowd chuckled good-naturedly with her and she bit her tongue to keep from apologizing for the porn e-mails many of these guests had received. It might lead to questions from people who hadn't been on the receiving end, or the mention could increase discomfort and . . . she took a breath and maintained her focus. "It's a testament to how much you love us that you're still celebrating with us amid all the hard things happening." People smiled back at her and lifted their Red Solo cups as though to toast her comments. "I'll also warn you that depending on what's taken place with Pete today, and what may happen between now and then, there may be some changes to the wedding." She heard a few expressions of surprise and tried to smile in an attempt to relieve the concerns. "Please stay by your phones so we can update you on what might take place, but regardless of what might happen tomorrow, we are so glad you're here and so grateful for your support, your love, and your well wishes. We hope that you enjoy dinner tonight and get a chance to meet everyone on whichever side of the family you don't belong to right now."

Her phone vibrated in her pocket again, and she quickly pulled it out, hoping it was Pete. It wasn't. The text was from an unknown caller, and Sadie stared at it a moment before she realized that everyone was still looking at her. She put a smile on her face and slid the phone back into her pocket without reading the message. "Sorry," she said, embarrassed. "Not Pete."

A few faces must have seen more in her reaction than she wanted them to: Jack, Shawn, Breanna, and Caro frowned back at her. Sadie didn't meet their eyes and faced the crowd of people watching her. "Anyway, Pete's children and their spouses have put together this *fabulous* meal. I'll have one of them tell you about it."

She stepped to the side and Brooke stepped forward to explain the history of Frikadeles with Ruskumsnuz. Everyone laughed at the name, and the mood lightened as Brooke shared accounts of camping trips and Sunday dinners where the meal served as a central point of their family time together.

Sadie was reminded of the sweetness behind Pete's children offering to share it with her family, each of whom were about to become their family too. But she couldn't stop thinking about the text message she hadn't read yet. Brooke took the lead in having everyone introduce themselves and how they were related, and Sadie decided to take advantage of the lack of attention being paid to her. She stepped to the side of the patio area and retrieved her phone from her pocket.

> *Unknown:* Tell me about your day, Sadie? Anything stressful happen?

It was easier to ignore this second text as Sadie could more clearly hear the gloating woven into the words. She returned the phone to her pocket and heard Maggie introduce herself as the only person not related to a member the wedding party. Another text came in.

> *Unknown:* You don't want to ignore me, Sadie. It's a very bad idea.

Sadie wanted to ignore Jane more than ever but she wondered if her silence would make Jane think that Sadie didn't have her phone with her. She wanted Jane to *know* she was ignoring her.

> *Sadie:* I talked to Professor Pruitt, Valerie. The gig is up. I will not be communicating with you again.

She hit SEND and got a response almost immediately—a derogatory term that made Sadie smile slightly. Not because she thought profanity was funny, but because Jane reacting with anger meant she wasn't getting what she wanted. Jane had been the focal point of Sadie's entire day. And as soon as she wasn't, Jane was mad.

Boy, did it feel good to make Jane mad.

Sadie's No-Fuss Sugar Cookies

1 cup butter, softened
¾ cup sugar
1 egg
2½ to 3 cups all-purpose flour

Preheat oven to 375 degrees F. In a large bowl, beat butter for 30 seconds. Add sugar and beat until combined. Add egg and beat until combined. Stir in 2½ cups flour until combined. Add additional flour slowly, a little at a time until a smooth dough forms; it should be soft but not sticky. Too much flour will result in a crumbly dough.

Divide dough in half and roll out on a lightly floured surface to ¼-inch thick. Cut with cookie cutter. Add cut trimmings to the second half of dough. Reroll and cut additional cookies. Place on greased cookie sheet. Bake 6 to 8 minutes or until barely brown. Cool 2 minutes then transfer to wire rack to cool.

Makes approximately 30 two-inch cookies.

Note: Can use powdered sugar in place of flour when rolling out the dough.

Glaze

4 cups sifted powdered sugar
¼ cup milk*
Food coloring (optional)

In a large bowl, combine ingredients. Stir in additional milk 1 teaspoon at a time until preferred drizzling consistency is met. Tint as desired with food coloring.

To glaze, hold cookie over the bowl of glaze. Use a small metal spatula or knife to cover the cookie evenly with glaze and remove excess. Glaze will harden as it dries.

*Evaporated milk makes for a smoother glaze than cold milk from the fridge.

Note: For more flavor, add ½ teaspoon lemon, almond, or orange extract to the cookie dough and ½ teaspoon of complementary extract to glaze.

Chapter 23

Sadie looked up from her phone to see Shawn approaching her while the introductions continued. "Everything okay?" he asked.

Sadie nodded. "Yeah."

"I've been watching you with those text messages you've been getting. They seem to be . . . thought provoking. Is it Pete?"

Sadie shook her head. "It's Jane, but I've decided not to play. I told her I won't be communicating with her anymore, and she didn't like that." Sadie smiled at him. "It felt good to make her mad."

"She's using a new number? Should we have the police track it?"

Sadie considered that but then shook her head. "None of the other four phones we've tracked have led us anywhere. She'll just ditch it and steal another one. Who knew phones were so easy to steal?" She held her phone out to him. "Anyway, I want to block the number but I don't know how."

"You sure?"

Sadie nodded. "Absolutely."

Shawn took her phone and started toggling. Twenty seconds later he handed the phone back to her. "Blocked."

"Thanks." She slid her phone back into her pocket. Brooke

waved Sadie over, and she asked Jared to say a prayer over the food that smelled so good. He did so, asking for God's grace to be upon both Pete and Sadie, which she appreciated. When he ended the prayer, Jared asked everyone to get in line for the grub, which everyone was more than happy to do.

Shawn stayed by Sadie while people fell into line, but Sadie followed his eyes to see he was watching Maggie talk to Caro.

"Maggie seems to be fitting in well," Sadie said. The girl was dressed in a silky red top that set off her dark hair and mocha-colored skin, white capris, and red platform sandals. Sadie watched Shawn watching Maggie for confirmation of what she suspected: he was head over heels for this girl.

"Isn't she great?" Shawn said with such wistful admiration that Sadie had to pinch her lips together to keep from chuckling out loud.

"She *is* great," Sadie said when she could keep her voice even. "And she's *hot*."

"Right?" Shawn agreed. "I can't tell you how glad I am she's not my sister."

Sadie did laugh out loud at that one, so did Shawn. The chime of his phone sounded in his pocket. He pulled out the phone and read the text message, his expression going from twitterpated to irritated in the space of a blink. Without explaining anything, he quickly started replying.

"What is it?" Sadie asked in concern.

"It's Jane," Shawn said without looking up. He'd mentioned before that she likely had his number since it was the same one he'd had two years ago, but until now she hadn't contacted him.

Sadie tried to see what he was typing, but he shifted so she couldn't read it. "What are you telling her?"

"I'm telling her exactly what I think of her," he said in tight words.

"Don't play into it, Shawn," she said strongly. "That's what she wants."

He stopped typing and looked up at her. "I so want to rage all over her."

"I know, but it won't help. She was far more affected by my cutting her off than she'd ever been by my responses." Finally, she felt as though she had pulled ahead. Even the Facebook post hadn't given her this same feeling of reclaiming her power. And it hadn't been so much about physically one-upping Jane as it was her emotional place. Interesting.

Shawn let out a breath and started typing again.

"Now what are you saying?"

"That my mom doesn't want me to talk to her anymore—but maybe not in those exact words. Have I told you how much I hate her?" He finished typing and sent the message.

"Yes, I think you have."

"Good, 'cause I really, really, *really* hate her."

"I bet I hate her more than you hate her."

"I don't think you have the capacity of hatred I have, so there's no way you can hate her as much as I do."

His phone vibrated, and he smiled at whatever response Jane gave him.

"Block the number," Sadie said, knowing he wanted to keep the angry text conversation going.

"Ah, do I have to?" Shawn said.

"No, but I wish you would."

Shawn grumbled but did as Sadie had asked, then slid his phone into his pocket. They looked out over the guests, half of whom had taken seats around the tables. The other half were still in line.

"We should get our food," Shawn said. They moved toward the line. "Will you guys still go to Costa Rica if everything goes okay with the wedding?"

"I don't know if we *can* go. I don't think Pete can leave the country until everything's cleared up. He's facing federal charges."

"Ridiculous," Shawn said, shaking his head. They stood at the back of the line, and Sadie conversed with Pete's brother until they reached the serving table where he began getting his food. It was as good as Pete's family had said it would be, and Sadie's mood was further enhanced by the enjoyment of a new recipe. She took a plate to each of the security guards, who thanked her and said they'd seen nothing out of the ordinary, which she was glad to hear.

It wasn't until dessert was served—a variety of ice cream novelty items alongside Rachel's sugar cookies—that Sadie got another text message. She had to stand in order to fish the phone out of her pocket. Would Jane have stolen yet another phone? But this time it *was* Pete. She told the people seated by her at the table—Jack, Carrie, Breanna, and Liam—then went into the house to read the text in private.

> *Pete:* On my way. Is there food left or should I grab a cheeseburger?

Sadie smiled and called him back for an update. The drug task force was looking into the situation, and Malloy had gone to bat for Pete, agreeing he'd been framed, but they'd found fourteen plants worked into the flowerbeds and Pete wasn't getting special privileges.

If anything, the task force would be more meticulous because of his connection to the Garrison police department. By following the advice of his attorney, Pete wasn't booked into jail.

"If Jane had any idea how much those pot plants would have benefitted this case *against* her, I'm sure she'd have come up with something else," Pete said after finishing his summary.

"That's not funny," Sadie said. "You just told me the charges weren't dismissed."

"But they won't be substantiated, and it pulled a federal task force into the situation. Shawn sent over that profile on Valerie, and there are cops in three states making contacts right now, gathering information that's going to lead us right to her. I hope I get the chance to thank her for framing me."

When he arrived at the dinner, he gave a shortened account to the group and assured everyone that he was not a drug dealer. He served himself some dinner and spent the next hour mingling with guests and acting as though everything that had happened was no big deal.

Sadie wanted to keep him to herself so they could discuss things, but she forced herself to be as optimistic and unruffled as he was in front of their families. It was getting dark before people started leaving for their homes or hotels; most of the out-of-town guests were staying at the Carmichael. The only other hotel in town was the Galactic, and Sadie never recommended it. The carpet had planets and spaceships on it that glowed in the dark, or at least it had when it was put in thirty years ago.

Sadie hugged and thanked and hugged some more, so grateful that everyone had come. To Pete's kids she gushed over the amazing meal and all their efforts to bring everyone together. What would she have done without them? They were equally gracious and sweet and wonderful. It was almost possible to forget about all the horrible things that had happened today.

Almost.

Sadie was saying her good-byes when she felt Pete's hand on her shoulder. She looked away from her cousin, Sandra, long enough to smile at Pete, but then saw the intent look on his face. "What?" she asked. He nodded toward her guests and she turned back.

"Thanks again for coming," Sadie said, then hurried through a hug and waved as Sandra headed down Gayle's front walk. Sadie turned back to Pete. "What is it?"

"They found her car."

"What?" Heat flushed her chest and face before she replayed Pete's comment in her mind. "Wait, just her car? Not her?"

Pete nodded. "The car's been torched, but she left a note for you. Malloy wants us to meet him at the scene—a campground by Walker Springs. Let's go."

Frikadeles with Ruskumsnuz

Frikadeles

1 egg
¼ cup diced onion
¼ cup diced green pepper
¼ cup oats, bread crumbs, crushed soda crackers, or flour
½ teaspoon salt
½ teaspoon pepper
1 pound hamburger

In a large bowl, combine all ingredients and mix well. (You can combine everything but the hamburger in a blender if you don't want chunks of onion and green pepper.) Mold into 4 to 6 patties.

Cook in a frying pan on medium-high heat until cooked through, about four minutes per side. Remove from pan and put on paper towel-lined plate to drain grease. (Patties can also be baked in the oven: 350 degrees for 30 minutes or until cooked through.)

Makes 4 to 6 servings.

Note: If hamburger mixture seems too crumbly, add another egg. Crackers and bread crumbs help it stick together better than oats do.

Ruskumsnuz

¼ cup butter
¼ cup flour
¼ teaspoon salt
¼ teaspoon pepper
2 teaspoon dried basil
½ teaspoon oregano
2 to 4 cups milk
1 to 2 pounds small red potatoes, unpeeled, boiled whole, and cut into 1-inch cubes
1½ cups sweet peas (fresh are best, but frozen works too)

In medium-sized frying pan, melt butter. Add flour and stir well until a smooth paste is formed. Add spices, mix well. Add 2 cups of milk and stir consistently until smooth sauce is formed, adding more milk as needed to make a white sauce about the consistency of a pancake batter.

Add boiled and cubed potatoes, mashing them slightly if desired. Add peas. (If using fresh peas, add them at the very end, so that they warm, but don't cook through.) Salt and pepper to taste. Keep sauce warm until ready to serve.

When ready to serve, place frikadeles on a plate and top with ruskumsnuz sauce.

Note: The best way to time the preparation of these two recipes is as follow: (1) Boil potatoes. (2) While potatoes are boiling, form meatloaf patties while frying pan heats up. (3) While meatloaf is frying, make white sauce. (4) After patties are fried, cover to keep warm. (5) Finish potatoes. Cook until a knife inserted into the center of a potato meets no resistance. Drain potatoes on a dishcloth for an extra light and flaky texture. Dice, add to white sauce with peas. Serve.

CHAPTER 24

Walker Springs was a campground located a couple of miles from Highway 14, on the edge of the Arapaho and Roosevelt National Forests. Sadie had never been there, though she'd passed the sign many times on her way to Denver. Pete explained that it was a small location—only four campsites and a single-seat outhouse. It had been built by the Civilian Conservation Corps back in the 1930s and 1940s but hadn't been expanded and facilitated for long-term use. In the winter, it was popular with snowmobilers. In the summer, it tended to attract travelers who would stop for a night before moving on.

"Why would Jane go there and light her car on fire?" Sadie asked.

"Why does Jane do anything she does?" Pete said with a shake of his head. They were on Highway 14, several minutes away from the life and lights of Garrison. The landscape was dark outside their windows, but the lingering heat of the day hadn't yet given way to the cooler temperatures of night. "The campground isn't far from the road. I can't help but wonder if she torched the car and then made it to the road where she caught a ride with someone passing by."

"It seems risky," Sadie said. "If someone from Garrison stopped, they might know who she is."

"So maybe the car is a diversion."

Sadie turned her head to look at him. "You think she planted it so she could lead the cops out of town and do something else?"

"Maybe," Pete said. "But our security is still at Gayle's, and it's not as though the entire Garrison police force responded to the car fire. Maybe the diversion is just to make us think she's gone."

Sadie faced forward again and let out a breath. "She texted me at the dinner—Shawn too—a couple of hours ago. I told her I wasn't going to talk to her anymore. Both Shawn and I blocked the number."

"Why didn't you tell me this earlier?"

"It's been a little busy," Sadie defended even though she hated the idea that she'd done something wrong.

"We can trace the call and find out where she made them from."

"Will that matter?" Sadie asked. "None of the other numbers have given us much to work with."

"It's still the only way we have of tracing her movements. Do you have the number? I'll call it in to the station and get them working on it."

Sadie got her phone from her purse and relayed the number to Pete once he had an officer on the phone with him. The road curved to the north, and red and blue flashing lights came into view. Pete slowed down and his headlights lit up the white lettering of the National Forest sign that read Walker Springs. He turned left onto the access road and rolled down his window to talk to the officer posted there. A few seconds later they were waved through.

Though the road was asphalt for several yards, it eventually turned into road base, necessitating that Pete slow down. They passed a day-use area with picnic tables, a restroom, and very clear signs indicating that overnight camping was not permitted. A mile past the day-use area, they saw the lights of the police vehicles that had responded. Pete pulled in next to a SUV from the Forest Service, and they opened their doors at the same time, equally eager to make their own assessment and get an update.

Sadie smelled burnt metal and rubber as soon as she stepped out of the car. Groups of officers stood around talking to each other, and an outdoor lighting system had been rigged up to illuminate something beyond Sadie's view. They bypassed some of the people and the fire engine and saw the burnt-out shell of a car parked next to one of the campground sites.

Some of the silver paint was still visible around the front fender, but most of the chassis was charcoal-black. The tires had burned, the windows had broken, and some trees nearby were charred. Though the fire was out, the trees and the car were still smoking. The bright lights lit up the front seat, and though Sadie was anxious about seeing evidence of anything gruesome, she wondered how the police were so certain Jane hadn't been inside the car. The thought made her shiver, and she looked at her feet instead of the car as she and Pete crossed the rest of the distance to Malloy, who was talking to a couple of Forest Service personnel.

"What do you know?" Pete asked as soon as they joined the other men.

Malloy updated them on what he had learned: the fire was reported around 9:00 by someone just arriving at the campground—there were no other campers. Forest Service was on the scene first with a water truck and worked to put out the car fire until they were joined by the Garrison fire department. There didn't seem to be anyone in the vehicle. Accelerant was suspected to be gasoline, though there would be an official investigation to confirm that.

"We'll be contacting all the gas stations in Garrison and Sterling for leads on anyone filling up gas cans tonight. The fire chief estimates it would take several gallons to burn this hot."

"You said she'd left something for Sadie," Pete said.

Malloy nodded and held up a Zip-loc bag, which Sadie knew meant they were trying to preserve the item for possible prints. "This was under a rock on the picnic table several feet from the car—out of danger of the fire."

Sadie leaned forward as Pete took the bag. Inside was a piece of lined notebook paper. One of the rangers took a flashlight from his belt and shined it on the bag so Sadie and Pete could better read it. Creases indicated that the paper had been folded in fourths at some point, but it was open now. On one side "Sadie Hoffmiller" was written in a feminine hand, and Sadie realized she'd never actually seen Jane's handwriting before.

Pete turned the bag over and adjusted it so the ranger's light made it possible to read without blinding them with the glare off the shiny plastic and white paper.

Sadie took a breath and read the words to herself.

You don't know me! No matter who you talk to or what you do you won't ever know me or what I'm capable of. I told you that you would never be free of me and I meant it! I'll come back and I will make your life a living hell!!!!!!!!!! Just wait, Sadie. JUST WAIT!

"She's insane," Sadie said after she read the note and found herself surprisingly unmoved by it. The words weren't those of a sane person—not that she had ever put Jane in that category.

"What do we do now?" Pete asked, looking at Malloy.

"We'll investigate, of course," Malloy said. "We got the profile Shawn worked up earlier." He cast a quick glance at Sadie that she thought might almost have been complimentary. "And I've assigned a team to expand on it. I've already contacted *The Denver Post* in hopes of keeping her in the public eye. We'll look for video footage from around town, we'll contact past departments that have worked with her, and we'll continue to work with the federal agencies. She's left a threat behind. We'll do everything we can to catch her before she can make good on it."

Sadie's attention returned to the car, lit up as though it were on a stage. She thought of the words of Jane's letter and considered what it meant. Maybe she and Pete should move away, go somewhere new and keep a low profile. Surely with enough time and manpower, the police would catch up with Jane and put an end to this. Tomorrow was her wedding day. Could she trust that Jane meant what she'd said about having left? Could Sadie believe that the wedding could take place?

She really didn't know—the day seemed to have sanded her emotional reaction to a smooth plane. Or maybe she had made the internal adjustments she needed to make to truly be free of Jane. Jack's words at dinner had made an impression on her. He'd pointed out that she'd had no outline for the other cases she'd been involved in, so she didn't need one now. Sadie herself had told Pete that she hadn't stopped hiding because she felt safe. She couldn't trust Jane's note—there was no reason to think that Jane had really left, and yet if she stayed, maybe they could handle it. Maybe, like Pete had said, everything really would be okay.

Chapter 25

It was almost midnight before Pete and Sadie returned to Gayle's house. The security company's vehicle was still parked in the driveway, and although Sadie had expected they would leave after the dinner, she was glad to know they were still watching over her family.

Breanna, Liam, Shawn, Maggie, as well as Brooke and Jared were in the living room—their families, as well as Michelle and her family, had chosen to call it a night after Pete and Sadie left. Despite the intensity of the day, Sadie loved that her children and Pete's children had been together for hours, talking and getting to know each other better amid missing furniture and the last of the sugar cookies.

They broke off their conversations when Pete and Sadie came in and then listened as Pete explained what had happened. Much of the same details Pete and Malloy had discussed were rehashed again. Hearing everything a second time didn't help Sadie make any decisions.

"She totally didn't leave," Shawn said, shaking his head, an expression of intensity on his face. "She's setting us up."

"Maybe she did leave," Brooke said. "She got blindsided pretty good today. She could have burned the car to make sure there wasn't any evidence left behind that would help people find her."

"Malloy would like to have a meeting at nine o'clock tomorrow morning," Pete said. "The police will know more by then, and we'll know if Jane tries anything during the night. Plus, he'd like to talk to our families about what to do tomorrow."

"So the wedding might still happen?" Breanna asked.

"We don't know," Pete said with a shrug. "There's so much we still don't know."

"But we'll talk about it in the morning?" Brooke asked.

Pete nodded. He, Jared, and Brooke discussed sleeping arrangements for Brooke since her family had returned to Fort Collins—both Jared and Pete had rooms at the Carmichael, and Maggie volunteered an extra set of pajamas.

Sadie went into the kitchen in hopes of finding something to clean up only to find it spic-and-span. She heard footsteps behind her and turned to see that Breanna had followed her, a look of concern on her face. "Are you okay, Mom?"

"I'm okay. I mean, I've been worse." She gave a smile. In truth she didn't really know how she felt, or how she should feel.

"Do you think she's gone?" Breanna asked, coming further into the kitchen and leaning against the counter.

"I don't even dare speculate," Sadie said, shaking her head. "Where are Gayle and Dr. McKay?"

"They went to the Carmichael."

Sadie frowned.

"We tried to talk her out of it, but she insisted. We got all the beds set up and everything so it's going to work for the four of us to stay here. Liam arranged for two of the security guys to stay here, one outside and one in—just in case. Maggie's staying at the hotel, though." She smiled. "I knew you'd prefer she and Shawn not sleep under the same roof."

Sadie smiled a bit sheepishly. "You'll make a wonderful mother one day, Bre."

"I learned from the best," she said with a quick shrug. "I thought maybe Maggie could drive over with Pete, and he could make sure she got to her room okay."

"Good idea," Sadie said. She yawned and reviewed the day in the space of it. It didn't seem possible that so much could take place in such a small period of time, and she resisted the urge to dwell on it in greater detail. "Sorry," she said. "I guess it's past my bedtime."

"Yours and mine both," Breanna said.

"Oh, I totally forgot about your jet lag. You must be dead on your feet."

"I've been drinking Mountain Dew like it's the fountain of youth, but, yeah, I could use some sleep."

"Then let's wrap things up and get everyone to bed," Sadie said. "Who knows what tomorrow will bring."

"There's just one thing we need to do before we turn in."

"What?"

Breanna grinned. "You need to choose a wedding dress."

She led Sadie into Gayle's room where six different dresses hung in the closet. Breanna called for Maggie and Brooke to join them and for the next twenty minutes, Sadie tried on the dresses Gayle had picked out. Three were either white or ivory, and she tried them first, liking the more traditional color. An ivory wrap-style dress stood out above the rest, and she set it aside before trying on the pale pink, ice blue, and sea-foam green options.

Though Sadie loved the fit of the blue one, and the girls agreed that it was best for her figure, her eyes kept going back to the ivory one she'd liked from the first set. She explained her dilemma to the girls and they all told her to try the dresses on again, back to back. She did so, finishing with the blue.

"They both look great," Brooke said, shaking her head. "I can't decide."

"Me neither," Breanna said. "They both work so well."

"Maggie?" Sadie turned her attention to the only one who hadn't expressed an opinion. "What do you think?"

"I'm not sure either, but I saw this trick on a TV show that might help."

She got the ivory dress, still on the hanger, and had Sadie face the mirror and close her eyes. Sadie could tell that Maggie was holding the ivory dress in front of her, but waited until Maggie told her to open her eyes before she looked. The ivory dress covered every bit of the blue, allowing Sadie to see how the color looked against her skin and with her hair.

"So, this is the more traditional one," Maggie said, then she took the hanger away, leaving Sadie looking at her reflection in the blue dress. "And this is the one with the fit we like."

The contrast was surprising as Sadie stared at herself in the mirror.

"Do it again," she said as she closed her eyes. Maggie put the dress in place again, then told Sadie to open her eyes, paused a few seconds, and then moved the dress away a second time.

"Which one makes you feel more like a bride, Mom?" Breanna asked.

Sadie looked up into her daughter's reflection over her shoulder, then moved her eyes to meet Brooke's on the other side. Brooke gave her a soft smile, and Sadie knew that for all her support and enthusiasm this was still hard for Pete's oldest daughter who missed her mother. Sadie looked back at her reflection in the blue dress.

"One more time," she said and closed her eyes for a third time. When she opened them, she looked at the ivory dress and remembered Gayle's words about the fact that Sadie and Pete *would* get married. If not tomorrow, another time. What did she want to be wearing when that happened?

"The ivory dress makes me feel like a bride," she said, the decision suddenly obvious. The girls agreed, hugged her in turn, and Maggie put the dress back in the plastic covering while Sadie changed out of the blue one.

When they returned to the living room, Brooke suggested a family prayer before they all parted ways for the night. Everyone stood in a circle, holding hands. Since she'd suggested the idea, everyone insisted Brooke also offer the words.

Sadie bowed her head and listened to the kind and heartfelt words of Pete's oldest daughter asking for the Lord's blessing to be upon them tomorrow, that hearts would be softened, spirits would be lifted, and lives would be protected. Sadie let every word wash over her and felt lifted up by the love of these people and the potential ahead of them.

"Amen," Brooke said when she finished.

A chorus of Amens answered her, and Sadie breathed in all the goodness of the moment and the hopes expressed in Brooke's prayer. She needed to keep those feelings close to her. She needed to remain mindful of God's eye upon all that may happen next.

They said their good-byes, and Pete, Brooke, Jared, and Maggie left. Shawn and Liam checked all the doors and windows of Gayle's house, and Liam had a final conversation with the security guard who would stay in the living room all night. Sadie got ready for bed and then waited for a text from Pete assuring her that everyone was safely at the hotel.

Sadie: Good. I'll see you in the morning.

Pete: I'm counting on it. Until tomorrow . . .

Sadie: Until tomorrow. Good night.

Chapter 26

Malloy entered the conference room of the police station, a sterile white-walled room located at the back of the building, at 9:06. Around the table were seated Pete and Sadie, Sadie's children and Liam, and Pete's children and spouses. Maggie was still at the hotel, even though Sadie had said she could come if she wanted to. She'd deferred, saying that this was a family thing. Everyone present was both eager and anxious as they watched Malloy take the empty chair at the head of the table.

"So," he said once he sat down. "Anything out of the ordinary this morning?"

Everyone looked at everyone else, waiting for someone to speak up but there was no response.

"I guess not," Pete finally said. "We've all been very vigilant but things seem to be . . . back to normal."

"Which is probably exactly what Jane wants us to think," Shawn cut in. "She hasn't left."

"She might have," Brooke said. "With the amount of pressure put on her yesterday, I can't imagine she'd still be here. The whole town is on alert, and there was an article in this morning's *Post*."

"She hid out for two years," Shawn reminded her.

"But there's nowhere left for her to hide."

"Maybe, but then again how did she get out of town without her car?" Shawn countered. "The woman's diabolical. Who knows how many contingencies she planned for."

Breanna cleared her throat and spoke before Brooke could continue the argument. "I think we can all agree that we can't know for sure whether or not Jane's still in town so we have to proceed as though she is."

As usual, Breanna was the voice of reason. Everyone nodded in agreement, though some were reluctantly offered. To plan with any other option in mind was foolish.

"So, how do we move forward?" Jared asked. "Is the wedding going to happen?"

No one spoke up right away, and Sadie met Pete's eyes across the table. It seemed no one wanted to be the one to take accountability for saying either yes or no. After a few seconds, Sadie cleared her throat. "That's such a hard question to answer," she said. "Of course we want the wedding to happen, but not if it's dangerous, and, like Breanna pointed out, we have to assume that Jane's still a factor."

"We have to further assume that if she's still in town and still determined to make good on her threats, she could very well be waiting for the wedding itself to make her next move," Pete said. "Since nothing else seemed to have worked for her the way she wanted to, this is kind of her last chance."

"Which means we can't have the wedding," Brooke added, shaking her head. "We can't risk it."

"No, we *have* to have the wedding," Shawn said, capturing everyone's attention and causing Brooke to frown. "If Jane's going to use the wedding as her big moment, it's our chance to put an end to this."

"At what cost?" Brooke said, sounding frustrated.

"At what cost do we cancel it?" Shawn countered. Sadie could tell he was trying to keep his tone conciliatory. "Using the actual wedding as her stage is exactly the kind of attention Jane wants, so let's give her the rope to hang herself with."

Brooke was shaking her head before Shawn even finished. "This isn't a game."

Shawn leaned across the table. "No, it's not, but—"

"What about a fake wedding?" Breanna broke in, sending Shawn a big-sister look that showed she was not impressed with the way he was handling the conversation. Shawn sat back but didn't push the issue, for which Sadie was grateful. She didn't want hard feelings between anyone here—especially soon-to-be stepsiblings. Breanna continued, "We replace the guests with police officers, but for all intents and purposes it's still the wedding—or, as Shawn said, the rope."

"We'd have this fake wedding at the same time and place?" Sadie asked.

Breanna nodded. "We'd want it to look as though nothing had changed, that we took Jane at her word and assumed she was gone so we kept everything as planned."

"Except that it's fake?" Brooke asked. She seemed open to the idea.

"It's arranged like a sting or something." Breanna gestured with her hands to indicate that she didn't know exactly what to call it. "With the hope that Jane shows up."

"And if she does, she's surrounded by cops," Shawn said, his face brightening with the prospect.

Breanna nodded. "Right."

"It's worth exploring," Malloy said, surprising Sadie with his agreement to such an unconventional idea. "Let's brainstorm some details of how it would work to see if it's a real possibility."

For the next half an hour they discussed details and options, and everyone seemed to be on board with the idea. Immediate family would attend for authentication purposes, though no children, as well as the police officers already on the guest list. Malloy felt certain he could find an additional forty cops to sit in as the other guests, and Heather and Michelle volunteered to call all the *real* guests and explain that the actual wedding would be held at a later date. People would be disappointed, but they all loved Sadie and Pete so they'd certainly understand. The caterers would still be on hand; the new cake Rachel had made would sit on the table in the corner just as planned.

Malloy would hold a special meeting a couple of hours before the ceremony where he could prepare everyone who was going to attend. Liam would coordinate with Allen Security to man the exterior since Jane would likely expect that. The excitement built and the plan came together rather seamlessly, but something ate at Sadie until she finally raised her hand to get everyone's attention.

"This is all great," she said with a smile. "And I so appreciate everyone coming together to plan this out."

"But?" Shawn prompted her when she paused.

"But, if we're going through all this trouble to stage a fake wedding, why not make it a real one?"

Everyone remained silent so she continued, "If we don't catch

Jane today—heaven forbid—we'll be right back where we are now, scared and worried about putting people at risk with another wedding." She looked at Pete who nodded to let her know he supported this idea. "We've paid for everything that will be utilized in this fake wedding and to make it seem real we'll have our closest family members there, we'll be saying all the same things we'd *say* for a real wedding, doing all the same things we'd *do* for a real wedding, and Jane might not show up at all. So, why not make it the real thing and avoid putting on a show with something this special?"

"With cops as the guests?" Jared asked.

Sadie nodded. "To make up the difference, yes. We still keep it to immediate family"—she thought of Gayle—"and a few select friends. We do everything we've discussed here: security, extra police instead of those guests who won't be there, same time, same place, videographer, lunch. But we have a real officiator, and we make real vows to one another."

"If we do a fake wedding and catch Jane, you could have the *real* wedding tomorrow," Shawn said. He was obviously unaware of the planning that went into a wedding, but the point he was making was a reasonable one.

"A real wedding consists of Pete, me, an officiator, and you guys," Sadie said, glad she'd had the chance to talk to Gayle yesterday and make that realization before this moment. "If we make the vows to one another, it's real. Quite frankly it feels extremely awkward to playact this in front of everyone only to do the real thing at a later date."

"And what if Jane shows up and turns your *real* wedding into a circus?" Jared asked. His wife, Heather, nodded in agreement. She wasn't the only one. But Pete and Shawn were watching Sadie carefully, and she could read that they were thinking deeply on her suggestion, weighing it out, and, she hoped, seeing the wisdom in it.

"If Jane shows up before we've taken our vows, we'll *have* to have another wedding later on. But Jane *could* be states away by now, taking satisfaction in the fact that she ruined the wedding without even having to be there to do it. I just think that if we're going to go to the trouble of a wedding, why not make it stick?" She looked at Pete.

"Dad?" Pete's daughter, Michelle, said. "What do you think?"

"I've never cared that much for the wedding part," he said with a shrug. He didn't meet Sadie's eyes, which was a good thing as she was mildly offended. "It's the marriage that matters to me and making this a real wedding takes care of that. I agree that playacting something so important is not something I look forward to doing. I think as long as Malloy's team is onboard and you kids will be there, this is a good solution."

"And hopefully Jane will stay away and everything will go smoothly," Liam said, sharing in Breanna's optimism. Breanna smiled at her new husband, and Sadie wondered if she and Liam were reflecting on their perfectly imperfect wedding, which had been thrown together in a matter of hours.

Sadie knew Shawn was right that the wedding was the perfect stage for Jane to get all the attention she could want, to claim all that power. Still, all the effort of going through with a wedding ought to at least have the potential of resulting in her and Pete becoming husband and wife. Even without birdseed party favors and monogramed napkins.

"I think it could work," Malloy said. "I know a few ordained officers who could conduct the ceremony."

"Could I ask my pastor first?" Sadie asked.

Malloy frowned. "He's not a trained police officer."

"But he is my pastor, and he's been planning to marry us. Let me at least explain the situation and see what he says. If he's the least bit uncomfortable with it, I'll ask you to help me find someone else."

Malloy didn't seem pleased, but Sadie was beginning to think he simply hated every idea she came up with so she didn't take it personally. And he was softer today. Ever since the showdown in Pete's backyard, things had felt a little different between them. He looked at the clock on the wall. "It's nearly ten," he said. "I'd like to have any civilian guests here at the station at noon where I'll brief them on what to expect. Does that give you enough time to inform your guests?" He looked at Pete, not Sadie, which was a reminder of whose opinion mattered to him the most, but Sadie let it go.

"We'll make sure it is," Pete said. He turned to his kids, who nodded their agreement to help.

"Alright," Malloy said with a nod. "I need to get some approvals, but I think we can make this work. Due to the time restraints, I feel we should proceed as though it will happen while I work on getting the clearances we need. Pete, why don't you stay here and help me get a wedding party together. We can put in a call to Fort Collins and Sterling; I'm sure they can make some officers available. Seeing as how the feds are already involved—thanks to Pete's drug charges—it shouldn't be hard to get some agents up here as well."

"And they get free lunch," Brooke said, looking between Sadie and Pete for confirmation. "The caterers are still onboard for lunch, right?"

"Yes," Sadie said. "Lunch will be provided. I have a couple more people to confirm with today, but everything seems to be ready to go."

"I'll confirm anything you didn't get to yesterday," Breanna said.

Malloy turned to Sadie. "You'll need to be careful for the next few hours. No taking chances."

"I know," Sadie said.

"We'll stay with her," Shawn said. "We'll make sure she's safe. No one's going to be taking chances this close to game time."

Malloy nodded. "Well then, I guess we're going to have a wedding."

Sadie met Pete's eyes and smiled. He smiled back and winked, then she looked at the clock and felt the first pre-wedding jitters start funneling in. "Oh my gosh," she said as everyone began to stand. Only a few of them heard her and turned with expectant looks. "I'm getting married today! I've completely forgotten to be nervous."

Breanna and Brooke looked at each other and laughed.

"In, like, four hours!" she added, feeling the blood drain from her face. "How on earth am I going to get ready in time?" She hadn't heard back from her hairdresser, but she was supposed to be there in ten minutes. And there were a hundred other things she'd need to do that hadn't even been thought of yet.

"Call Gayle," Breanna suggested. "You did say she was your fairy godmother, right?"

Sadie relaxed a little bit. Gayle could work miracles, and there was still time for Sadie to make the hair appointment. Pete and Malloy would fill the seats, and the kids would inform the guests and take care of the last few confirmations. All that was left for Sadie to do was get herself ready—Gayle would help with that, too—and be to the reception hall on time.

It's happening, she thought as she stood. *It's really happening.*

CHAPTER 27

The clock in the foyer of the North Hampton Reception Center said 1:59 when Sadie put her right arm through Shawn's and her left arm through Breanna's. She looked between both her children and blinked back the tears that would ruin the makeup Gayle had so perfectly applied. "I hope you two know how much I love you," she said, trying to keep her wobbly voice under control.

Shawn gave a dramatic eye roll. "We know," he said like a petulant child, then smiled at her and patted her hand on his arm. He looked fabulous in the suit Maggie had chosen for him online almost a month ago. It was a similar color to Pete's, but with a pinstripe and longer coat that helped balance out his shoulders.

Breanna, dressed in a plum-colored dress, leaned in and touched her cheek to Sadie's. "We do know, Mom, but today is about you and Pete."

"And most of the Garrison police department," Shawn said, cocking his head to the side as though deep in thought. "Some retired cops, a few from Denver and—"

Breanna reached across Sadie and slapped Shawn's arm. "Stop it. It's Mom's wedding regardless of who's here."

Or why they're here? Sadie thought. Ever since Pete's proposal in Ketchikan, Alaska, she'd envisioned getting married in front of lifelong friends, not a room of strangers, but she wasn't really grieving, not after all that had happened. Rather, she vacillated between hoping Jane would show up so they could put an end to the years of living beneath the threats, and hoping that Jane *didn't* show up, thus keeping this day beautiful.

Sadie had to keep reminding herself that despite all the complications, she *was* getting married today. Pastor Donald hadn't hesitated to agree to perform the ceremony despite the unusual circumstances. Apparently he'd been a military chaplain before taking over the church in Garrison. He even owned his own bulletproof vest and a handgun he could wear beneath his suit jacket. Sadie was in the minority not having a weapon on her person during the event.

The music started up on the other side of the door; the jazzy version of the wedding march had been Gayle's idea. Sadie was grateful for the energy of it and smiled at the quick tempo. She was glad so many of her favorite people were in attendance despite the risks. Each of them had gone to the briefing at the police station and promised that if Jane showed up, they'd not be a hero and would let law enforcement do their job. To say the whole thing was unprecedented was a laughable understatement—part ploy to lure Jane in, part defense to protect the wedding party. Allen Security guards were at every door and watching closely.

The double doors at the back of the reception hall were pulled open by the security guards acting as ushers. Every eye inside the room turned her direction as Sadie and her children moved through the doors at a regular walk rather than the traditional step-pause-step cadence of a bride. *A bride!*

The room was set up with sixty chairs divided by a wide aisle that led to a slightly raised platform where Pastor Donald waited beneath a tulle-wrapped archway. It was backlit by a frosted window that allowed the natural light of the beautiful summer day into the room. Several round tables were set around the perimeter of the room; after the ceremony, they would be moved to accommodate the luncheon. Sadie's eyes took in every detail until they focused on the man in the dove-gray suit standing at the head of the aisle. Once she saw Pete, she had eyes for nothing else.

This is my wedding day, Sadie said in her mind and pushed all the other thoughts and fears and tactical procedures from her mind. She was wearing the ivory dress with the flattering drape and soft lines Gayle had picked out from Coldwater Creek and the matching kitten-heel shoes that only pinched her toes a little bit. She wore her mother's pearls around her neck and the diamond studs Neil had given her on their tenth anniversary. Her hair was perfect, her head was clear, and Pete awaited her at the threshold of their lives together. It was unreal. It was overwhelming, and Sadie took satisfaction in the knowledge that while Jane had severely complicated things for her, she hadn't ruined this. The trained officers in the room were here to be watchful and mindful and protective, which meant Sadie could stay focused on the beauty of this day. And it was *so* beautiful.

When the three of them reached the end of the aisle, Breanna and Shawn leaned in to kiss her on the cheek, before sitting in the empty chairs next to Maggie and Liam on the front row.

Pete extended his hand, and Sadie eagerly took it. As his hand wrapped around hers, the circumstances of everything melted away a little more. They walked up the three steps of the platform hand in hand, facing Pastor Donald and ready to commit their lives to one another.

Someone sniffled behind them, probably Gayle.

Pastor Donald smiled at them and immediately began the ceremony as though this were any other wedding. Sadie listened to the words, nodded when it was appropriate, and squeezed Pete's hand now and again when a passage of scripture or bit of advice struck her as particularly poignant.

When Pastor Donald turned to her, she said, "I do." When he turned to Pete for the same commitment, he gave the equally agreeable response. Sadie's body was flushed with excitement and confirmation of how right all of this was as the moment of completion drew closer.

She thought of the Christian pop song "God Bless the Broken Road" and how well it related to the journey she and Pete had made to reach this point. They had had so many difficulties and flat-out perilous circumstances to overcome throughout the years they had been together. Even today things were not exactly as they should be. There had been several coming-togethers and then pulling-aparts between them for a variety of reasons. More than once Sadie had wondered if those things were signs that spending their lives together wasn't meant to be. And yet they were here, in this moment, together. She could see how their hardships had strengthened them and that realization helped her believe that even this trial would work toward their good somehow.

"I now pronounce you man and wife."

Sadie caught her breath as Pete stepped toward her and put a hand alongside her face, smiling sweetly at her as he came in for their first official kiss as a married couple. Their lips met with a sweet softness of promise and commitment for all the years they had left to love each other. Sadie felt enveloped in the profound beauty of it for the space of a heartbeat. Two. She heard people begin to applaud, adding their confirmations to the one she felt so deeply in her heart.

Pete pulled back and smiled even wider. "We did it," he whispered.

Sadie nodded and blinked back tears. They turned to face their guests, and Pete reached for her hand as they stepped down from the platform. They would greet their guests while the room was transformed into the luncheon portion of the day. It had happened! It was done! Pete was Sadie's husband, and she could scarcely wrap her head around it.

Pastor Donald followed them to the edge of the platform. He held a hand out toward the couple as he looked over the room. "May I present to you, Mr. and Mrs. Cunningham."

The applause increased; guests came to their feet.

Sadie squeezed the hand of her new husband.

Pete squeezed the hand of his new wife.

And then the window behind Pastor Donald exploded.

Chapter 28

Pete reacted impossibly fast and pulled Sadie to the floor as a million shards of glass shot toward their backs. Sadie hit the floor hard and was immediately dragged to the side as a roar filled her ears and the room seemed to scream of one accord. Sadie lost seconds and space until she realized Pete had pulled her toward the north side of the room. He let go of her hand long enough to flip one of the round reception tables on its side, creating a kind of foxhole in the corner, then he grabbed her around the waist and pulled her behind the upended table.

Sadie huddled against the wall, trying to catch her breath and make sense of what had happened. The window exploded? *Really?*

Pete crouched behind the tabletop and pulled his gun from the holster at his side. He couldn't stand completely upright and remain protected, never mind that a round table left much to be desired considering its gaps and spaces.

"You're okay," he said to her as though issuing a command but his words were muted by the ringing in her ears.

Sadie nodded. She *was* okay . . . she thought. But what had happened? She could smell something burning, she could hear the muffled sound of tables and chairs crashing and footsteps making an exit. *Shawn!* She thought. *Breanna!* Liam and Maggie and Pete's children! Were they okay?

Pete peered around the edge of the table, his gun pointing toward the ceiling. Sadie got to her knees and crawled over to inspect the room. Every table around the room had been flipped on its side and pulled close to the wall just as Pete had done. Had that been part of the procedure the police had discussed with the guests while she was getting her hair done? Upended chairs were scattered across the floor along with tablecloths, napkins, flatware, flowers, and broken centerpiece vases. Water from those vases was everywhere while officers dressed as wedding guests rushed out of the room with their service weapons drawn.

Sadie looked toward the window that had exploded. The sheer drapes were shredded and charred. Something outside the broken window casing was on fire; she could see flickers of bright orange flame amid the black smoke. Thick clouds of smoke were coming inside the building through the broken window—that's how close whatever had exploded was to the building.

Movement to the side of the platform drew her attention, and she gasped as Pastor Donald tried to push himself up to a sitting position. He held the back of his head with a hand covered in blood.

Sadie moved toward him but Pete pulled her back behind the table. "No," he said while shaking his head. "Stay here."

His voice sounded like it was at the far end of a tunnel. "But, Pastor Donald?" she asked. The table blocked her view.

Pete peered around the table himself, giving Sadie a view of the back of his coat, which was torn and singed and showed blood seeping through in spots. He pulled back behind the table and looked at her. "We can't go for him now. We don't know what we're up against."

"You're hurt too," she said, pointing toward the back of his coat.

"I'm fine." Pete pulled his phone from the inside pocket of his mangled coat, then holstered his weapon for the moment. "I need to check with Malloy."

Had Malloy made a plan for such a catastrophic event as this? As Pete made the call, Sadie inspected herself and found that her dress was also torn in places. She could feel stinging in her back and a rather sharp pain below one of her shoulder blades, but the injuries weren't serious.

Pastor Donald hadn't been so lucky, and Sadie had to clasp her hands together to keep from running for him again. He'd volunteered to officiate, and it may have cost him his life. The thought made her throat thick, and her thoughts moved to the other people who may have been injured. Their guests had been an additional ten to fifteen feet from the window, but they'd been facing it. What had happened to them? This was Sadie's worst nightmare, and she could scarcely stand to think of what she'd done in agreeing to go through with this at all. She clenched her eyes against the accountability she felt glaring at her.

"Okay," Pete said into the phone. "Right . . . at least one in need of an ambulance."

Sadie knew that allowing the emotional onslaught threatening to descend upon her would be more than she could handle. Pete would tell her this was not her fault and the only way she could remain free of Jane was to put the responsibility where it belonged—on Jane's heartless shoulders. And he would be right.

The ringing in her ears dissipated, and Sadie heard voices from outside the window, shouting and giving orders. Was it Malloy? The fire continued to roar, and she heard sirens in the distance. Whatever law enforcement hadn't already been at the wedding was coming now.

Pete dropped his phone back into the inner pocket of his jacket. "Car bomb," he said. "Parked right outside the window. So far the fire hasn't spread beyond the car, and Malloy's working on a plan to evacuate the building." He glanced at the blackening smoke spreading across the ceiling, then looked at Sadie. "They're searching for Jane, but we need to be on guard. She could be in the building or she could have triggered the explosion remotely. We just don't know."

Sadie nodded to tell him she'd heard what he'd said and understood. She kept to herself how often in the last two days she'd taken comfort in the idea that Jane was gone, only to be reminded that she hadn't in fact left at all. Had her torched car at the campground last night been a trial run of *this*?

Pete pulled his gun from the holster under his arm again and pressed his back against the underside of the table. He turned his head toward the room.

"Guests of the Cunningham wedding," he yelled. Sadie hadn't realized how many voices she'd heard talking in the room until everyone stopped to listen. "Remain where you are. The explosion we've experienced was from a car bomb outside the window. Help is on its way, but I need an accounting of injuries in need of attention."

There was a pause as though people were waiting for someone to speak, finally Jared's voice filled the room. "From those on the south side, we have a possible broken arm, a sprained ankle, and multiple lacerations, nothing critical, however." Jared was a doctor in his first year of residency; thank goodness he could help those injured. "Are you alright? The angle of the blast seems to have been towards the south."

"Minor injuries for Sadie and me," Pete said. "However, Pastor Donald has been severely injured. He's on the north side of the stage. Can anyone help him get behind a table? He needs medical attention, Jared."

"I can get him," Shawn yelled.

"I'll go with him," Jared added.

"Bert Lipton—deputy from Sterling—will cover," said an unfamiliar voice.

"Good," Pete yelled back, then poised to provide additional cover to the rescue. "Proceed on three. One—two—three."

There was the sound of quick footsteps, a moan from Pastor Donald, and then more movement.

"Clear," the deputy called out about thirty seconds later. Pete returned to his place behind the table

"He's not in good shape, Dad," Jared called out. In a quiet voice not meant to carry as well he said, "Hand me those napkins, Shawn. Help me straighten him up but keep his head elevated. Miles, help Shawn hold him."

Sadie could barely breathe. *Please don't let him die,* she pleaded with the One she knew appreciated Pastor Donald even more than she did. *Please let all of us get out of this alive.*

"What other law enforcement officers are still here?" Pete called out.

"Sharon Jacobsen from Fort Collins," a female voice yelled from the back of the room.

"Ernie Blacktree, federal agent," said another voice from a similar location.

Only three? Sadie thought.

Pete continued, "I need the officers to gather all remaining occupants into one location and provide cover and protection."

All three voices answered in the affirmative. Sadie heard the sound of movement and tables rolling for a couple of minutes. She remained between the north wall and the table, trying to control her breathing and her panic, wishing she and Pete were with the others instead of on the opposite side of the room.

"Are our families still here?" Sadie asked Pete.

Pete nodded to show that he'd heard her but kept listening until the movement stopped.

"Clear," one of the officers reported. "There are seventeen persons gathered near the southwest doors. It seems to be everyone."

"Is there anyone else in the room?" Pete asked, addressing his comment toward the back of the banquet hall.

The silence made Sadie nervous. She couldn't help but picture Jane crouched behind a table somewhere, undetected and waiting for another opportunity to exact her twisted revenge.

"Jared, how is Pastor Donald?" Pete called after several seconds of pause.

"He's losing a lot of blood, Dad," Jared said, concerned. "I don't dare remove the glass in his neck, but it interferes with our ability to apply pressure. He needs to get to a hospital quick. Two of the additional guests have injuries as well—heart palpitations and what seems to be another sprained ankle. The smoke is triggering Michelle's asthma, and we need to get her out of here. She doesn't have her inhaler with her."

Pete's mouth tightened, overwhelmed by the news. "Help is on its way," he said again. "We need a roll call to see who else is here. Starting with the farthest southwestern individual."

"Jared Cunningham and Pastor Donald," Jared called out.

"Shawn Hoffmiller."

"Rex."

"Caro."

"Breanna."

"Liam."

The names continued to be called out and with each name of someone Sadie knew and loved she felt herself relax a little bit more. They were okay. They were safe.

"Excellent," Pete said when they finished. "Sharon and Ernie, clear the rest of the room. There's an equipment closet in the far northeast corner. It was checked before the event but should be checked again. Throw the tables not being used for cover topside down to remove potential hiding places."

They both agreed to the task, and there was the sound of shuffling feet.

Pete explained the protocol for evacuation, which would start as soon as Malloy told him the officers and evacuation location were ready. Pete paused each time a table made a thwack sound as it was laid flat. "We'll evacuate two people at a time every thirty seconds on my count—*thwack*—Jared and Pastor Donald will exit first, Bert will facilitate—*thwack*—there will be—"

Another explosion came from the direction of the already burning car.

Screams and the sound of bodies hitting the floor again filled the room.

Sadie covered her head with her hands and pressed herself into the corner, not realizing she was screaming until she felt Pete's hand on her arm to stop her. His eyes were not hiding his own fear any longer.

"That one was further away," Pete said, but she could tell by his tone that the fact gave him little comfort.

"All those officers are out there," Sadie said.

Pete gave a single sharp nod. The officers out there were Pete's friends. Men he'd worked with for years. Were there more explosions to come? She looked toward the ceiling, which was now hidden by the black smoke still pouring into the room. She could feel the thickness of the toxic fumes and worried about Michelle's ability to breathe.

Pete reached for his phone and put it directly to his ear. Sadie hadn't heard it ring, but of course he'd put it on silent for the wedding. *The wedding.* She looked up at her new *husband*—holding a Glock 9mm in his hand. This was not what she imagined the minutes after her marriage would be like. Even with the fear that Jane may have chosen the wedding as the forum for her revenge, no one had anticipated explosives.

"Yes," Pete said into the phone. "We can't wait, Pastor Donald needs immediate attention. . . . My daughter's having trouble breathing. . . . There are nineteen of us." He paused to cough behind his hand. "The smoke is thick. . . . Okay."

Pete put his phone away. "A second car," he explained. "Malloy has secured an office in the building we can remove to for now."

"What if there are more explosives?" Sadie asked.

Pete didn't have an answer. What if there *were* more? What could anyone do about it? "The officers that went out of the building have been evacuated away from the parking lot. Malloy's sent half a dozen back to help us."

The sirens were louder—maybe right outside. Would the fire truck be allowed to put out the burning cars?

"Is everyone okay?" Pete called out from his side of the table.

"No further injuries," Jared called back. "But Pastor Donald has lost consciousness. It is *critical* that he gets to a hospital as soon as possible, Dad. Michelle's struggling but is still breathing. The smoke is getting worse."

Pete's intake of breath was staggered, as though it was all he could do not to bolt across the room to help his daughter. But part of his training was to follow procedure, and he'd been given his orders. "There will be a knock at the southwest door. As soon as officers are in place, they will help get the pastor from the building. Will you attend him, Jared?"

"Yes," Jared said with anxious frustration. "When will they be here?"

"Anytime," Pete said. "Bert, can you cover their exit to the ambulance?"

"Affirmative," Bert called back.

"I need help to carry him out," Jared said. "I need him in a low Fowler's position as much as possible. Shawn can attend, but Miles is helping Michelle."

"Bill McKay, will you attend?" Pete asked.

"Yes," Dr. McKay called back.

Pete continued. "After the pastor's removal, everyone stay where they are until I give the signal to begin evacuating every thirty seconds on my count with Michelle and Miles to remove next. Sharon and Ernie, will you assist by pairing each injured person with someone who can assist them from the room?"

"Affirmative," the officers called back in tandem.

Sadie coughed behind her hand and looked at the ceiling. How much longer could they safely stay here?

"How could she do this?" she asked out loud. The level of trauma everyone was experiencing overwhelmed her. Had this been Jane's plan from the beginning? Had everything Sadie had done led up to this moment just as Jane had expected it would?

Pete tried to wrap his arm around Sadie's shoulder, but she winced as he touched what she feared was a shard of glass imbedded in her back. As the adrenaline wore off, the pain became more pronounced. Several areas on her back and head, arms and shoulders stung. Pete pulled his hand away and touched her chin instead, looking her in the eye.

"Our children are okay," he said. "We're okay. Everything will turn out alright."

"They aren't going to find her," she said as guilt, panic, and hopelessness spread throughout her body. "She'll get away with this and come back to do it all over again."

"Not a chance," Pete said with resolution Sadie appreciated more than she could say. "She's left us her car and two car bombs' worth of evidence against her. She has made herself some powerful enemies through the officers who were here. We can trace parts on something like this. I guarantee we'll find her."

"There's the knock, Cunningham," Bert called out.

"Wait for my count," Pete yelled as he flipped back into cop mode and resumed his position against the table with his head turned to the side. He pulled his phone from his pocket and dialed a number Sadie guessed was Malloy.

"We're ready," Pete said into the phone. "Okay."

He hung up and slid his phone into his pocket again. He turned his wrist so he could see his watch. "On my count. One—two—three."

There was the sound of movement and hinges, but it was quickly gone. A few seconds later, Sharon called out, "Clear."

"Michelle, you go next, sweetie," Pete called out to his daughter.

"She's ready," Miles answered, perhaps because Michelle couldn't speak for herself. Sadie's chest constricted in response.

"On my count," Pete called out loudly. "One—two—three."

Shuffling. Muted voices. Seconds ticked by. "Clear," the female officer called out.

Pete checked his watch, waited fifteen seconds or so, and called out, "The next two injured to exit. . . . Ready. One—two—three."

Over the course of the next five minutes, the pattern of counting and "Clear" sounded over and over until Sharon said only she and Ernie were left.

"We're ready for your exit, Pete," Malloy's voice called out from the direction of the evacuation door.

Pete reached his hand to Sadie and they stood up together, crouched down even though they were in full view of the room.

Sadie scanned the chaos and destruction that had started as her wedding ceremony. She wondered if Jane was watching them, waiting for her final moment of triumph. Standing brought them in contact with the thicker smoke, and Sadie coughed, feeling the burning fumes in her lungs. She covered her mouth and looked at the door that seemed so far away.

Malloy was at the southwest doors conferring with a man and woman Sadie assumed were Sharon and Ernie. They stepped out, leaving only Malloy to supervise Pete and Sadie's exit.

Pete tugged on Sadie's hand and led her around the edge of the table. They stayed to the perimeter of the room and went the long way around, avoiding the gaping hole in the west wall. Halfway to the door, they reached a jumble of tables that cut off their route.

After a moment's pause, Pete pulled her with him as they cut across the corner of the room toward the southwest door. Sadie looked over her shoulder. With so many tables still on their sides, the room was full of hiding places. Somehow, the cake and the table it was on had survived the melee, standing unscathed and untouched in the northeast corner, near the equipment closet Pete had mentioned earlier.

Sadie's eyes lingered on the lavender tablecloth that pooled on the floor, creating another hiding place, and she thought she saw the cloth move. She told herself she was seeing things. Sadie gripped Pete's hand tighter and coughed as she faced forward, anxious to get out of there as quickly as possible.

The door was only twenty feet away when a single shot rang out. Sadie felt Pete's hand shudder before it slipped from her grasp and he crumpled to the floor.

Chapter 29

Sadie screamed and fell to her knees beside him.

Pete rolled onto his back, his teeth and eyes clenched shut. Blood poured from a wound just above his knee—*It's his leg,* Sadie thought, relieved—that he held with his left hand. With his other hand, he tried to pull himself behind one of the reception tables still on its side, using his good leg to push against the floor.

Sadie kicked off her shoes and moved to his head. She grabbed under his arms and pulled. He moaned in pain, but she kept pulling, determined to get him behind some kind of cover as absolute dread filled her head.

Jane's here!

"Put the gun down!" Malloy yelled.

Sadie looked toward the sound of his voice, thirty yards or more to their left, but she couldn't see him from where she and Pete were hiding. She assumed Malloy was talking to Jane. She hadn't left town or detonated the explosives from a distance. She had been *right here* all along.

"No one's been killed, yet," Malloy continued. "We still have some options."

Another shot rang out. Sadie ducked and gasped as the sound of a heavy body—too heavy to be Jane—hitting the hard wood. *Malloy*. Sadie thought of all the news stories she'd seen of someone going on a shooting spree and killing multiple people in a matter of seconds. It was all happening so fast. Pete's face twisted with pain but was also hard with the same fear Sadie was feeling.

"Come out, come out, wherever you are, Sadie." The sound of Jane's voice caused Sadie's whole body to recoil.

"If I come to you, I do it with guns a'blazin'!" Jane called out, her voice closer.

Sadie's eyes moved to the leather holster Pete wore beneath his jacket. The handle of his gun stuck out over the top of the brown leather.

She reached for the gun.

"Sadie," Pete said quietly. She met his eyes for just a moment, but still pulled the gun from his side. He didn't try to stop her.

Her hand wrapped around the grip, warm from having been nestled at Pete's side while they promised to spend the rest of their lives together. She held the gun firmly as she peered around the edge of the table. Jane was only about forty feet away from her, dressed in a pale yellow dress that made her look like a wedding guest and holding a gun at her side. Had she run in when the officers had run out?

She was walking quickly toward them from the direction of the wedding cake, and though Sadie pulled behind the table, she could hear Jane's quick footsteps getting closer. Would she ambush them? Come around the table and finish the job she'd started when she'd shot Pete in the leg?

There was no time to argue with herself about her options so Sadie took a breath and came to her feet, pointing the gun at Jane, who stopped fifteen feet away, her gun pointed at the floor. She had shoulder-length dirty blonde hair, curled into soft spirals. Her eyes were hard and sharp behind her glasses. She smiled at Sadie in a way that made Sadie's blood run cold. *You'll never be free of me,* Jane had said all those months ago. Sadie had had no idea how far Jane would go to make good on that threat, but she refused to be held captive by it.

A quick glance toward Malloy's large body lying in a heap on the other side of the hall made Sadie's breath catch in her throat. He wasn't moving and Pete was injured. It was down to Sadie and Jane.

Sadie steadied the gun with both hands and stepped around the edge of the table, stopping once she was in front of it. The smoke nearly gagged her but she couldn't release the gun so she coughed toward her shoulder. No way would Jane get past her. She locked her elbows and pointed the barrel directly at Jane's chest.

"You're going to shoot me, Sadie?" Jane said sarcastically, raising her eyebrows. "You're ready to watch me bleed to death right in front of you?" She coughed as well, not immune to the acrid air that was only getting worse.

"If it spares the lives of the people I love, you bet I am," Sadie said.

Jane laughed—*laughed*—and shook her head, the honey-colored curls of her current wig moving a half second behind. "You'd never do it," she said, wrinkling her nose in a sneer. "It's against your moral code."

Sadie clicked off the safety as though to prove that she would shoot if she had to.

Jane's gun was still at her side, but her finger was on the trigger. She was not surrendering either.

"Why are you doing this?" Sadie demanded, unable to keep the emotion down. She blinked quickly, wanting to keep the tears away but unable to do so. Her body shook with both adrenaline and fear. Maybe she could hold Jane off long enough for help to arrive. "What did I do that made you so angry?" The rising emotion made her coughing worse. She had to release the gun with one hand to try to keep from taking in a mouthful of the smoke each time she coughed.

"Everything," Jane said in a harsh tone. The smile finally fell from her face. "You give so much, but not to me. You comfort and help, but not me. From the first moment we met, you measured me and saw me as missing pieces, and no matter how hard I tried to convince you that I deserved your attention—the same attention you give to everyone else so freely—you have refused it."

Jane had said similar things before, but Sadie hadn't understood it. She understood now, though. After learning Valerie Smith's history of finding and fixating on motherly figures in her life, Sadie understood that she had become Valerie's next attempt at that kind of connection. But Sadie had never played into it. Not the way the others had. Not the way Jane—Valerie—wanted and expected her to. Sadie had not allowed Jane to get her fix, so to speak, and Jane was punishing her for it.

"Obviously, I was right not to trust you, *Valerie*," Sadie said. She worked hard to keep the fear out of her voice. *Cough.* She needed to be strong, needed to take control of this situation somehow.

Jane narrowed her eyes at the sound of her real name. "You think you know me?" she said, a hiss in her voice. "You think that digging through my past and talking to people as idiotic as yourself gives you any kind of upper hand?" She started to lift her gun, and Sadie was suddenly and completely focused on her opponent again. "I'm the one in charge here, Sadie, not you. Not Pete. Not anyone!"

"You're right," Sadie said, her voice shaking as the gun continued to rise. She did not want to shoot Jane—how would she live with that? "Which means you can stop this."

"Why? So I can spend the rest of my life in prison? You think I don't know what happens next? You think I would put this amount of time and planning to simply let you go on with your life?" Jane leveled her weapon at Sadie.

Sadie looked between the barrel and Jane and put both hands on the gun again. She put pressure on the trigger of Pete's gun, and her mouth went dry. Her heart rate increased. Would she really shoot Jane? Pete had told her that every gun's trigger had a different pressure point. That was why it was important to know your gun so that you knew where that pressure point was. Sadie had never shot Pete's gun; she had no idea when she would pull a millimeter too far and fire a bullet.

"I'm not going to prison," Jane said.

"You can get help. There are—"

"I don't want help!" Jane screamed, her hand shaking. Sadie took an involuntary step back and hit up against the table. "I'm not crazy, Sadie. I don't need to work through my choices, and I'm not going to get stuck on something as juvenile as regrets. But I made you a promise. I promised that you would *never* be free of me, and if it means you live with the knowledge that you killed me, so be it. It will destroy you."

"No, it won't," Sadie said, shaking her head even though she couldn't imagine the effect killing a person would have on her. She watched Jane's finger closely. Jane still had the gun's safety on; she wasn't committed to this path . . . yet. "I'll learn to live with it, and I will know—without a doubt—that I did everything I could to avoid it. You said I would never be free of you Jane, but I will be—I already am. I'm not running from you. I'm not hiding. I'm facing you with my own weapon drawn, and I'm not backing down." She coughed and then blinked; the smoke was making her eyes water. She couldn't afford to lose sight of her target.

Jane's eyes narrowed, just enough for Sadie to know she'd made her point. She coughed, but didn't seem to be having nearly the trouble Sadie was.

Sadie continued, "My heart makes me free of whatever you may want to burden me with. I will not question whether or not I could have done something different because I will know you are the one who created this situation. If you choose, we can end it a very different way and neither of us has to—"

The safety on Jane's weapon clicked off, and Sadie's heart tripped. She squeezed the trigger a bit more and felt the resistance increase, reminding her that this action was a final one. Another ounce of pressure could fire a bullet Sadie wouldn't be able to call back. Would she fire a shot to kill, or could she aim slightly to one side and risk missing? The chest was the largest target, the easiest place to hit. If she missed, what would Jane do?

Jane took a step toward her.

"I'll do it!" Sadie nearly screamed, lifting her hands higher. She moved her feet apart in the A-line stance Pete had taught her for balance. It pulled the skirt of her dress tight against her legs, and for the first time she noticed Pete's blood on the three-quarter sleeve of her wedding dress. The thought made her stomach roll but also reminded her what was at stake. "But I would really, *really*, rather not."

Something about Sadie's words made Jane smile a little. Her eyes narrowed and a new intention entered her expression. She shifted her arm to the side, moving slowly enough for Sadie to know exactly what she was doing as she turned the gun toward Pete's hiding place.

Pete was still behind the table—could a bullet go through the plastic top?

"Don't," Sadie warned, watching Jane's finger carefully, not letting go when she had to cough yet again. The shaking of each cough terrified her. What if she pulled the trigger on accident? She blinked as quickly as possible to keep her vision clear. How long would Sadie consider her options before she could no longer protect either one of them?

Sadie would not live with the regret of choosing Jane's life over Pete's—such a thing would be impossible to cope with. She had to act. She closed her eyes and squeezed the trigger just a little more, unable to breathe. Unable to think. Unable to—

A shot rang out. Sadie opened her eyes in time to see Jane's body jolt before she fell backward, the gun falling from her grip. It hit the floor and clattered away, useless without a hand to make it lethal.

"Sadie!" Pete called out.

She looked at her hands holding the gun, her finger still poised on the trigger she hadn't pulled.

She turned her head toward the doors on the southwest side of the ballroom and her eyes locked with those of Detective Malloy, lying on his side several yards away. One hand was covered in blood, holding his side. The other hand held his service revolver still pointed at where Jane had stood a moment earlier.

Chapter 30

Sadie!" Pete called again. He'd pulled himself around the edge of the table and was looking at her with wide eyes. He blinked and then looked at Jane, who was lying on her back, kicking at the floor as though trying to push herself up.

Sadie dropped the gun; it clattered to the floor as uselessly as Jane's had. She looked from Pete to Jane, and then to Malloy, who had rolled onto his back.

"It was Malloy," Sadie said in answer to Pete's unspoken question. He looked past her, and she finally broke through her shock to admit what had happened. *Malloy shot Jane.*

Everything was frozen for a beat and then a rush of adrenaline pushed through her as a thousand thoughts slammed into her brain all at once.

Pete was hurt.

Malloy was hurt.

Jane had been shot but she wasn't dead.

The room was filling with smoke.

They needed to get out of here.

Sadie grabbed several dinner napkins off the ground, handing them to Pete before she ran in the other direction and fell to her knees beside Detective Malloy.

"Someone help us!" she yelled toward the closed doors, then coughed into her shoulder. Why was no one was coming? Had it been only a minute since Jane shot Pete? It seemed as though it had lasted forever. "Help us!" she yelled again. "The shooter's down." A door opened and she yelled, "Two officers are down."

"The shooter?" the man asked without coming in. Sadie glanced at Jane, she wasn't moving.

"I don't know," she said.

The man nodded then waved over his shoulder as though beckoning people to follow him. Sadie returned her attention to Malloy. There was so much blood. She looked around and found some napkins that she balled up. She moved Malloy's hand out of the way so she could press the napkins against the wound in his side.

"I'm so sorry," she said, feeling tears finally overflow as she took in how pale he was. *So much blood.* "I'm so sorry for all of this."

"Not . . . your fault." His voice was raspy and his eyes were closed.

Sadie felt someone's hand on her shoulder and looked up as Jared knelt beside her. "He's lost so much blood," she said to him.

Jared nodded and rolled up the sleeves of his shirt. He'd already removed his jacket and tie.

"He saved your dad's life," Sadie said.

Jared met her eyes, then scanned the room. "Where is he?"

There were a dozen or more officers swarming the area where Sadie had left Pete. "Over there," she said, waving a hand in that direction.

"Go to him," Jared said, taking over the pressure Sadie was applying to Malloy's injury. "I've got this covered."

Sadie got to her feet, wiping her hands on the front of her dress. She hurried toward the table where Pete had hid, and couldn't help but glance toward Jane. Two SWAT members were attending to her. That meant she wasn't dead, right? Did Sadie want her to die? She knew in an instant that she didn't, not really. But did she believe Jane could get well and not be a threat?

"Sadie?"

Pete was lying on the floor, a blood-soaked napkin tied tight around his knee. He reached a hand toward her, and she hurried the remaining distance. She fell to her knees and took his hand; both of their hands were covered in blood, dark and drying. She buried her head in his chest, sobbing and coughing against him in relief that he was okay and trembling with the shock of all that had happened.

"It's okay," Pete said. She could feel his other hand in her hair as he consoled her. She couldn't stop sobbing, completely overcome. Thoughts moved in and out of her head faster than she could focus on them, swirling and pushing and pulling at her.

"Ma'am?"

Pete shook her shoulder, and Sadie lifted her face, looking up at a middle-aged woman dressed in a paramedic's uniform.

"We need to get him on a stretcher, ma'am."

Sadie looked at Pete's face that was contorted and pale. She straightened. "Of course," she said, embarrassed to be in the way of Pete getting the help he needed. She moved to stand up but Pete grabbed her hand.

"It's over, Sadie," he said, squeezing her hand. "We're going to get through this, and we're going to be okay, but I need you to understand that it's over. Malloy did what he had to do. She wouldn't have stopped."

Sadie looked toward Jane again—a paramedic had joined the SWAT members attending her. She couldn't tell what they were doing. "I don't want her to die. She's sick, Pete, and maybe—"

"Sadie," Pete cut in, drawing her attention back to him. "Sick or not, she made the choices that put all of us in this situation. Whatever the result, it's going to be okay. I need you to understand that."

Sadie nodded, realizing he needed the assurance that she would work toward believing what he'd said. She moved aside so the paramedics could lift Pete onto the stretcher. She followed behind them and was shortly joined by Shawn, Breanna, Liam, and Maggie, each of whom hugged her in turn and asked if she was okay, trying to hide their shock at her appearance: barefoot, her dress smeared with the blood of three different people.

Breanna was crying; Liam and Shawn were keeping a brave face but were obviously shaken. She looked into their faces and understood why Pete had been so insistent on what he'd said before they took him away. She looked toward Jane, lying still on a stretcher, an oxygen mask over her face. The flurry of activity around her meant her injury was serious. There was nothing Sadie could do to help her, but she knew that if she could have, she would have done anything in her power for a different result than this.

"It's going to be okay," she said to her family, echoing what Pete had told her, but feeling it for the first time. They would cope with whatever came next—the physical and emotional recovery—but it was going to be okay. "It's over," she said quietly, feeling those words seep into her bones. "It's finally, horribly, over."

Epilogue

Two months later

Sadie let herself in to a charming three-bedroom, cottage-style house near Old Town in Fort Collins, Colorado. "I'm home," she said as she closed and locked the front door behind her. "Pete?"

"On the phone," he said from the third bedroom that served as his office. Sadie made a face, she hadn't meant to interrupt. He'd recently been hired as part of a tri-county cold case unit, and she wasn't used to him being on "work" calls. She hung her purse in the entry closet and headed for the kitchen to boil some water for cocoa. It was mid-September in the Rocky Mountains, and the glorious heralding of autumn was right on time, but she hadn't been ready for the chill in the air when she'd left for her therapy appointment that morning. Plus, it was never a bad time of year for cocoa.

After everything that had happened at the wedding, she and Pete had decided to make a *fresher* start than previously anticipated by moving closer to Pete's daughters in Fort Collins. Sadie had no expectation that either of her own children would settle down anywhere near Colorado, and there was nothing left in Garrison for her other than a handful of good friends who understood her need to live elsewhere. She enjoyed being a grandmother to Pete's grandchildren and had come to genuinely love his daughters who had embraced her as she had always hoped they would.

For the most part, life had gone on with relative normalcy after the "Bombed Wedding," as it had been dubbed by *The Denver Post*, who, with the help of the Garrison police force, put together the details of Jane's plot.

After Boston, Jane had attempted to start a new life in Nebraska. She'd used her real name again since all it had was an expired protective order connected to it, and she managed to keep herself out of trouble. After a year of losing track of Sadie, she had joined an online group of Garrison mothers, which is where she'd "met" a member of Sadie's church. Jane claimed to be a former student of Sadie's now living in Wyoming but hoping to return to Garrison soon.

The woman hadn't thought twice of giving her an update about Sadie whenever Jane asked how Mrs. Hoffmiller was doing—which Jane did every few months. She didn't participate in the group otherwise, simply lurked and absorbed information as needed. When she asked for an update on Sadie in June, she'd learned about Sadie's engagement, and it had triggered her old obsession more deeply than ever.

She came to Garrison and rented two different storage units where she stored her more incriminating possessions, including the receiver for the listening device she had routed to an app on her phone. The cars she later blew up had been stolen and re-plated. She'd moved in to her apartment in July, keeping a low profile and using a variety of personas when she had to go out. It was so orchestrated, so premeditated. So sick.

Sadie shook her head, clearing her thoughts. She hated thinking about Jane and let her mind move to the other things that had happened after the wedding. Happier things that lifted her mood instead of depressing it.

The living liver transplant Shawn had participated in for his birth mother had gone well, and Sadie had been able to be with him. Pete insisted Sadie go to Alaska while he recovered from his injuries—which had led to emergency surgery on his knee the day after the wedding—at Brooke's house. After the transplant and requisite recovery, Shawn had started working for an investigation firm in Sacramento and had rented a studio apartment not far from Maggie. Sadie expected an official announcement from the two of them any day now.

Jane's storage unit had supplied proof of her fraud against him, but it would still be some time before everything was cleared up on his credit. Being distracted by his relationship with Maggie was probably the best thing for him right now.

Breanna and Liam had returned to London and hinted that they might be looking for a vacation home in the Fort Collins area when they came back for Christmas. Sadie had already sent them half a dozen property listings as encouragement.

"Sadie," Pete said from behind her. She turned to see him leaning on his cane with one hand, his other hand on the counter. While she'd been seeing a psychologist every week—including today—Pete had been seeing an excellent physical therapist three times a week and steadily improving.

She had stopped expressing out loud the guilt she felt at what had happened to him—to everyone. Her therapist was helping her separate the things she was accountable for from the things that belonged on someone else's shoulders. Someone else's cold dead shoulders.

Jane had been pronounced dead on arrival at the hospital that day. Malloy's bullet had hit its target, and Jane had not lived to face the repercussions of her actions. Some said it was a blessing—the toll of a trial and the possibility that Jane wouldn't have served much time for destruction of property and assault against Pete would have been too much for Sadie to carry.

For her part, though, Sadie wished things had ended differently. She hadn't needed Jane to die to be free of her; she'd found that place before Malloy pulled the trigger. And yet, she could admit relief at not having to worry about Jane ever coming back.

Sadie forced her thoughts away from Jane for the second time since coming home. "Who was on the phone?"

Pete moved a few steps past her and sat on one of the kitchen chairs.

Sadie pulled another chair around in front of him and lifted his foot onto her lap. She couldn't massage his knee, but a foot rub now and again at least made her feel as though she were helping where she could. Pete relaxed and leaned against the chair back. "It was Malloy."

Sadie's attention perked for a very different reason. Before the wedding they were silent enemies with one another, but the mandatory investigation that followed the shooting was far more intensive for Malloy than it would have been had Sadie pulled her trigger first. As an officer-involved shooting, there was a lengthy protocol that had to be followed to determine whether he acted appropriately. Because of the investigation and the need to recover from his injuries, Malloy had been on administrative leave since that fateful day nearly two months ago. Pete's drug charges and Sadie's breaking and entry had already been dropped, but Malloy's future had hung in the balance with far more potential difficulties.

"How is he?" Sadie asked.

"Good," Pete said with a smile. "Better than good, in fact. The DA wrote the letter."

Sadie let out a breath of relief and her hands stilled. It was what they had all been waiting for, an official letter from the district attorney stating that Malloy had been cleared of any criminal charges. Due to the personal attacks Jane had made toward Pete—a friend of Malloy and a former Garrison police officer—and the unprecedented choices Malloy had made regarding the wedding operations, it was essential to prove he had no personal interest in shooting Jane.

Sadie certainly didn't understand the intricacies, but she did understand that each week that went by without a decision increased the pressure Malloy felt regarding his future in law enforcement. "And he's cleared?"

Pete nodded. "Of *all* criminal charges. The letter has been sent to the chief of police and the city and county council members. Malloy could be back to work as soon as next week, assuming his doctor will allow it." As a result of the gunshot, Malloy had lost his spleen and a section of large intestine, but he'd recovered well and lost twenty-five pounds in the process.

"I am so relieved," Sadie said, taking another deep breath and letting it out, releasing with it the pent up anxiety she felt for Malloy's situation.

"Me too," Pete said. "As is Malloy and his family. I think his wife is more excited than anyone else. He's driving her crazy kicking around the house all the time now that he's feeling better."

Sadie smiled. "Malloy being cleared breaks one more hold Jane had on us," she said. Pete's words from their wedding day came back to her. "It's over," he'd said before being loaded on the stretcher. And while Sadie wasn't sure it would ever be truly *over*, it was easier to deal with today than it had been yesterday and that was a good feeling. "We can all focus on our own recoveries a little more now that Malloy's future is clear."

They talked a few more minutes about Pete's hope that Malloy would receive the Distinguished Service Star for his actions. Sadie agreed. He'd saved both Pete and Sadie through his actions, and she would forever be grateful.

"How was your appointment this morning?" Pete asked. Sadie hadn't realized she'd stopped rubbing his foot so she started up again and watched his shoulders relax. Pete loved a good foot rub.

"It went really well," she said. "I bounced an idea around with Dr. Kim that might not be as ridiculous as I first thought. She was leading me through a free-thinking exercise of goals and ambitions."

"I hadn't imagined you needed much help with goals and ambition," Pete said with a smirk as Sadie knuckled the ball of his foot. "You're always coming up with new things to do. I'm still not quite recovered from those amazing homemade noodles you put in the chicken soup last week; they were out of this world."

"I'm glad you liked them," Sadie said with a smile. All these years and she'd never made homemade noodles. Now that she had, she couldn't believe how easy they were, and so good she might never put store-bought noodles in soup again. "But this idea is a little bigger than finding a new recipe. In fact, it's different from anything I've done before."

"Really?" Pete said, arching his eyebrows.

Sadie nodded with enthusiasm. "I'd need a clever pen name to really pull it off, though."

Pete pulled his eyebrows together. "A pen name?"

Sadie's smile got even wider. "I'm thinking of writing a book. Well, actually, a series of books about my experiences these last few years."

"Books?" Pete said. "Like, self-help?"

Sadie shook her head. "Novels."

Could he furrow his brow any deeper? "Novels?"

Sadie wriggled forward in her chair as the excitement took an even stronger hold. With Malloy cleared, she felt more free than she had in a long time. Free to plan her future again and free to think fantastical thoughts that a short time ago seemed both silly and impossible.

"Think about it. A series of mystery novels about a woman who uses the skills she's gained through living a relatively normal life to help solve murders and missing person's cases. Dr. Kim said there's a whole genre of mystery novels that even involve recipes as part of the plot. She called them 'culinary mysteries' and apparently they're quite popular. She thought they'd be just the genre for my stories."

"Have you ever written . . . anything?"

"Well, I have extensive notes about all the cases I've worked and, though I've never pursued writing as a career, I did very well in all my writing classes in college. And I attended a few writing conferences as part of my continuing education before I retired from teaching. I've also *read* thousands of books so I'm betting I have a pretty good sense of structure."

"You're going to write novels," Pete said. His look of confusion made way for surprise.

Sadie scowled at him. "You don't have to act quite so shocked."

"I don't mean to," Pete said, leaning back and putting his hands behind his head. "I've just never thought I'd one day be sleeping with a novelist."

Sadie laughed.

"And you'll be writing about your own cases?"

"Well, sort of," Sadie said with a noncommittal shrug. "I'll have to disguise certain details, of course, and exaggerate other ones—change names and things to protect both the guilty and the innocent—but it could be fun. It's probably a lot safer than the way I've spent the last few years." She paused as she thought of a few more details. "You'd have to play the part of a cop or something to explain why you're there, and I'd need to disguise my own character enough that no one would guess it was really me I'm writing about, you know? I could have a signature recipe for each book that would work for the title—desserts, I think. Everyone loves desserts, and they'd make fabulous covers."

Pete shook his head again. His expression had turned playful. "My, my, you are a woman full of surprises."

Sadie eased his foot to the floor and got up from her chair. She gently set herself down on his lap and put her arms around his neck. He wrapped his arms around her back as she ran her fingers through his hair and continued to contemplate how her plan would work. She'd need to attend some additional conferences to learn more about the craft of writing, and with a little luck, maybe she could find an excellent editorial team that could smooth out her rough spots. She'd heard over and over again that when contemplating a book a would-be author should write what they know. It was beginning to feel like wasted knowledge if she *didn't* write her stories.

Pete's lips on her neck brought her back to the present, and she decided she could work out such details later. Amid everything else that had happened these last two months, perhaps the very best thing was that she and Pete were together, legally and lawfully married and as committed as ever despite what some might call a rocky start, muddy middle, and terrifying end to their courtship. They had postponed their honeymoon to Costa Rica until Pete was more fully recovered but enjoyed the casual interactions of marriage . . . not to mention the intimate ones.

"When did you think you might start the actual writing of these books?" he asked, his breath tickling her ear and making her whole body shiver.

Sadie gave him a coy smile as she stood, then took his hand and pulled him to his feet. He shifted his weight to his good leg and his cane. "I was thinking of getting started on an outline for the first book later this afternoon." The sparkle in his eye made her stomach do that zingy little flip-flop she hoped she would never get used to.

"Do you think you could start in, say, an hour or so?" Pete suggested.

"An hour?" she said, raising her eyebrows. "Wouldn't that be something?"

He laughed, pulled her close, and kissed her soundly. When he pulled back, he looked her in the eye and lifted a hand to stroke her jaw with his thumb. "Oh, Sadie, Sadie, married lady. You have a way of keeping me on my toes, don't you?"

"Well, once you figure me out, I'll be boring."

"Oh, I'm not worried about that," he said, lowering his face toward hers for another kiss. "Not the least little bit."

Chicken Soup with Homemade Noodles

2 tablespoons butter
½ onion, diced
4 chicken breasts, cooked and diced
4 (14.5-ounce) cans chicken broth (approximately 8 cups)
½ cup water
1 teaspoon kosher salt
¼ teaspoon pepper
½ teaspoon poultry seasoning (or Italian seasoning)
½ teaspoon basil
1 bay leaf
4 carrots peeled and sliced
2 ribs of celery, sliced
2 cups medium-sized egg noodles (or homemade noodles)

Melt butter in a large pot over medium heat. Sauté onion for 3 min. Add chicken and sauté 2 more minutes. Add broth, water, spices, carrots, and celery. Bring to a boil. Cover and simmer 30 minutes.

Add noodles and return to a boil, cooking 15 to 20 minutes or until noodles are cooked through. (Watch carefully to keep noodles from overcooking.) Salt and pepper to taste before serving.

For added flavor, top soup with grated Parmesan cheese.

Note: Adding a dash of nutmeg with the other spices gives great flavor.

Homemade Noodles

2 cups flour
½ teaspoon salt
½ cup melted butter
2 eggs
3 tablespoons milk

In a large bowl, mix flour and salt. Add butter, eggs, and milk.

Mix together with a wooden spoon or rubber scraper until dough forms a ball. Turn dough out on a floured surface. Roll out dough very thin—⅛ of an inch or so. Using a sharp knife or pizza cutter, cut dough into strips, the length and width desired (thinner is usually better).

Lift noodles with the blunt edge of a knife, one small section at a time, allowing pasta to drape over the edges of the knife without sticking together. Drop separated noodles into boiling soup one at a time so they don't stick together. Continue adding until all noodles are in the soup. (There will be a lot of noodles.)

Add additional broth if needed to accommodate the noodles, returning soup to a boil before adding additional noodles. Cook an additional two or three minutes to make sure the most recently added noodles are cooked. Remove from heat and serve.

Serves 10.

Note: Noodles can also be frozen. Cut as directed, then flash freeze on a cookie sheet. Store in an airtight container (a plastic zip-top bag works great) and freeze for up to six months. To use, add frozen noodles to soup as directed.

Acknowledgments

I'm writing this right after finishing my final revision of this, the final book in the Sadie Hoffmiller Culinary Mystery Series. What started as one chapter for a writing contest has ended with twelve books and a cookbook.

To bring it to an end is a little sad (I'm going to miss Sadie), a little bit relieving (I'm ready to write something new), and a little bit scary (will I ever write something as enjoyable for me and my readers as Sadie and her misadventures?). Regardless, as I look over this series, I am stunned at the growth I have had personally, the impact Sadie has had on readers, and the amazing experience it has been. When I think of all the people who made this possible, I am truly overwhelmed and find it difficult to know where to start.

There's no way to prioritize who should come first in my thanks, so please don't try to instill some kind of importance to the order of this list—I didn't.

Jeff Savage (J. Scott Savage, *Zombie Kid,* HarperTeen, 2013) inspired that first chapter that led to *Lemon Tart,* and I will be forever grateful for his friendship and the simple opportunity he created that led to this.

Lisa Mangum (*After Hello,* Shadow Mountain, 2012) and Jana Erickson have been the dynamic duo from day one—carrying each book through the internal processes and producing a quality final product. Multiple people have worked as assistant editors, typesetters, designers, photographers, online coordinators, printers, shippers, etc., and most of them I have never met despite them being such an important part of this process.

Specific people who have made ongoing contributions include Shauna Gibby (design), Rachael Ward and Malina Grigg (typographers), Kenny Hodges (audio producer, Kenny Hodges Productions), and Diane Dabczynski (voice talent for audio). Everyone at Deseret Book and Shadow Mountain has always treated me so well and believed in this project. Thank you, from the bottom of my heart, for everything.

My test kitchen has been incredible—all volunteers, all wonderful cooks, all sharing in the responsibility of making these recipes work. For *Wedding Cake,* specifically, I was blessed by the talents of Whit Larson, Lisa Swinton (*Fallen Angel,* Createspace, 2014), Danyelle Ferguson (*Sweet Confections,* Wonderstruck Books, 2014), Megan O'Niell, Laree Ipson, Annie Funk, and Sandra Sorenson. With each book I've requested more and more help with recipes, and I appreciate all the contributions toward this final volume. They provided several more which will be available in the cookbook.

In addition to my cooks, I had some recipe help from a few others. I fell in love with my sister-in-law's homemade noodle recipe; thank you, Crystal Schofield, for allowing me to include it in the book. I borrowed the Rice Pudding recipe from *The Lion House Cookbook* as I have made the recipe for many years and never found one better. The triple chocolate cake is another recipe I have made for years, thanks to Joyce Elliott, and Lenny Barker gave me the recipe for lemon water and shared her father's experience with it regarding kidney stones. Frikadeles with Ruskumsnuz was the favorite recipe of a past resident at one of my husband's Assisted Living Facilities. I was able to find his daughter, Brenda Wedgwood, who gave me permission to use it in a book and helped me understand its history.

My writing group was priceless throughout this series, helping me keep Sadie true to her character: Nancy Campbell Allen (Isabelle Webb series, Covenant, 2009–2013), Becki Clayson, (*Disengaged,* coming in 2015), Jody Durfee (*Hadley, Hadley Benson,* Covenant, 2013), Ronda Hinrichsen (*Betrayed,* Covenant, 2014), and Jennifer Moore (*Becoming Lady Lockwood,* Covenant, 2014). Thank you, thank you, thank you, ladies, for being so good to me.

Gregg Luke (*Deadly Undertakings,* Covenant, 2012) once again helped me with some pharmaceutical brilliance. As he likes to say, it's nice to have a drug dealer on speed dial. ☺

And finally, my family. They are my happy place, my softness and my joy. My older daughters have become women through the course of this series, and while I hope that my writing is a blessing to them, I know that it has also at times interfered with them establishing their own identities. I want them to know how much I love them, how I regret any negatives left behind for them to balance, and how much I appreciate that, despite those hard things, they have supported and encouraged me. My youngest daughter read her first Sadie book not long ago, and her excitement at knowing I wrote the story will forever be imprinted on my heart.

As for my son—my favorite boy in the whole wide world—I am very grateful to have him as a fan even if he hasn't read a single word.

My biggest fan has always been my sweetheart, Lee. From the time we first met, he has always seen the very best in me and helped me learn and grow in ways that fifteen-year-old girl could never have imagined. I owe him everything and am without words to express how grateful I am for his friendship and his love.

There are many things about the universe and this life that I do not understand, many questions I am still looking to answer, but there are a few things I know. I know that we are all children of a loving God who wants us to be the best we can be. I know that hardships refine us and that nothing is as good or as bad as it seems in the moment we find ourselves within it. I know there is purpose in my writing beyond the stories that come of it, and that my novels have been a part of me becoming who I am.

I believe in life missions. I believe in the power of families. I believe in the joy that pursuing our talents brings to our lives. And I believe in finding a purpose in life worthy of the difficulties and struggles and heartache that grow us into the people God sent us here to become. I am forever in debt to my Father in Heaven and my Savior, who have laid a path before me that has brought so much joy and peace into my life. May any achievements I make reflect well on Them.

About the Author

Josi S. Kilpack began her first novel in 1998. Her seventh novel, *Sheep's Clothing,* won the 2007 Whitney Award for Mystery/Suspense and was the Best of State Fiction Winner in 2012. *Wedding Cake* is Josi's twenty-second novel and the twelfth book in the Sadie Hoffmiller Culinary Mystery Series. Josi currently lives in Willard, Utah, with her husband and children.

For more information about Josi, you can visit her website at www.josiskilpack.com, read her blog at www.josikilpack.blogspot.com, or contact her via e-mail at Kilpack@gmail.com.

IT'D BE A CRIME

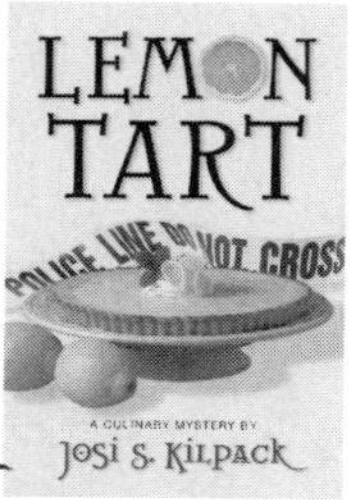

ISBN 978-1-60641-050-9
$17.99

ISBN 978-1-60641-121-6
$17.99

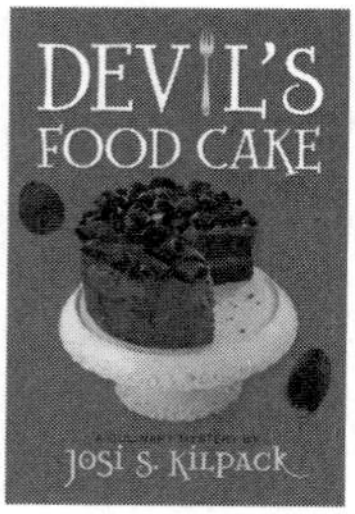

ISBN 978-1-60641-232-9
$17.99

ISBN 978-1-60908-903-0
$18.99

ISBN 978-1-60907-170-7
$18.99

ISBN 978-1-60907-328-2
$18.99

BY JOSI S. KILPACK

www.shadowmountain.com • www.josiskilpack.com

SHADOW MOUNTAIN

TO MISS THE REST OF THE SERIES . . .

ISBN 978-1-60641-813-0
$17.99

ISBN 978-1-60641-941-0
$17.99

ISBN 978-1-60908-745-6
$18.99

ISBN 978-1-60907-593-4
$18.99

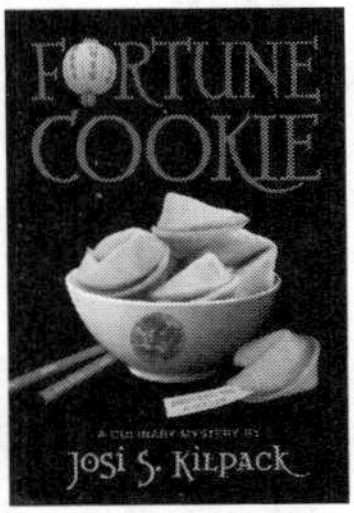

ISBN 978-1-60907-787-7
$18.99

Available online and at a bookstore near you.

Available on audio.

DON'T MISS

SADIE'S LITTLE BLACK RECIPE BOOK

A CULINARY MYSTERY COOKBOOK
BY JOSI S. KILPACK

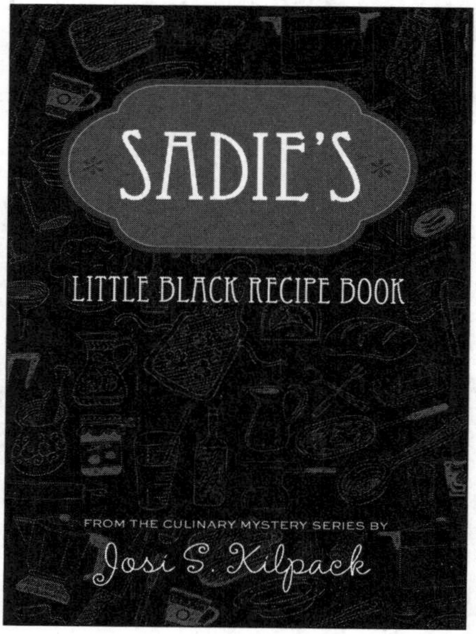

All the recipes from all of the books!
More than 120 recipes

ISBN 978-1-62972-020-3 • $15.99
Available in bookstores and online

SHADOW
MOUNTAIN